the (fake)
DATING
game

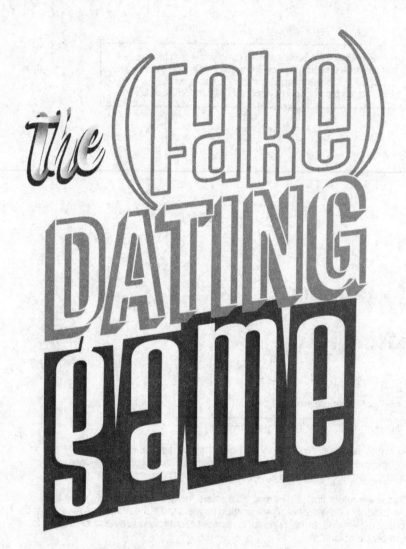

TIMOTHY JANOVSKY

Recycling programs
for this product may
not exist in your area.

ISBN-13: 978-1-335-04155-5

The (Fake) Dating Game

Harlequin Enterprises ULC
22 Adelaide St. West, 41st Floor
Toronto, Ontario M5H 4E3, Canada
www.Harlequin.com

Printed in U.S.A.

Author Note

This story contains the (off-page) death of a parent
and frequent discussions of grief and healing.
I hope I have handled these topics with care and grace.
As such, I hope you, dear reader, will give yourself the same
when choosing whether this romance is for you.

If you or someone you know is struggling with grief,
please visit my website, timothyjanovsky.com,
for a list of support resources.

Much love,

Timothy Janovsky

One

Amber bulbs dangle on white strings above our heads, making everyone in the restaurant look like a cartoon character with a bright idea. I, however, feel like an absolute fool for coming here tonight.

It's crowded, loud, and overpriced. Three things Buckley hates.

Buckley, my long-term boyfriend and college sweetheart, sits across from me looking pensive in a brand-new shirt, a crisp oak color, that's too snug around the collar. I bought it for him this afternoon as a surprise from the athleisure boutique I work at.

I always forget Buckley's neck size. Shoe size: ten and a half. Pant size: 30x32. Dick size...a gentleman never tells. But, somehow, I always screw up his neck size. It's wider than the rest of his parts.

(No, I'm not talking about *that* part, which has plenty of girth, thank you very much.)

(I, Holden James, never said I was a gentleman.)

When he got home from work at the accounting firm, I had this fresh outfit laid out on the bed for him, flashed him a pair of train tickets, and told him we were having dinner in Manhattan tonight.

If Buckley had it his way, we'd never leave our town. It has a Whole Foods! We're within driving distance of *two* IKEAs! Both of which we can only shop at because he brings home the bacon, and by bacon, I do mean the organic smoked turkey bacon I attempt to fry on Sunday mornings while he sleeps. Unimaginably, I always set off the smoke detectors, and he wakes up to open all the windows, reasonably grumpy.

But tonight, he didn't protest the trek into the city because I told him it was my treat.

Though, this treat turned out to be more of a trick.

Gwendolyn, my boss and the woman who owns the boutique I work at, recommended this place. "It's divine," she'd said, while watching me fold ugly pairs of patterned leggings for the fashionably indiscriminate who frequent Fab Fitness Flair. (Try saying that five times fast.)

The Yelp listing made this restaurant seem like a lavish, dimly lit dining establishment with olive accent colors and old-world charms. A good place for important conversations like the one I'm hoping to have with Buckley tonight.

"Your boyfriend will love it," Gwendolyn had reassured me when I clocked out this afternoon.

Now here we are and, judging by the disgruntled look on Buckley's face, he is *not* loving it. He's the embodiment of the anti-McDonald's slogan right now.

Not that I blame him.

Our light wood table is smashed up against our neighbor's—a short, bald agent talking career trajectory with a young blonde. She's probably a singer judging by her wacky outfit, a neon bucket hat and Edward Scissorhands–esque nails. How she picks up her wineglass is above and beyond me. I watch in abject horror, hoping she doesn't spill the dry red all over her white crop top.

I'm fixating on the excess of stimuli around me because I'm more nervous than I've ever been before. A big question hovers just behind my lips. I'm holding it back until the right moment. During dessert, probably. Right after Buckley's first bite of cake. I'm trying to sweeten him up so he's sure to say yes when I pop the question.

The plates we've been served so far were small. Each tasting has been just that—a bite of bliss that escaped my palate before it even settled. The pear salad was exquisite with a refreshing pink dressing—pomegranate, maybe?—that I was afraid to ask the fussy waiter about since he was already annoyed with us for our (*my*) stinginess.

We've ordered the cheapest drinks and the least expensive plates because the boutique doesn't pay me that well, and my side hustle of teaching Cardio Dance Fit classes isn't much better. This outing tonight is being bankrolled by a Capital One credit card limit I have no idea how I got approved for.

"Thank you for coming here tonight," I say to Buckley,

sounding small. My heart is skittish. Here's the only man I've ever loved sitting across from me, the man I live with, and despite the small distance of white tablecloth between us, it feels like I'm shouting at him from the other side of the world given the noise around us and the chasm of emotions I'm afraid to fall into. "I know it took a lot for you to get off from work early since you're still the new guy and, yeah, it means a lot to me."

"Sure, Holden," he says, and my chest contracts.

He never calls me *Holden*. Since forever, he's called me H.

One night, when he was really drunk, not long after we first met, he went on a rant at an ABC—anything but clothes—party about how Holden has no immediate nicknames. "Hole?" he goofed. "We can't call you hole!" The room lit up with laughter from every corner, and even though it was at my expense, I didn't care. His attention had that spectacular effect on me. "I'll call you H. Short, simple, eighth letter of the alphabet. H is like a house, dependable and sturdy, right? Like, two I's connected together."

Then, when we started dating, he told me H was more like a home, still dependable, still sturdy, but he and I were the two I's and the line connecting them was our love.

It was over-the-top, but I rolled with it, enjoying that I could be someone worthy of romantic words, no matter how cheesy. For once, I didn't feel reduced to the-guy-whose-mom-died at the end of high school.

"I bet you're wondering why I chose to trek all the way out here tonight." I muster up a prizewinning smile, shucking the bad memories I almost let infiltrate our night. I've got to sell this.

The waiter, a handsome guy with piercing hazel eyes, comes by with our entrées, interrupting my flow. There are approximately four truffle raviolis on a large pewter plate topped with green leaves and a measly amount of sauce. I already know I'm going to be starving when we leave. As if my stomach weren't already in nauseated knots.

"Thank you," Buckley says almost too congenially to the waiter. His eyes drift down the waiter's ass as he walks away. I normally wouldn't mind Buckley checking out another man. Looking is fine. Touching, within the express bounds of our open relationship, is fine, too. But to do it so brazenly in front of me when I'm obviously trying to talk to him about something significant is more than grating.

"I didn't really give tonight a lot of thought," Buckley says when he finally tears his eyes away and picks up his utensils.

"Well, it's actually because..." I sip my watered-down cocktail to steel my nerves. "There's something I wanted to ask you. Something important."

It might be the swaying lights, but I think I spot a bead of sweat trickling down the side of Buckley's face.

"Uhhhh, okaaaaaaay." Buckley's eyes dance away from me.

"Are you all right?" I ask, handing him my napkin because he is already sopping. He blots at his suddenly shiny nose.

"Did it get hot in here?" he asks, fanning himself with his hand.

The agent from the neighboring table leans over: "I've been asking myself the same thing." But the agent looks like he's a smarmy ball of sweat all the time, so I don't consider his opinion relevant.

"Do you think it's something you ate?" I try to flag down the waiter so we can see a list of ingredients. Buckley doesn't have any known food allergies, but of course, tonight of all nights, he might as well go into anaphylaxis. I bring the bad luck with me wherever I go it seems.

"No." He glugs back his water. "No, I'm fine." The water dribbles down his chin and onto his lap. My worry mounts.

I haven't seen him this nervous since the day he asked me out. We were at an amusement park, we'd just stepped off a roller coaster, and the exhilaration of the ride mixed with the worry about my answer caused him to faint. In the nurse's station, mostly filled with children who ate too much cotton candy and retched on the Tilt-A-Whirl, he grabbed my hand like a patient on their death bed and asked, "Will you go out with me?"

He was so pale and clammy, yet still so sweetly beautiful. I sighed and said, "Of course. You didn't need to do all this to guilt me into it. I would've said yes no matter what."

Once again, over-the-top, but we laughed for a good five minutes. It felt good—better than crying—so I decided it was right.

"Go on," he says, roping me back into the moment. A moment I'd honestly like to forget about at this point. None of this is what I planned for, and now I'm worried this whole night has been ruined beyond repair.

"Really? I think we should see what was in the salad. Maybe it was the dressing? You don't normally eat pomegranates. Was that even pomegranate I was tasting?" I'm half stalling, half trying to make sure he's okay.

"No, I'm fine," Buckley snaps. Snapping seems to be his favorite way to speak to me these days. When did that start? And now that I think of it, why did I assume this was a good idea in the first place?

Oh, right. Because of what's currently hidden in my pocket.

"If you're sure," I say, fortifying myself once more. I clear my throat. "I brought you out here so I could ask you to be my—"

"Don't propose to me," he whispers quickly with deadly seriousness.

"Huh?" His words bounce around inside my head like a pinball, launched and looping.

"Don't propose to me." He looks like he's about to cry. His eyes dart around the restaurant making sure nobody is peering at us. I haven't just lost the thread of this conversation. The whole thing has unraveled like a Forever 21 scarf at this point. "I won't say yes if you do."

Stunned laughter bursts out of me when his words decode themselves. Heads turn in our direction. Even the agent is put off by my performance, and he seems like he'd represent just about anyone. I don't mean to make a show of myself but this is too rich. When I calm down enough to speak, I say, "I wasn't going to *propose* to you."

"You weren't?" he asks. He appears almost embarrassed—for his assumption or by me? I can't tell. "Then what was all that about?"

"I wanted you to audition for *Madcap Market* with me."

Other people love *Wheel of Fortune* or *Who Wants to Be a Millionaire?* Some worship at the altar of *Jeopardy!* Thanks to my late mom, I grew up grinning ear to ear while watching teams of two race down the aisles of a fake grocery store looking for specific products and trying not to fall into waiting pools of Reddi-Wip or aged barrels of baked beans. It's slapstick at its finest. God Bless America.

"When I was reminded on Instagram about their open casting calls for the show, I knew we needed to be on it," I tell him, excitement cranking through me. I conveniently leave out the part that I had seen the post while drinking. I don't know what it is about spiked seltzers, but they always lead to financially unwise decisions.

From my pocket, I pull out two plane tickets to Los Angeles that I impulse bought courtesy of black cherry White Claw.

"What?" Buckley mumbles, looking over the tickets I've handed him.

"It's *Madcap Market*," I say. "We leave four weeks from today!"

My heart drops another inch into my stomach for every silent second that goes by. For every new crease across Buckley's forehead and beside his frowning mouth.

"You and that show." Buckley shakes his head in visible disbelief. "It's an unhealthy obsession."

This is far from the reaction I was hoping for. It's been forever since our last vacation. Dovetailing a TV game show into one seemed like a good idea. Or, at least, not an awful one. I blink back my panic and immediate hurt. "Obsession? You know what *Madcap Market* meant to me and…"

My sentence trails off as my lip quivers. I can't spit out *my mom* no matter how hard I try.

"It's been six years, Holden," he says as if grief, like the Greek yogurt he buys in bulk from Whole Foods, has an expiration date.

My center of gravity is out of sorts when I ask, "What is that supposed to mean?"

"You've got to move on already, Holden. It's not healthy," he says, completely lacking sympathy and maybe showing me his true colors. I didn't expect them to be so bleak and off-putting. "And, frankly, neither is that show. It's everything that's wrong with American TV."

My sadness mutates into anger because anger is far easier to express and less quicksandy. "Just because I don't binge the BBC every free-bloody-wanking-minute I have doesn't mean I have poor taste." I don't care about magical doctors or abbeys or emotionally distressed women who hit on hot priests! I don't watch *Madcap Market* to *care*. I watch it to de-stress, to enjoy, to forget. All the things I've been trying and failing to do since Mom passed away from a freak blood clot after she beat cancer. A shock that tore my tiny family apart right before I graduated high school and left home for the first time in my life for college.

There's this supercharged second where the agent leans over and whispers, "Are you two filming test footage for a reality series? Because, if so, this stuff is really juicy. This is my card and—"

"Not now!" I swat at his hand and the business card goes flying, landing in a nearby soup bowl, soaking up bloodred broth. "Why do you think you're better than me just because you have a boring office job and a snobbish taste in TV?"

His nostrils flair like a dragon's in one of his ridiculous fantasy shows. "Because, Holden, getting your shit together is not as hard as you so claim it to be. It's called being an adult. How about you try it sometime?"

"Try it? I live it. I breathe it. I am it! What are you even talking about? I have *two* jobs. I pay *half* the rent." I struggle to do it, but I don't voice that part. After Mom died and we became a one-income household, I had to take out a mountain of student loans to still go to my dream school, which didn't even land me a good job. A waste of time and funds. I'd say it was worth it solely for my relationship with Buckley, but his glare reads like a countdown clock—detonation imminent.

"You don't pay half the rent," Buckley says gravely.

I rock back in my seat. "Yes, I do. Where else is my money transfer going every month if not to our rent?" I ask. We're amassing more attention the longer this spat goes on. Nobody is even tasting their tastings. Their mouths are too busy hanging open as they try not to stare.

"You pay a *quarter* of our rent," he whispers. "You pay a quarter of our rent, and I pay the rest. How else did you think we afforded such a nice place?"

My neck grows hot. "What? Since when? When we signed the lease, you told me what the rent was and we agreed that we'd each pay half." I knew it would stretch my bank account thin, but I was young and "in love" and desperate not to move in with Dad lest I be reminded of

Mom's absence every time we sat down to a meal. Desperate to make this—with Buckley—work.

Even if, in the back of my mind, I know I rushed into it and then contorted myself into a pretzel at his every whim so he couldn't see my mess or my pain.

"I lied! I made a sacrifice. Like an adult. I wanted to live there and, at the time, I wanted to live there *with you*."

"At the time?" I ask, my voice breaking, reduced to a deflating tube man outside a car dealership at the end of a shitty sales day. Nothing but a cheap heap of synthetic fabric flattened to the pavement.

"I've been trying to tell you." He wrings his wet napkin.

I blink back at him, not computing this, wondering how one evening can fly so far off the rails. "Been trying to tell me what?"

"That—" he looks away "—I don't think this is working anymore."

His words pin me to the chair. "What are you talking about?" I'm hoping the question dulls the sharpness in his voice. That his answer is: this date isn't working for him or our apartment isn't working for him, not...

"I'm talking about us. I don't think *we're* working anymore." His brown eyes are a mudslide after a rainstorm. "I want to break up, and I want you to move out."

Words drain out of my mind; blood drains out of my face. "You don't mean that." He can't mean that. People don't just decide to unlove you, do they? We don't live in a world cruel enough to take away moms too young and ruin love this suddenly, right?

"I do mean that," he says in a monotone. "I'm sorry, Holden." Abruptly, he stands, places his napkin on the table and grabs his coat from the back of the chair. I'm tempted to snatch the fluttering sleeve, tug it back, and beg him to stay, even if I sort of hate him right now.

Instead, as he's walking off, some demonic spirit possesses my body and throws my anger into the spotlight. I stand and yell after him, "You're a coward! You're selfish! Just because you have a full-time job, and health insurance, and can pay three-fourths of the rent on an apartment I don't even like doesn't mean you're better than me! You would've held me back anyway!"

Turning around, his visage is twisted and devilish. He says through gritted teeth, "I would've held *you* back?"

I cough into my hand, not having expected a response. "Yeah, I never could've won the show with you. You're all work and no play. I don't need you."

He laughs an angry, watery laugh. "Okay, Holden. We'll see about that."

"What's that supposed to mean?" He walks away, not even flinching at the booming sound of my voice. "What's that supposed to mean?"

I'm left answerless, with a broken heart and a massive bill.

Two

FOUR WEEKS LATER

I hop off the plane at LAX with a dream and my mending heart.

Not exactly a Miley-worthy moment, but I'm manifesting a positive outlook, shoving down the sad shit for the sake of palm trees, hot locals, and my favorite TV game show. Buckley, who?

As I strut through the airport—trying to summon pop star in a music video confidence—I adjust the quarter zip with a wrap component in a bright green mesh-like fabric that I'm wearing. It's very sporty, and I got a hefty discount on it so I'd stop playing breakup jams over the boutique's sound system during my shifts. Heartbreak has its perks sometimes, I suppose.

Gwendolyn practically insisted I go. I already had the time off approved and the plane tickets and hotel ended up being nonrefundable, so with the glitz and glam of LA just outside this airport terminal, I couldn't be readier to forget about my unfeeling ex and the breakup that tore my life asunder.

Los Angeles will rejuvenate me.

It has to.

Who cares that I couldn't find anyone to take Buckley's place on my cross-country adventure? Apparently cold-texting old acquaintances *would you want to appear on a TV game show with me* is not the best way to find an audition partner for *Madcap Market*. Even with the added bait of a free vacation.

I shake away the negative thoughts because I still have one final lifeline: Alexia Morozov, one of my closest college friends.

Technically, she was Buckley's friend first, but we became tight separately when we took the same gruesome ballet class as an elective our senior year, and she's an actress, so there is no chance she's camera shy. As I last heard, she's just returning from a contract on a rinky-dink cruise ship where she sang Celine Dion covers to overtanned tourists with barely any cell service. She's agreed to meet up for drinks tonight and I doubt she's going to say no to me because she lives to be in front of the camera.

We'll have to fudge our friendship history a bit at the audition. *Madcap Market* only casts couples with fun back-stories for the prepared package videos that they show prior to the final competition, but that shouldn't be hard. Alexia has improv training, and I'm a good yes-man. As proved by how I'm saying *yes* to this trip and all the restorative energy it's going to bring me.

I cling to this surefire hope at baggage claim where the carousel goes around and around with a plethora of over-stuffed bags on it. Strangely, I don't see the navy blue bag with the sparkly Holden James luggage tag on it, though, no matter how hard I look. No matter how much time passes. No matter how impatient I grow.

Turning to the woman in the neon visor next to me, I ask, "Is this the baggage claim for the flight from Newark?"

"Sure is, dearie," she says. "Lloyd! Lloyd! That's it. That's my bag. Grab it for me, will you?" The portly man in the floral shirt beside her struggles to haul the bag over the lip of the conveyor belt. It lands on its wheels with a groan.

"Forget what your luggage looks like, son?" the man asks with a huff, still waiting for his own suitcase to come around.

"No, I just don't see it." I'm not a frequent flier—not a fre-quent traveler, period—so I don't know how long this usually takes but the man begins growing visibly frustrated beside me as the minutes tick by, which makes my stomach sink.

"Not seeing mine now either," he says, folding his arms, tone suggesting that I somehow had something to do with the delay. As if I pulled the luggage from the plane's un-dercarriage as a fun prank—masterminded an unfortunate meet-cute between me and this married middle-aged man.

"Oh, Lloyd," the woman says, patting his arm. The ges-ture is so sweetly reassuring that I have to look away. It's been a minute since I've experienced physical comfort like that. It's a craving you can't quit—like chocolate even after you find out you're lactose intolerant. "It takes them a while to unload all the bags from the plane. This isn't like Aruba again. Losing your luggage is a fluke. It happens once in a lifetime."

Forty-five minutes later, I realize I'm having my once-in-a-lifetime moment, today of all days. With Lloyd and his wife long gone, I stand there, alone, sneering at the empty carousel before trudging over to the long line at the customer support counter to fill out a missing luggage form.

As I inch ever closer to the counter, to keep my cool, I list out all the positives about this trip that I can think of:

I get a break from the store. After college graduation, I sent my résumé to anyone who would have it, hoping and praying my communications degree would turn into something fruitful overnight. When the only interview I got was for Gwendolyn's Lululemon knockoff boutique, I had no choice but to take the $15 an hour position. Then, two days into the job, when Gwendolyn asked, "Holden, you *do* have a fitness regimen, right? I can't have nonfit people working at Fab Fitness Flair. It's bad for the brand." For a split second I debated a class action lawsuit, then I signed up to get certified in Cardio Dance Fit.

Oh, there's that, too.

I get a break from Cardio Dance Fit classes. It's not Zumba. No. Zumba is for advanced dancers who can afford their steep registration prices and boot camps. I teach Cardio Dance Fit. It's Zumba's homely half sister. Instead of hip movements with a Latin flair to contemporary songs, we do step touches and grapevines to songs that are just current enough that you recognize them, but just irrelevant enough that you have absolutely no idea who sings them.

I get to make good on my promise to Mom. Madcap Market was the show we shared for over seventeen years. Laughing and pointing and snacking on break-and-bake Pillsbury chocolate chip cookies. We'd strategize like we had an audition coming up, even though I wasn't old enough to compete yet.

Then, when she was sick and the outcome looked grim, we'd watch episodes I saved to my iPad while she received chemo, and I promised that one day I'd win *Madcap Market* for the both of us. That always made her smile.

Even remembering that now sends a jolt of longing through me. I wish she were here right now. She'd make a game out of us waiting in this lengthy line. She'd force me to laugh by doing a silly voice.

I stuff those memories into my backpack beneath clean underwear and toiletries. No sense dredging that up. Positive outlook. Shoving down sadness. All is okay. Los Angeles will help me forget.

I notice the strong-jawed, blond-haired man standing behind the airline's desk, waiting expectantly for me to speak. I hadn't realized it was my turn, and his handsomeness startles me a moment. It's been a while since I've been anywhere besides work, so I'm surprised when my dust-collecting libido clicks on for the first time in quite a while.

"Lost baggage?" he asks in a bored monotone when I've clearly taken too long for his liking.

"Yes, I—"

He doesn't let me finish before he asks for my ID and baggage claim tag and then assaults me with paperwork and a promise that the bag will be delivered to my hotel once it arrives. I want to ask clarifying questions—maybe even ask for his number if I could be so bold—but I'm staring at a multipage document, being handed a pen, and being grunted at by annoyed people behind me, so I smile, say thank you, and step aside to get this over with.

A short time later, the blinding sun spotlights the pickup area at LAX, which is colored Nickelodeon slime-green— from the sidewalk paint to the square umbrellas. Even the overcrowded trolley I need to take to Terminal 1 to grab a Lyft is a giant rolling booger.

The AC must be broken on this one because it's ungodly hot. There are very few seats which are already taken, so I end up standing, holding the handrail for dear life. The driver is acting like he's Sandra Bullock from *Speed*, making me nauseated.

So nauseated, in fact, that by the time I make it to the Toyota Camry I pre-booked to take me to the hotel, the driver takes one look at me and says, "No throw up in my car. No ride." And proceeds to cancel on me, which is how I find myself in the back of an ancient cab, stuck in traffic, hanging my head out the window like a dog, pleading with my stomach to cooperate, due to the oppressive heat and overwhelming smell of leftover fast food lingering in here.

This is decidedly not the glitz and glam I was hoping for.

"First time in LA?" the cabbie asks over the sound of Beyoncé on the radio and horns honking around us.

"Yeah," I say.

"Traveling alone and no suitcase?" he asks, suspicious eyebrow raised, which I spot in the reflection of his rearview mirror. "You in witness protection?"

"No."

"You a spy?"

"No."

"Running from the law?"

"No," I bark, growing frustrated by this incessant and ridiculous line of questioning. This day is already proving awful, and my patience is cracking like an eggshell.

"Jeez," he says with an offended *pff*. "Just trying to make conversation."

And I swear he hits every pothole on the rest of the drive just to spite me.

Let's do tapas tonight! Pick the place and send me the deetz, Alexia texts me as I'm riding in an elevator with an overly chatty man in a polo who doesn't seem to notice I've stopped listening to his rant about the ice machine being out of order. My brain is like the ice machine—unable to do its basic functions at present.

I reread Alexia's text to fully understand. Tapas was not in my budget for this trip, but I figure if she is my ticket to a one-hundred-thousand-dollar cash prize and televised revenge against my ex on *Madcap Market*, then I can spare fifteen bucks on teeny-tiny empanadas. The investment will be recouped.

Refreshing my phone, I switch apps to see if there are

any open reservations for two at some of the top Google hits, but sadly, everything looks booked. While the elevator groans upward, I check my other notifications. There's still no word from the airline on the status of my suitcase, and my mood has soured even more, which I didn't believe to be possible.

I want to take a shower as soon as I stumble into the hotel room, needing to wash off the stench of travel, but I reconsider when I see what awaits me.

The room is decrepit and smells faintly of mothballs, and the shower is clean—you can smell the bleach—but, against all logic, still appears grimy. I didn't notice the hotel's star rating when I booked it. I was roped in by the cheap price tag.

Even the lobby has a *Tower of Terror* vibe, overused and disused at the same time. I try not to think about it as I take the elevator back down to it and cross to the concierge desk.

Behind it stands a man with thick jet-black hair that's slicked back to look professional. His skin is pale with darker hues around his eyes. His nose is slender across the bridge, but widens at the bottom like a hand bell. There's a delicate handsomeness to him that all but disappears when he crinkles up his face at the computer monitor.

"Die!" he whisper-shouts.

"Excuse me?" I ask.

The man's eyes flick up. "Oh, no. Not you. The zombie."

The computer screen reflects in the shiny black walls behind him. In the reflection, I notice he's playing *Minecraft*. The boxy people and landscapes sprawl across his monitor.

He fiddles with his mouse, changing the perspective. It's trippy from my vantage point.

"Got it," I huff. "Anyway, I was hoping you could help me. I'm getting tapas tonight with an old friend, Google was no help, and I need a recommendation—"

"Fuck. Not a spider!"

"Where?" I jump away from his cart. Arachnophobia runs in my family. Anything with eight legs can't be trusted.

The man—Leo as per the engraving on his scratched-up nameplate—laughs. "It's on the screen." In the reflection again, I see he's shooting a spider and it's hissing and turning red. He clicks his mouse, pausing the game. "What can I do for you?"

I regain my bearings, the tired frustration from earlier rearing its ugly head once more. "Tapas restaurant recommendation for tonight, please." I know my tone is clipped, but this day has been pressing on me, testing my patience. He lackadaisically shows me a laminated list in a falling-apart binder, and I pick the one that has the coolest name because I think it will impress Alexia who is notoriously hard to please.

"You want to spend a lot of money on little plates of food?" He judges me from beneath exceptionally long eyelashes. "Sushi? Seafood? Caviar? I'd understand. But tapas? That's just a fancy way of saying 'eat before you get here.'"

"Don't you get some sort of kickback for booking reservations at fancy restaurants? I feel like you're being bad at your job right now," I crow.

"Touché." He raises one well-sculpted eyebrow before

crinkling his face again when he looks back at the computer screen. "It's all booked. For weeks. Do not pass GO. Do not collect $200."

"Is that a Monopoly reference?"

He smirks. "You like games?"

"Yes, as a matter of fact, I do like games. I like board games and game shows, though, not whatever game you're playing right now. Why would you recommend a restaurant that doesn't have any available reservations?" If I was annoyed before, I'm downright vexed now.

Everything is riding on this dinner, and I won't have a repeat of what happened in Manhattan. I won't let Buckley's dismissal rain on my promise to Mom.

"Because, don't you know I get a kickback from booking reservations at fancy restaurants?" He's still smirking. It's like he can't move the musculature anymore. He's forever stuck looking smug and sexy.

His sexiness is a sudden surprise. Though, it's not unfounded. He's got pouty lips, bedroom eyes, and nice, veiny forearms emerging from the rolled-up sleeves of his white shirt, which should be against dress code and the law, maybe?

My libido, which revved up after a long period of disuse at the airport, is purring at full throttle now. This man is eye candy—sickeningly sweet to look at. The urge to taste him overcomes me.

Shocked at myself, I hush the horny drone inside my head.

"Are you serious right now? I thought concierges had special priority when it came to booking reservations." Somehow, frustration is the emotion nearest to horny, and I can't stop it from coming out in droves.

"Chill," he says, the smirk growing wider, defying the foundation of the ends of his face. "I'm fucking with you. I know the hostess. She owes me a favor. I'll give her a call. They always have one table set aside in case somebody famous shows up. So, unless Rihanna is in town, I think you're good."

He holds up his right pointer finger as he grabs the phone with its curly black cord. When the person on the other end of the line picks up, he begins speaking in what sounds like Korean. I take my iPhone out of my pocket.

Still no word about my luggage.

That means I probably won't have it today.

I shouldn't dip into my trip money for clothes, but I can't show up to meet Alexia in my *athleisure*. That's not the kind of outfit you wear to woo someone. Once I'm done here, I'll grab my wallet and run out to a nearby store to pick up something nice and inviting. I'm sure there's a fast-fashion store somewhere close that I can pop into quickly.

I glance up and Leo is still on the phone, still speaking in hushed Korean. His eyes flick back down to his desk when he notices me looking. Was he staring at me? The idea of it makes me a little hot under the collar of my quarter-mesh wrap.

"Bad news," Leo says when I slide my phone away from googling nearby H&Ms. "Rihanna's in town."

"You've got to be kidding m—" I pause, inspecting his face closer. "You're fucking with me again, aren't you?"

He nods with so much arrogant pleasure. "Table for two tonight."

"Do you do this to all the guests?" I ask. Though, after I say it, I look around and it's not like this place is crawling with clientele.

"Get them highly coveted reservations at hip eateries?"

"Play games with them," I correct. After spending the entire night alone on a red-eye—the empty middle seat mocking me the whole way—all I want to do is lie down and then go beg my friend to be on national TV with me. A tension headache begins to form around my temples.

"I've got to pass the time somehow," he says. "But if you're unhappy with my service, you're welcome to file a formal complaint with the hotel manager. Just so you know, though, I don't actually work here."

"Wait, what? You just go around pretending to be a concierge?" This situation keeps getting weirder.

He laughs. It's unexpectedly breathy and light. "No, I'm a concierge. That's my job. But, I'm a floater. My company rents out space in the lobbies of hotels all over the country. Sometimes, I'm here. Sometimes, I'm not. If you file a complaint here, it'll never make it back to my supervisor."

"And why's that?"

"Because he's vacationing with his family in Amsterdam as we speak. He won't have a second to set down his *stroop-wafel* and check his work phone, and by the time he gets back, the complaint email will be long buried in a series of Out of Office autoreplies." It's as if he takes some perverted satisfaction out of gaming the system. "And even if he did read it, I wouldn't get in trouble because there's two other biracial men around my age who work for Traveltineraries, and the supervisor mixes us up all the time. Even if I've worked for him the longest."

I stammer for a second. "That's...troubling. Well, then, fine. I'll share my feedback to your face." I'm on the verge of a sleep-deprived breakdown. A post-breakup breakdown.

A missing Mom and being alone in an unfamiliar city breakdown. "All I wanted to do was book a nice place for my friend and me so I can convince her to audition for a prime-time TV game show with me, prove to my ex that I'm not ridiculous, and be able to pay off my student loans. On top of that, the airline lost my luggage and my room smells like farts, so please, *please*, just give me the time of the reservation so I can go."

He stares at me, blinking rapid-fire. It's like he's short-circuiting. But then, he clicks a pen, writes languidly on a piece of hotel stationery, and presses it down into my waiting hand. An olive branch.

"Finally," I huff before I start crying from exhaustion. Maybe he wasn't so bad after all. His job seems tough, this place seems awful, and maybe I was being snippy first. *Maybe.* I turn on my heel to go.

"Aren't you forgetting something?" he calls after me.

My brow furrows as I wipe away the tears. "What?"

"A thank-you?" His sexy, alluring, infuriating smirk materializes once more.

"Why would you thank m—" Oh. Now I feel like a major ass. I gulp back my pride. "*Thank you*," I say, head dipped in apology. I pivot once more and beeline toward the elevator bay, upset fizzling out in every step.

I won't let my feelings get the best of me.

I adopt a new mantra: "Nothing else will go wrong on this trip." I whisper it to myself repeatedly until I believe it. Mostly.

Three

Alexia is two glasses of wine late.

I'd be able to calculate that better if I had carbed up on the charcuterie board in front of me before downing my first glass, propping up my nerves on heaven in a bottle, but I'm jet-lagged and didn't have the foresight. I'm wine tipsy and still sitting alone.

As the minutes turn to a half hour or more, I start receiving pitying looks from my fellow diners out on the patio at this lush Spanish establishment where the outdoor seating spills into the street but is tastefully cut off from the traffic by tall plants. There are white flowers in a small vase on the table beside a lit candle, and I spend a while trying to decipher the type of flower it is—carnation? Chrysanthemum?

Just as I'm about to google it, I'm overwhelmed by a blur of movement in my periphery.

"Sorry, sorry!" comes a familiar voice.

When I turn, I spy Alexia snaking her way through the

crowded tables trying not to hit anyone with a duffel bag. She's got reddish-brown hair pulled back by a large clip, and she wears a scoop-necked red shirt and a pair of black leggings. *Athleisure.*

You've got to be kidding me.

Alexia drops into the chair across from me, forehead dewy, and I can't believe I spent major money on dressy trousers and a button-up when I could've worn my Fab Fitness Flair ensemble.

"Long time, no see! Sorry I'm late," Alexia says. "I had to get a workout in because I have an audition in the morning, and I knew the gym would be closed by the time we finished, but then I lost track of time chatting with this new, really cute personal trainer named Stu—I know, Stu is kind of any icky name, but he was hot, I promise—and I haven't seen a new hot guy since I boarded the cruise six months ago, so yeah, but I'm here and you look cute and I'm hungry." It all comes out in a single breath before she helps herself to a heap of cheese.

"Wine?" I ask, holding out the bottle of red that I've been downing. It's shaking in my tipsy grip. *Keep it together, Holden,* I think.

She declines. "No, I don't want wine-face at my audition tomorrow."

I should probably ask what wine-face is, but I go for the easier question instead. "What's the audition for?"

"Some app-based trivia thing? I don't know. My agent is sending me everything possible right now." She fills her wineglass with water and gulps it down. "The cruise was a good experience, but now casting directors have completely forgotten about me. I'm just desperate to book something ASAP so I don't get dropped."

"Anything?" I ask, sensing my segue while pushing away my wine, which I need to be cautious with. I've still got my bearings right now, but if my bloodstream becomes entirely merlot, I might lose them.

She nods with her mouth full, hand politely covering her puffed-out lips. "I would take any credit for my résumé and any paycheck I could get at this point. Los Angeles is a dog-eat-dog world and, yeah, I saved a bunch while on the cruise ship but living here—living here *right*, I mean—is expensive."

I know by *right* she means stylishly, leading the life people go nuts over on IG. It's nothing like where I'm at right now: heartbroken, trying my best, and looking for a financial lifeline. "What if I said I had an opportunity that could net you fifty thousand dollars?" Her eyebrows fly up. "Well, a bit less after taxes and everything, but yeah. It would come with a TV spot."

"Tell me more," she says, leaning in. Her hair nearly catches the flame from the candle between us. I scoot it out of the way. My luck she'd leave our tapas date singed to the root.

I fiddle with the bottle on my right. "Would you consider auditioning for *Madcap Market* with me?"

My question lands like a paperweight dropped from an impossible height. Her face contorts into an unnatural grimace. "Is that the show where people run around like children trying to grab coupons and stuff?"

"It's a lot more than that," I say, possibly losing her interest and maybe slurring a bit but I can't tell. I grab at a piece of bread in the hopes I can reverse the buzz. "There's a trivia element and we get to design our own team sweatshirts."

"Not only do you want me to do cardio on TV, but you want me to wear a polyester blend? I get hot too easily. Hard pass," she says.

"It's light cardio at best!"

Alexia shakes her head again, more seriously this time.

"But it's one hundred thousand dollars!"

"For sixty minutes of on-screen humiliation!" Her voice is a little too loud for my liking. I'm having flashbacks to my breakup with Buckley. I've spent four weeks trying to block out those all-encompassing feelings of dread. Four weeks crashing in Dad's guest room, trying to plot out my life without routine or order.

A one-hundred-thousand-dollar cash prize could help me get out of debt and start a new, single life. Aside from miraculously winning the lottery, this is the only solid thought I've had in ages for how to pull myself out of this dank, dark hole of despair without a rope.

"Look, it's not just that," she says before blotting her lips with her napkin and setting it on the table, which seems like a bad sign. "If I audition for a TV show with *you*, what will…what will Buckley think?"

His name is a bullet that lodges itself inside the weakest chamber of my heart. "Nothing," I choke out. "He didn't want to do it. He didn't want to be with me. Why should he care?" The sharp pang of missing him even if he's blocked me on all social media and sent me packing strikes my stomach.

She cringes, but it doesn't read like sympathy. "As a friend to you both," she says, not entirely sounding like she means the *both* part, which causes my whole body to tense. "I can't pick sides. Doing this with you would be like kicking Buckley in the balls and laughing in his face. Completely unfair."

But isn't that what Buckley did to me? Leaving me all by myself in that restaurant was a brutal blow I haven't completely recovered from. Perhaps I should've known college sweetheartdom was an unsustainable sugar rush.

"I get it," I say, resolved because I tried to fight the inevitable in Manhattan, and it blew up in my face, and sad because what she's trying to say in as little words as possible is that she was Buckley's friend first. Her allegiances are with him. No matter how convincing and rehearsed my argument may be, she's not going to switch sides all of a sudden. In the breakup battle, Buckley won her.

It's time to face the facts: I'm a loser. I lost Mom, I lost Buckley, I've lost Alexia, and now, by default, I've lost *Madcap Market* by not even getting to audition. Failure sits on my shoulders and announces itself to all the other diners in our vicinity.

"Thanks for understanding. I'm glad we did this," she says with a slightly condescending lilt, placing her hand on top of my balled fist on the table. I shrink further into myself. "Now, let's get the bill. I'm beat."

I've massacred the minibar.

Empty tiny bottles are spilled all over the floor. They tell you not to mix your medicines but I'm self-medicating with vodka, rum, and scotch tonight, mixing and matching at will, and nobody is going to stop me!

I'm sitting propped up against the bed on the gross, scratchy carpet that probably hasn't been steam cleaned in centuries. The muted TV is set to the Game Show Network. Not that I'm fully watching a rerun of *Baggage*, a dating show where three potential suitors open suitcases containing their emotional secrets, but it would feel apt if I were, wouldn't it? Isn't that why Buckley left me and Alexia turned me down? Too much baggage?

There is a basket of snacks on the work desk with a price guide stuck in a stand in front of it. I peer at the list, which is frustrating since I'm tipsy and the letters are blurry. What I can see is outrageous. $5.00 for a snack pack of Goldfish. What, are they plated in actual gold?

I bite the bullet and use my teeth to rip open the pack. The cheesy crackers spill out all over my stomach. I snatch them up before they hit the ground like a ravenous dog. This is what it's come to: me, alone, drunk, on the floor, eating an entire pack of children's crackers.

"All Too Well (Ten Minute Version) (Taylor's Version)" by Taylor Swift starts back in on its loop. I've lost count, though I'd say this is the fifth time it's played tonight. It's the perfect soul-crushing soundtrack for a romantic breakup and a friend breakup in the matter of a month.

Alexia didn't say as much when she left me outside the tapas restaurant, but there was finality in the air when she hugged me. Without Buckley in common, she wordlessly said, we are better off as strangers. At least that's how it felt. Especially when I suggested we get together once more before I fly home since I'm touring the town solo and she said, "I'll text you."

I know that text is never coming just like I know Buckley isn't coming back and Mom is gone and *Madcap Market* is completely out of the question. All my best-laid plans drowned with tiny bottles. What joy.

Around midnight, the phone on the bedside table rings. Its trill is jarring. I fumble to pull it from its cradle. "Hello?" I groan.

"Sir, we've gotten several noise complaints about your room. We're going to need you to stop blasting sad bops on a loop. It's disturbing the other guests," the oddly familiar voice says from the other side.

"Sorry my sorrow is so *disturbing*."

"Great song choice, though," the man says. "Guessing the tapas didn't pan out?"

"Leo?" I place the voice even in my dazed state. "Why are you calling me? You said yourself you don't even work for this hotel." I take the handset off the table, cradling it like it's a baby, propping the phone between my ear and my shoulder.

"I was just about to leave when the receptionist asked me to do her a solid and call the sobbing sad boy in 412. I had a feeling it was you." I hate how validated he sounds for having perceived my inevitable upset. Should I have seen it coming, too? Should I have seen Mom's death, my and Buckley's breakup? Is everyone else clairvoyant but me?

"Were you all placing bets or something?" A coating of dust flies up off the handset making me sneeze. Leo blesses me. At first, I think it's a kindness, considering the way I'm feeling, but then I realize that's what normal humans say to other humans when they sneeze.

I'm a goddamn mess.

"Whether I won twenty bucks or not is not the problem. The problem is that you're blasting music and other guests are trying to sleep. It's late. You sound drunk. You should do the same." His voice has mollified. If I listen hard enough, I might even hear care in the pauses between words.

Fighting the whole way, I climb up on the bed, flop onto my back, and stare at the gross popcorn ceiling. I swear a fleck of it falls into my partially open mouth. I spit it out before saying, "Can't you just give all the other guests complimentary earplugs? I'm unraveling. Let me have this." I know it would be easy enough to slip on headphones. I don't want to. If I'm miserable, everyone else should be, too. "Plus," I glance over to the desk, "I'm out of good snacks and alcohol."

When he doesn't say anything right away, I fear he might've hung up on me. This is the first human interaction I've had since jogging through the lobby hours ago. It's semi-soothing, feeling like I'm not completely alone.

"I can help you out with one of those things," he says finally. "There's a 24-hour pizza joint nearby. If I bring you a pie, will you pipe down?"

"Do they have sausage? Oh, and roasted red peppers? If they have sausage and roasted red peppers, then yes, I'll pipe down." I know I'm being demanding, but my shattered heart is piercing me from the inside out. Besides, Leo fucked around with me earlier. Now, it's my turn.

"I'll see what I can do," he says. The line goes dead. My hand goes limp. The phone flops out of my grip, and the off-the-hook beep blares in a steady monotone against Taylor's croons. I turn off the song and lie there in silence, buzzing, hoping he comes through.

When I find the strength to open the door twenty minutes later, Leo stands in the hall holding two boxes. His smile falters when he sees my disheveled state—shirt half unbuttoned, hair sticking up at all angles, Goldfish dust crusted under my fingernails.

Truth be told, he's not looking any better. His untucked shirt goes down past the edges of his thighs, making him look like a child playing dress-up in his dad's work clothes. I hadn't noticed how cartoonishly large it was on him earlier today, probably because I was too busy staring at his forearms and being frustrated.

"What's that?" I point my chin toward the second box. "Can I eat that, too?"

"It's Monopoly, so no, please don't eat anything in here. It says not to right on the box. The pieces are choking hazards. Of course, that warning is for *children*." The hot pizza box gets thrust in my hands as he pushes his way inside. He peers around like he's never been in one of the rooms before, which I guess could be the case considering he bounces between stations.

I shut the door. "Why did you bring Monopoly?"

"You said you liked games." He raises an eyebrow at me as if this should've been obvious. "Figured you could use something to take your mind off whatever happened." I set the pizza down on the bed, while he opens his box and unfolds the game board on the dinky table with not one but two wobbly legs.

I'm half-heartedly touched by this gesture, though I'm afraid I'm in no state to play a game, especially not one where I have to make smart decisions and be careful with my money. That's paper, play stuff. My real money was all tied up in this trip, which is imploding more every second.

In a saintly act, Leo lets me be the Scottish terrier. After a period of deep decision, he decides on the battleship. I'm tasked with setting the tokens on GO. It takes three tries, but I finally get it right. As Leo counts out our personal banks, he asks, "So, 'All Too Well,' huh? It was that bad?"

"Let's just play," I sigh and roll the dice.

Four

An hour later, I'm in jail, desperately attempting to roll doubles so I don't have to pay bail. I'm low on funds (the irony) after collecting three properties and placing houses on them. Wishful thinking only gets me so far.

"Pay up," Leo says with a wicked smirk, gesturing to the pot in the center of the board. Begrudgingly, I slap down my $50 and roll again. "Do you want to talk about it?"

"Do I want to talk about the fact that I flew all the way out to LA because I booked a nonrefundable trip for me and my now-ex, and then I feebly convinced myself our old friend might be willing to compete on a TV game show with me?" I ask stiffly. "No, sorry. Not looking to play a round of 20 Questions over my many miscalculations."

"Woof. That's—Wow." His concentration face becomes more compassionate. Maybe it's a trick of the light, but I swear he's experiencing empathy, especially by the way his pupils dilate as they land on mine.

There's genuine connection here, as tangible as the plastic pieces in front of me. It's so unlike all the disengaged conversations I had with Buckley before the breakup and all the frustrating interactions I have with customers at Fab Fitness Flair who routinely treat me like their personal assistants.

Leo is seeing me. Granted, he's seeing me at my worst, but that's not what matters right now. What matters is that Leo doesn't have to be doing this. Any of this. And yet he is. Whether it's out of pity or kindness, who cares? His presence is more than appreciated. I obviously misjudged him.

Leo forces me to drink more water. I'm two glasses in and my bladder is near bursting, but I don't want to get up. I'm afraid if I do, I'll miss something. If I disappear for a second, Leo will be gone by the time I get back. Loneliness is a monster lurking under the bed, and Leo is the light here to scare it away.

Gradually, I realize that since we began playing, I stopped stewing. I don't have the urge to cry or blast breakup anthems. The foremost thought in my mind is beating Leo—smugly sexy Leo whose forearms are not-so-secret weapons which I think he realizes judging by the way he rolls up his sleeves a little more each time I land on a property he wants. Is it flirtation or a tactic? I can't tell, but the distractions of this game and his strong-looking, flexed hands are welcome.

I wonder, only momentarily, what those hands might feel like bracketing my waist.

"You really came all the way out here to audition for a game show when you didn't even have a partner?" He fin-

ishes off the burnt crust on his last slice of pizza, crumbs
tagging themselves to the edge of his pale pink lips.

"What can I say? I'm an optimist." I shoot him with my
best half-hearted sneer.

"I can tell."

"I guess I was hoping people would surprise me," I say,
resigned.

Leo lands on one of my properties and curses under his
breath. "In my experience, surprises aren't all they're cracked
up to be."

It's clear he's speaking from experience. I'd ask clarifying
questions, but it doesn't seem like he's open to exploring the
topic further by the way his features pinch and his eyes dip
back down to the board. He nudges the dice toward me.

I wonder, once again, about those fingers. Long, boney,
soft-looking. How would they feel tracing down my jaw?

"What were you doing here so late anyway?" I ask, pushing off my attraction to him. "A faux concierge seems like
they'd be off much earlier than midnight."

"I got off at 7:00 p.m., but my mom works as a housekeeper here, and she's got the overnight shift today. I like to
stick around until she gets her room assignment for the night.
Get her settled with her suitcase and everything. Then, I
grabbed a late dinner and drinks at the adjoining bar. By
the time I was closing out my tab, Annabelle, the woman
on the desk tonight, asked me to call you." The stuff about
his mom is lovely. It punctures my sternum and injects me
with just enough grief that I have to get up.

Four weeks ago, Buckley told me that my grief was one

of the reasons he was leaving me. That it was unhealthy after all this time, but what he failed to see was that Mom's absence reverberates through every one of my decisions. I'm reminded of it every time I make a student loan payment or talk to Dad or watch my favorite show. It's horrible when someone is both everywhere and nowhere all at once, and there's nothing you can do about it.

I scrub my face with the back of my wrist. "That's really sweet. Most guys would be embarrassed to be working the same place as their mom."

"Yeah, well. I'm not most guys," he says. And I believe him because he's here playing a game with me and eating pizza and not making me feel bad for how awful I look right now. Most guys would've run for the hills as soon as I opened the door. He came inside with a mission: to make me feel better, maybe? "Plus, my mom sacrificed a lot for me. Being a single parent and all."

"For the last six years, I've only had my dad," I say, a second sudden ripple of connection running through the room. My throat becomes a trash compactor filled with unspoken words. I can't tell him about Mom. I can't get that vulnerable with this sexy stranger. I don't even know his last name.

The sound of rustling paper signals he's paying me rent even though I haven't asked for it and have almost entirely lost track of the game. My heart keeps hiccuping. I pop a TUMS to stop the acid reflux from commandeering my night. Despite my ugly countenance, Leo doesn't seem fazed by my obvious undoing.

He offers me a lukewarm smile. "Should we count out our banks and call it a night?" he asks, voice slightly wavering.

The chalky medication makes me cough before I can say, "No need. You win."

In a strange display of...*something*, he does a victory dance. His hands are on his knees, swiveling in and out to the funky electronic theme music to a late-night airing of *Whammy! Press Your Luck* on the Game Show Network. "I never win things!" Goofiness glides across his face.

He's got moves. He'd far surpass even my best student in Cardio Dance Fit classes. "What about *Minecraft*? Seemed like you were doing pretty well at that this afternoon." I remember how coldly I treated him. "Sorry about my attitude when we met. It was wrong of me to speak to you like that."

"Thanks, but that's customer service for you. I've dealt with worse," he says, waving it away. I can't tell if he's unfazed or he doesn't want to think about it. "But there's no winning in *Minecraft*."

"What's the point of the game, then?" My love of old game shows stems from the adrenaline of rooting for my favorite team. It's stimulating yet comforting to experience a high-stakes, no-thought competition from the comfort of my couch or my bed. A way to unplug from the world and then devolve into a ball of catharsis when someone's life changes by winning a massive jackpot or a new car or a lavish vacation.

It was escapism. Escape from questioning my sexuality, Mom's diagnosis, the world at large.

"There is no point to *Minecraft*. That's the point."

"So, you just roam around shooting things?" Sounds maddening to me, but I don't say that because he clearly enjoys it, and after Buckley's mean words, I never want to judge someone else for their interests.

"Pretty much. It's like virtual LEGOs. It's an open world where you build things and adventure and survive. It's about imagination and creativity and free thought." He cocks an eyebrow at me. "You've never played before?"

"I wasn't much for computer games," I say. "Never did *The Sims* or anything like that."

His hand flies to his heart. "You mean you never made the two boy Sims kiss for...research?"

"Uh, no?" My cheeks flush. I pop a second TUMS just to be safe, and to stop myself from choking with excitement on his words. He's confirmed he's some form of queer, which charts a couple new directions this night could go. Maybe, by the end of the night, those hands I've been admiring will be all over me.

Leo must notice my shifting, wistful expression. "Can I say something?" he asks as he sorts the game pieces into their proper, plastic slots.

"Sure."

He slides the lid back on the box. "Someone else's shitty decision doesn't reflect back on you. You know that, right?"

My eyes fall from his eyes to his bare feet. How is he okay being barefoot on this disgusting carpet? I can't even think about the kind of fungus he must be picking up without the acid reflux returning. Defensively: "I don't even know what you're saying." Because him being here and sexy and *thoughtful* is so much to process. One good quality too far for my addled brain.

"I'm saying your ex is an idiot." His toes wiggle for the sole purpose of making me smile. It works. "You're not broken just because you were broken up with, Holden James."

My full name presses me to the wall. What I wouldn't give for a little physical comfort right now, arms and hands and warmth and breath ghosting across my cheek. Why am I so inconveniently horny?

"How do you know my last name?" I ask, more confused and aroused than before.

"I booked your reservation, remember?"

Ah. Duh.

He's moving to the door, searching for his socks and shoes. I can't let him go. I just can't.

"Are you here again tomorrow?" I ask, trying not to sound too leading.

"Yeah, I think so."

I perch on the edge of the bed, pretending to be nonchalant, looking at the TV but not absorbing the image of the woman with a blunt bob slamming down on her big red button. *Whammy!* The red monster dances across the screen the way Leo was dancing minutes ago. "What time is your shift?"

"Why? You coming to harass me again?" That patented smirk lifts his cheeks. I want to kiss that smirk right off his mind-bogglingly symmetrical face.

"No, I was..." Rethinking everything, I change my mind. I can't ask a stranger to spend the night with me in this hotel. Again, I don't even know his last name. He might not be interested. On top of everything else, I don't need to be saddled with further disappointment. "Forget it. Get home safe."

He's deciding what to do with the pizza box when he narrows his eyes into slits. "Oh, save it, what is it? What other demands could I possibly appease for you this evening, sir?"

"Sir?" My brows lift; fresh sparklers lighting off in my pelvis. "Kinky."

He chucks the empty pizza box at me. I'd be worried about grease splatter, but this room is one giant grease splatter as it is. What's a little burnt cheese to round out the mess?

"Stop deflecting."

"Fine. Deflection mode deactivated," I say with a sigh, remembering the loneliness monster under the bed building back my courage. "I was just thinking that if you had an early shift, you could, maybe, possibly, I don't know, stay."

I think about all I wanted to accomplish with this trip. No closure. No *Madcap Market*. I could, at the very least, sleep with someone new. And Leo's here and he's handsome. He brought pizza and he played a board game with me, and he's kind. What's sexier than kindness?

"Stay." He says it like a song lyric he's misheard for years. "Stay here? With you?"

"See? This is why I said forget it." I build my metaphorical wall back up to ward off rejection. I have had enough to last a lifetime this past month. "Forget it now. Forget I said anything. Go home. Leave me to wallow in peace."

Like he's reading my mind, he challenges jokingly, almost seductively, "If I leave, are you going to start blasting Taylor Swift again?"

"Ding, ding, ding!" I flush with a light, flirty laugh. "But if you're here, if you *stay*, I could… I don't know, show you my gratitude."

Leo's posture changes. "By which you mean…"

"You know, reward you for winning Monopoly." I inch closer to him, dropping my shoulders and broadening my chest to match his stance. Fuck it, I want him. I want to taste him and ride him and smell like him in the morning.

I want him to fuck me so hard that I forget about the last month, the last six years, anything before this second and his dark brown eyes piercing into mine.

"How so?" he asks, standing his ground, making me come to him which turns me on to no end. Sends my nerve endings into a titillated frenzy.

"I could start by giving you a kiss," I suggest, moving so that we're toe-to-toe, nearly chest to chest. It would take little more than a tip to push my body weight into him. Have him catch me and kiss me and take me to bed. Ravish me with the lights on or off. His choice.

His eyes, which have grown darker with desire, drop to my lips with an audible gulp. "That sounds like a good start."

With his permission, I cup the back of his neck and press in, allowing our lips to touch. A shiver races down my spine at the kiss. There's a passion radiating from his end, cutting through the taste of pizza, that shocks me. Buckley hadn't kissed me like that in months.

Leo's hands possess an assurance as they wander across

my back, eradicating any thought of Buckley, anything but this scorching moment.

One button at a time, I fumble with the front of Leo's shirt, desperate to make closer contact. To run my fingers along the ridges of his ribs and watch him react. To nibble on his erect nipple and make him shudder.

But these damn buttons are getting in my damn way. "This," I say breaking the kiss. "Off. Now." I tug at the overly baggy shirt which is doing nothing to highlight the hard, gorgeous physique I can sense beneath it.

"You're awfully demanding for someone who's asked for a favor," he says, nipping at my bottom lip, making me groan with intense pleasure. I use my palm to pull him closer to me as he charts a trail of playful bites down my jaw and my neck, shedding his shirt like I asked.

Through the pleasure, I retort, "You're awfully demanding for someone who's getting a free night in a two-and-a-half-star hotel."

At this, he snaps back. "Who said I was staying?"

I stammer, both from the question and from seeing his naked torso for the first time. He's toned, cut, and smooth. Even in the unflattering light of the bedside lamps, his skin is airbrushed perfection.

What cruel world forces a man who keeps up appearances like this into faux concierging? It's oxymoronic. He belongs on billboards, bus stickers, eye candy on a prestige miniseries.

I want him to destroy me in every way imaginable.

"I repeat, who said I was staying?" His shirt is a pool of

fabric at his feet, and as my eyes scan back up, they land on a prominent bulge presenting in the front of his work slacks, which causes my own groin to ache. How long had it been since I'd done something daring like hookup with a near stranger?

"I thought..." My sentence trails off because I'm finally hearing him, and I worry that we've somehow crossed a boundary. Because he kind of, sort of works here, and maybe fraternizing with the guests is a nonstarter.

"You thought that I was the kind of guy who brought pizza to strangers, played board games with them, and then railed them within an inch of their life?" he asks, and I swear he flexes his abs which...holy mother of God. I'm distracted again.

"Admittedly," I choke out. "Yeah."

"Well, then," he says with an apparently offended snort as he bends down to pick up his shirt.

My chest heaves with embarrassment. "Oh, my God. I'm so so—"

"You'd be right," he says, head snapping up while wearing a shit-eating grin. "I'm fucking with you."

I sigh with a unique mixture of relief, horniness, and annoyance. What is this man doing to me? "Okay, well drop the *with* from that sentence, please."

I go to kiss him again, but he holds out a firm hand. "While I may be that kind of guy, I'm also the kind of guy who only rails men within an inch of their life when they're *sober*."

It's right as he says this that I notice I'm listing a bit to the

left. I had been so caught up in the excitement and the forgetting and the sexiness of it all that I forgot I'd already had
a threesome this evening with Jack Daniel and Jose Cuervo.

"Fair," I say, agreeing that I'm not in my best shape right
now. Disappointed in both myself and the situation, I cross
over to grab the water glass Leo had brought me earlier and
drink from it. There's no shaking this away right now. As
much as I want to.

Which means Leo's not getting his reward tonight, and
he no longer has a reason to stay, so I'll go to bed alone like
I have for the last four weeks, except this time I'll do so in a
grody hotel room in the middle of Los Angeles. Lucky me.

I never should've come, I think, turning so I don't have
to watch him leave.

But then Leo says, "I need the left side of the bed."

I could crumble like a breakfast bar right now.

"You bring an extra toothbrush?" Leo asks as he starts
making himself comfortable. It's possible, but I can't remember. "What kind of traveler are you? Don't you know to always pack a toothbrush in your carry-on *and* your checked
bag just in case?"

I fumble around in my backpack. In the dig, I latch onto
a pack of winter mints, shaking them in the air like I've
found nuggets of gold.

"Ah, candy. The epitome of oral health."

"Just use mine. It's new. It's right from the dentist's goody
bag."

"Your dentist still gives you a goody bag? Does he give
you stickers and a paddleball for being such a good boy, too?"

I know he knows what he's doing by saying that. Goose bumps crop up across my red-hot skin. I'm still yearning to taste him. Every part of him. Several times. I'm sweating again.

"What can I say? I get rewards as good as I give them." Just because he pumped the brakes on tonight doesn't mean this wasn't a teaser for what's to come later in this trip if we're both lucky.

"Oh, yeah?" he asks, standing in the doorway to the bathroom, half his still-shirtless torso beamed with fluorescent light. "Well, then, the kiss was a good start. We can iron out a full repayment plan in the morning."

He winks at me and then his laugh echoes in the bleachy bathroom as he shuts the door.

Five

There's a banana on my back.

Firm, curved, pressed upward into my sacrum like a silly morning surprise. I must've fished it out of the not-so-complimentary snacks last night and discarded it on the bed. Potassium was not what I wanted to quell my tidal wave of emotions after my awful tapas date with Alexia. However, now that I think about it, I don't remember there being any fruit in that basket at all, so unless a banana from the sad-looking continental breakfast spread grew legs and…

Legs. There are a second pair of legs in this bed. They stir and snuggle against the backs of mine. For a fraction of a heartbeat, I'm back in New York and Buckley's behind me. "I'm sorry, H," he'll whisper any second now, morning breath, disgusting but semi-endearing wafting over me. "I'm so, so sorry. You're my home."

Except a sleepy arm drapes over my side, pulls me close. Dry lips smack together next to my ear. When I finally find the nerve to open my eyes, I notice a practically hairless, defined forearm; pronounced veins snake in braided twists up its interior. That's not Buckley's freckled limb. That's the arm of another man entirely.

That's when last night with Leo returns to me, which means, that's not a banana on my back, that's...

Nice.

It's strange to admit, but it is.

Not only is it nice, but it's *exciting.*

Leo's morning wood and warmth and slightly oaky scent all pleasantly combine to stir my own arousal until last night's tension is mounting again, swirling low in my gut, and Buckley's ghost gets banished to another hellish realm.

I hear a sleepy grunt behind me. Leo's waking up—I can sense it. His breathing against my back grows from slow and lax to full and measured. A yawn tickles my ear as his grip around me becomes tighter, tugging my body toward him like I'm a pillow. His strength entices me.

Last night, my overzealous drinking got in the way of any fun, but right now, I can't stop myself from grinding back into his erection, allowing my ass to slope against the gentle curvature of him. I let the electricity jolt through my body and wake me up even more.

Leo grunts again, but this time there's nothing sleepy about it.

He's awake too and that grunt is more of a growl. A hungry, needy growl that starts in the base of his throat and spurs me to grind back harder. My skin grows hotter.

"What a lovely alarm clock," he whispers into my ear as

he matches my pressure. The oppositional rock of our pelvises becomes rhythmic, until the bed springs are squeaking softly beneath us.

"You tried to kabob me in my sleep so…" I joke, but only half-heartedly. I'm too turned on. I'm reaching a hand down the front of my sleep pants and brushing my thumb against my slick tip. My quick laugh morphs into a self-inflicted moan.

He whispers playfully, "I wanted you so badly last night. I guess little Leo couldn't restrain himself."

Hearing those words causes me to glow from the inside out. I roll over to face him, ignoring morning breath and bed head and any other number of insecurities that may hold me back. I've had a shitty run of it this last month, and suddenly this gorgeous man with dark brown eyes is hard for me and fuck if I'm going to let that opportunity run away.

"I'm sober now." There's need laced in my voice. My chest bubbles with anticipation.

His warm right hand wanders down my stomach and stops just above the waistband of my pants. "And hard, too, I bet." His tone is slow and deliberate and delicious.

"Why don't you find out?" I dare, quirking a brow, radiating seduction.

He takes no time plunging his hand below the waistband of my lounge pants. He, too, finds the head of my cock leaking. The pad of his pointer finger swirls across the sensitive skin, making my whole body shudder as he skates across the slit and down the engorged underside.

When I open my eyes, he's holding that very finger up to his mouth. "Any STIs?" he asks.

I shake my head. "Tested just last week. You?"

"Last month, but haven't been with anyone in…" His eyebrows scrunch up like he's doing the math. "A while." Then, he looks right at me as he sucks his finger, licks me off him. Pressure builds beneath my balls as I imagine him doing that but to my dick. The fantasy of him bobbing up and down between my thighs is almost too much for me.

"I find it hard to believe," I say when he stops. "That a hot guy like you hasn't had any in *a while*." Someone like Leo would clean up on the apps back home.

He kisses the tip of my nose, then chuckles and shrugs. "Maybe I'm picky." But his voice betrays the sentiment fully. I can tell there's more to the story than that, however, I'm far too horny to press it, so I press into him instead, inhaling his musk.

I kiss him again and he pulls me on top of him so my knees are straddling his waist. He's already shirtless so I run my palms along the length of him, stopping to trace the divots below his pec muscles with my thumbs. He's chiseled marble made flesh, heat lapping off him and making my erection throb.

Leo raises his arms and knots his fingers behind his head, revealing twin patches of dark hairs. I tilt down and flick my tongue across his right nipple which makes the cocky expression on his face slip, become far less controlled.

I do it again. And again. Until he's writhing underneath me, bucking his hips upward toward my still clothed ass.

I take my tongue on a trip down his abs before hiking my head up. "Is it time for the second installment of the repayment plan?" I ask, mouth watering, heart leaping.

He nods. "Yes, please." He digs his heels into the mattress and lifts his hips, giving me enough leeway to shimmy down and slip his eggplant-purple boxer briefs off his lightly dusted thighs and fling them away.

Leo's penis stands at attention, inches from my mouth. It's a good size with a nice thickness that curves slightly upward toward his belly button, resting in a patch of neat pubic hair. Just the thought of that domed head hitting my prostate…woof.

"What are you waiting for?" he asks, staring down at me with visible anticipation. Taking on a domineering tone I wouldn't have expected from him, but I love instantly.

My tongue finds the taut area of skin between the head and the shaft and performs the flick that made his nipples perk up. He jolts at that. "Teasing you," I say. "You're not the only one who likes fucking with people."

"Oh, yeah?" he asks with a grumble. "I thought you were going to reward me, not mock me." And with that, his large hand finds the back of my head and with gentle force, he guides my lips to the top of his penis where I all too willingly swallow him whole. Not even a struggle, which isn't like me. I must be really relaxed, gag reflex turned off, mind flung into another dimension.

His other hand rakes through my unruly hair as he repeatedly tells me how good my mouth feels. Gradually, he thrusts deep, Magic Mike–ing the hell out of the back of my throat. I start to hum, lightly, a little trick that never ceases to make my partner exhale hard.

"Fuck yes," Leo moans, his head flopped sideways almost hidden in the pillow I slept on. He might even be sniffing it, taking a hit of the scent of me. Hot.

As I pleasure him, I grab myself between my legs, finding a wet stain saturating the fly of my pajama pants. In a Cirque du Soleil–level move, I keep Leo in my mouth as I wiggle my way out of the pants, freeing my erection.

I slip the sheet and duvet off, giving Leo an unrestricted view of my Cardio Dance Fit ass, up in the air, back arched. When he opens his eyes and sees this, his chest hiccups and he bites his knuckle. "Oh, damn. Slow down. I don't want this to be over too soon."

Teasing him still, I don't slow down in the slightest. Instead, I flaunt my ass in the air more while massaging his balls, feeling as they grow tighter and tighter under my confident touch. I'm edging him and I know it.

"Fuck…" he groans. "You!"

At that, I slow and slow, and then slide off all together. "That's sort of where I hoped this was going," I whisper, wiping my mouth with the back of my hand before mimicking his special smirk.

He leans forward quickly, enrapturing me with a kiss and then biting my bottom lip playfully before leaning over to the nightstand where I hope he's looting out a condom. I'm disappointed when he grabs for his phone instead. Whatever he sees on the screen makes his face fall, but his penis doesn't flag for a second.

"Fuck," he says, wiping a hand down his face.

"What is it?" I ask, sitting back on my heels, penis pointing up at the popcorn ceiling. Still slick. Still eager. Still overriding my every thought.

He turns the screen to me. "My shift starts in ten minutes."

My hope falters, but my fingers brush the inside of his thigh feebly. "Can you be late?"

He grabs my hand, stilling my fingers. "I wish, but I'm not financially stable enough to lose this job right now, so as much as it fucking pains me." He looks down at his flexing dick. "I gotta jet."

Even as he stands and starts collecting his clothes from the chair in the corner, I can't help but stroke myself. Just the sight of his toned, firm ass bouncing as he walks turns me on and reminds me how long it's been since I've truly let go.

"Hey," he says, once he's back in his briefs and his pants. "Stop that." It comes out as a command. A stimulating one.

"Why?" I ask, not knowing what to do with my hands when their impulse is to simultaneously touch him and touch myself. "We can accomplish a lot in ten minutes." I imagine unzipping those slacks, pulling his boner back out, and sucking him to completion, leaving him to go to work lighter and focused.

"Because," he says, pressing one knee onto the bed, taking my hand, and pressing it to his still solid bulge. "When I promise to rail someone within an inch of their life, I mean it." His eyes are hooded as they gaze down at me. "I go on lunch at noon. I expect to find you here just like you were before, facing the headboard with your ass in the air. Can you promise me that?"

I shrug innocently. "Depends. Is that your final request as part of the repayment plan?"

He's got his oversize shirt on now. He's retying his orange tie in the reflection of the black TV screen and he meets my gaze, shaking his head. "No, my final request is to watch you unravel."

"Haven't you seen me unraveled enough?" I joke, nodding over to the destroyed minibar and snack basket, thinking back on last night and my messiness.

He turns back to the bed as he puts on his watch. "Holden James, you haven't experienced unraveled until you've had me inside you."

My full name and his dirty poise spills anticipation through my veins. "Noon?" I ask.

"Noon, sharp," he says, toeing on his shoes and tying the laces while I'm still exposed and naked on the bed, watching him. Not wanting him to go but excited to sit with this swelling eagerness, which I know is likely to end in immaculate fireworks.

I flop back on the bed, flushed. "What am I supposed to do until then?"

"Refresh. Eat some breakfast. Grab a drink," he says.

"The minibar is all out of—"

"*Water*," he insists. "A hydrated body is a happy body." Well, he would know. His body looks ecstatic, the rippled emotion I'm sure most of his lovers experience when running their hands along his well-worked lats. I can't wait to tongue those later.

"Fine," I groan. "But what am I supposed to do after that?"

"Miss me," he says, then gives me one last, sumptuous kiss to remember him by.

Six

When I get out of the shower, my phone chimes from the charger on the bedside table.

Madcap Market Audition. Three Days Away.

I sigh, disappointed that that part of my trip has completely fallen apart. I can't go audition for a paired TV game show alone.

At the very least, the forgetting part of my trip is off to a spectacular start thanks to Leo and our late-night/early-morning shenanigans.

Even without an orgasm, Leo's kisses and caresses were more satisfying than most of my sexual encounters combined. Sex with Buckley became rote and after a while, I stopped wanting it. My sex drive dimmed until it was a barely there gas lamp on a cobblestoned street at midnight. Now I stop in front of the mirror in the bedroom and I'm glowing. The full brightness I exude is more than enough to keep me from wallowing in any unwanted emotions.

Smelling fresh and feeling clean, I throw on a pair of ass-hugging pants and a gray T-shirt and call myself a Lyft. If I can't be on *Madcap Market*, I at least want to see Pat Crumsky's star on the Hollywood Walk of Fame. Pat Crumsky is the aging host of *Madcap Market* and has been since the show's premiere. A photo with that star will be a good way to commemorate this trip, my time here, and what could've been.

But I won't mope about that too long because the excitement of Leo's and my lunchtime playdate is still surging through my body. Post-orgasm, those intrusive thoughts might return, but I'll cross that bridge when I get to it.

When I pass through the lobby, a brunette girl is standing at Leo's counter chatting with a middle-aged couple who have a line behind them. The whole lobby is more bustling than I'd expect it to be. It's a Friday, so there must be two concierges on to manage the crowd since Leo is MIA. While I had hoped to flash Leo a flirty parting shot of my ass, I beeline for the rideshare and head out instead so I have enough time to myself.

I'd read enough travel blogs to know that the Walk of Fame is no longer an illustrious symbol of Hollywood glamor. Instead, it's more of an overpriced, dirty set of streets you'd do well not to traverse alone at night, but when the Lyft drops me off outside a burrito shop and I see Pat Crumsky's name emblazoned onto the sidewalk inside a red star with a tiny TV medallion below it, I tear up anyway.

Mr. Crumsky may well be into his seventies now, but his white-haired grace and congenial sense of humor always comforts me. Whenever he steps foot onto my TV screen, I know I can tune in and turn my mind off.

After Mom died, I thought this show might be too painful to continue watching, but instead, every hour spent binging old episodes felt like an hour dedicated to remembering her. Like if I closed my eyes she'd somehow materialize on the other side of the couch with a glass of wine and a too-loud-for-her-small-body laugh.

I snap a picture of the star on my phone before lifting my head up to the blazing Los Angeles sun and let the rays warm my face. For a moment, each of those beams is Mom sending me a message from beyond. A fresh set of tears flows in but I swipe them away.

Coming to, I ask a hostess from the burrito restaurant behind me to take my picture. Happily, she gets me from all angles as I squat next to the star, pointing and smiling, laughing and fighting off a third round of tears.

"I took a few," she says, handing the phone back. I swipe through them, grinning. "You know this dude?" she asks.

"Yeah, he's a famous game show host," I say, trying to sound casual but hearing my voice excitedly pitch without my control.

"Like, on Netflix or something?" she asks, clearly in no hurry to get back to her post.

"No, on cable," I explain. "The show's been on since the eighties."

"Oh, tight," the woman says, throwing her curly brown hair over one shoulder and unwrapping a piece of spearmint gum. "I don't have cable, so wouldn't know a thing.

When I started working here, I always wondered but never bothered looking it up." She shrugs. "You coming in for something to eat?"

I look up at the sign and think: Why not? Something light and small to tide me over until Leo's and my afternoon delight couldn't hurt.

At a table near the window, I order chips, salsa, and a non-alcoholic frozen drink because I'm on vacation—I want to have fun—but I told Leo I'd hydrate in a healthy way. Even if a virgin strawberry margarita in a shapely glass with a tiny umbrella in it probably wasn't what he had in mind, the first sip cools me down and makes me smile. "Thanks," I say to the server who disappears into the back while I type out a text to Dad along with one of the photos the hostess took of me.

Minutes later, my phone lights up with a call.

"Holden," Dad says as soon as I hold the phone up to my ear. "You look so happy in that picture! Made my day. How's LA?"

Dad's always been a chipper optimist. When Mom went into remission while I was in middle school, he was adamant that the dark cloud over our family was gone. And then when she died, he made sure I understood how much of a gift it was that we had her in our lives, even if only for a short while.

"Great, yeah, solid," I say because as soon as Leo showed up at my room last night this whole trip took a complete one-eighty. "The weather is beautiful."

"Looked like it," Dad says. In the background, I can hear the crew at the furniture store he manages unloading a new shipment of sectionals from the grunts and shouts and Dad offering helpful instructions to "pivot!" before returning to our conversation. "Where was I? Oh, yeah. Pat Crumsky. So great you could visit his star!"

"Yeah, even if I can't audition," I say sounding less upset than I would've been yesterday when I was still clinging to the false hope that Alexia would save my plan. Back when I never expected a faux concierge with late-night pizza hookups could save my trip.

"Maybe you can still go to the live taping," Dad offers kindly.

That thought hadn't occurred to me. "Oh, maybe. I should look into that." It could be a nice consolation. Seeing the show tape in person, even if I don't get to be on it, sounds fun. It's not like I had any concrete plans. I thought Alexia might show me around town, I'd do the Warner Bros. Studio back lot tour, and, if I was feeling sporty, I'd hike up to the Hollywood sign.

All of those sounded so solitary, even if I'm making peace with my shifted expectations for this trip, but being an audience member might just be the way to feel like I'm a part of something.

It would be a better use of my time than anxiously pondering what waits for me when I return to New York—still broke, still aimless.

"I'm glad you went, Holden," Dad says. It's quieter where he is now like he's stepped inside his office and shut the door.

"Why?" I ask. "Because I'm out of your hair for a while?" Dad's guest room was the only place I could go after the breakup with Buckley who never came home. I quietly packed up my life the next morning and left.

Dad's place came fully furnished—the kind of unit meant for men like Dad, widowers who don't have an eye for interior design and prefer to leave behind the couches and end tables that remind them too much of the people they loved and lost.

Dad's only qualifications when picking a new place to live after selling our family home were two bedrooms, running water, and a wood shop. He makes his own furniture and knickknacks in his spare time, which is why the twin bed frame was super basic, but the dresser that barely fit was handcrafted from fine wood, finished to perfection.

So, in some ways, for the last four weeks, it felt homey, but it certainly never felt like home.

"Not at all. You know I love having you around," Dad says, and I know he means it. "I just mean you're having an adventure! Getting out of your comfort zone is a good thing." There's a muffled knock somewhere on the other end of the line. "Listen, they need me back out on the floor, but send more pictures, okay? I love you and be safe."

"I love you too, Dad."

As soon as I hang up, I'm graced with a plate of fresh tortilla chips and homemade salsa verde.

Seven

When I return to the hotel with a pep in my step, Leo's still not behind his concierge desk. The brunette from earlier stands where he and I bantered yesterday. She's smiling and waving at me as I pass. Decidedly *not* playing *Minecraft*, which seems smart.

The crowd from earlier has dissipated, clearly all out on their excursions for a fun-filled day in LA—business or pleasure, whatever their purview. My mind is firmly fixated on *pleasure* right now. All the different definitions of that word I plan to play out with Leo on that hotel bed, on sheets I won't have to wash in a city I'll leave soon with nothing but hot and heavy memories.

The dirty imagery fades when I step off the elevator on my floor and hear familiar subdued croons emanating through the wall a few doors down. I'd know that melody anywhere. It's "All Too Well (Ten Minute Version) (Taylor's

Version)." As if I hadn't just been reprimanded for doing this exact thing from my own room last night.

The closer I get, I realize it *is* coming from my room again. I can't swipe my key card fast enough.

Pushing my way inside, I find Leo sprawled out in the spot I resided in on the floor last night, eating a bag of Fritos, eyes closed, head swaying to the music. His orange tie and the top buttons on his shirt are undone, revealing a small stretch of smooth, taut skin.

"Hi?" I call into the room. He startles, opening his eyes. I hold my stance in the hall between the bedroom and the bathroom, perplexed. "You're early." The time on my phone reads eleven twenty. I thought I was going to have a little more time to prepare before he showed up.

"I'm already on lunch," he says, emptying the crumbs from the Fritos bag directly into his open mouth. His body does not look like the kind of body that ingests Fritos, so I grow steadily more concerned by this uncharacteristic display. "I'm on lunch forever now."

I shake my head. "I'm sorry. What?"

He looks me dead in the eyes and says, "I got fired."

My chest contracts. Immediately, I go and sit beside him. "Shit. I'm—I'm sorry. That's awful. What happened?"

"I got my dates wrong, that's what happened," he says, reaching toward the bedside table. I notice he has a whole mountain of vending machine snacks nestled up there, each crinkly bag seconds from toppling over. "I didn't double-check my schedule last night when I said I was working here this morning. Really, I was supposed to be working across town."

"That doesn't sound like the worst offense in the world." I try to be comforting and resist the urge to place a hand on his arm to soothe him. We're still strangers. I'm not sure how he feels about this or what kind of attention he needs right now. My only hint is the song, which I turn down once I find his phone by his foot in the mess of empty wrappers.

He sighs. "It wouldn't be the end of the world if this wasn't a common infraction of mine." He says *infraction* like the kind of person who heard that word a million times in the principal's office while in school; a casual contempt rolls naturally off his tongue.

"I'm—I'm sorry," I say again, at a loss.

"Why are you sorry?" he asks, looking at me as if I hold more answers than I feasibly do.

I shrug. "Because if you weren't here last night..."

He sits up from leaning against the bed and squares off to me, showing weak signs of the assured Leo from last night. "No, that has nothing to do with it. If I had wanted to check, I would've. Yeah, sure, I was—" he gestures to me "— distracted, but the truth is... I hated this job. Actually, I've hated the last four jobs I've had, but apparently being a functioning member of society means holding one which sucks major ass."

"I see," I say, starting to understand.

"By the time I got to the hotel I was supposed to be at, the front desk staff had called to get a replacement and, of course, my boss just happened to come back from his Amsterdam trip early because his kid had a bad ear infection so he was in a foul mood and now I'm canned and in deep shit," he says, mirroring me from last night. "Sorry I crashed your room. I've been telling my roommate for a while now that I'm saving up to get my own place, and I was a couple months away from being able to afford one. Now, I'm going to need to drain my savings to float myself until I can find another job."

Ever since Mom passed, I've been hapless when it comes to emotions, uncertain how to handle other people's feelings when mine were so all-consuming. Right now, though, it only feels right that I be as present for Leo as possible. He saw me at my worst last night and stuck around anyway. It's the least I can do in return.

And I know what it's like to not want to be home. That urge snaked through me when I rolled over the morning after the breakup to find an empty half of the bed. Confrontation can be scary, especially when the venue of that confrontation is the one place in the world you should be allowed to let your guard down.

"Is that why you came here?" I ask, finally. "You don't get along with your roommate?"

He looks stricken. "It's not that I don't get along with my roommate. It's more that it's time that I don't have a roommate at all. I'm twenty-six. If I don't go out on my own now, I'll... I don't know."

"I get it," I say quickly. "I broke up with my boyfriend about a month ago. He was supposed to come on this trip with me. We'd been living together, and when we split, I didn't have the money to swing my own place. I ended up moving in with my dad, which is a whole thing." I don't bring up Mom because I know if I do, I won't be able to stop the flow of words and this isn't about me right now. I'm only trying to relate, so he knows he's not alone.

His eyes widen with intrigue. "I guess I can drop the word *roommate* then."

"Huh?"

"I live with my mom," he says resolutely. "I'm twenty-six years old and my mom is my roommate. There, I've said it."

The sharp pang from last night when Leo mentioned his mom worked at this hotel returns. Despite his interest in moving out, there's a softness to the way he says *my mom*, as if she holds prime real estate inside his heart, while mine inhabits a haunted Victorian mansion overstuffed with history.

I fight off the complicated feelings with a rueful laugh and a deflective joke: "Wow. Look at us. *Thriving.*"

"At least you'd moved out once."

"You haven't? Not even for college?"

He hangs his head. "I didn't go to college."

"Oh, I'm sorry. I'm an asshole. I shouldn't have assumed," I say, mortified.

"It's okay. My mom was a first-generation immigrant who never went to college, so she really wanted me to go at first but I never cared much for school and it's not like we had the money. I convinced her we needed the income more, that I should start working full-time instead. But, I guess, maybe I should've gone. Maybe I wouldn't feel so directionless if I had listened to her." He stares wistfully into the middle distance.

"I think it's cool that you didn't go to college," I say sincerely. "Making the choice to do what feels right for you means you know yourself. Not many people can say that."

"I don't think *knowing myself* is a skill I can boast about in a cover letter."

"Look, I went to college, took out a massive amount of loans, and I still feel directionless. I got a degree in communications and instead of getting a job in my field, I work in an overpriced boutique and teach cardio dance classes to women who are constantly telling me how much I *slay* while wearing shirts that say *Strong Mother Flexor*, so believe me, you're lucky not to be buried under a mountain of student debt, where your only hope to pay it off within the next ten years is competing on a TV game show and winning one hundred thousand dollars."

Those words detangle a traitorous knot that has been plaguing my brain. All those wires have been plugged into the wrong neuroreceptors. What was I thinking, coming all the way out to Los Angeles following a pipe dream?

"Wait." Leo's entire body shakes as if he's just hopped up onto a lakeside dock; I can imagine thoughts like water droplets flying into the air around us. "You win one hundred thousand dollars if you win *Madness Market*?"

"*Madcap Market*," I correct. "But, yeah. If you make it to the finale, you race against the clock to win the grand prize. They bring out a big check and everything." How many nights had I spent imagining the moment when Pat

Crumsky passed off that cartoonish piece of cardboard to me? When I was young, I stood beside Mom, grinning for the cameras. Then, when Mom passed, I substituted Buckley into the preexisting fantasy. Now the whole conceit feels hollowed out like a post-Halloween jack-o'-lantern, rotting and ghoulish.

Leo's brow is crinkled. "That's major bank. I could afford a pretty plush place with that kind of cash."

"Yeah," I say with a sigh. "But it's such a long shot. Not only do you have to audition but you have to get cast, and then once you're cast you have to beat two other teams at the mini challenges and trivia. Once you've done that, there's still giant hurdles between you and one hundred grand. It's taxing to say the least."

Leo stands and crosses to the mirror, stops to check himself out. His expression shifts slowly from deep thought to open expectation. "Are the auditions still happening?"

"Yeah, they're on Monday. Why?" I ask, getting off the floor and sliding onto the bed.

"Because we should audition," he says.

I laugh, not taking him seriously in the slightest. "I thought we went over this. No more fucking *with* me, only *fucking me.*"

"No, I'm serious," he says, voice firm and composed, a sharp change from the self-pitying rasp I heard when I arrived.

My heart shocks itself into a state of frenzy. Auditioning was the only thing I wanted to do when coming out here, but rejection after rejection dulled the sparkle of that idea.

Hearing those words from someone else's mouth causes a traffic jam inside my head.

"Didn't you hear me? It's not guaranteed," I say, finally voicing one of the cons for taking this trip in the first place. The column in my mind I'd conveniently erased from the whiteboard when booking those blasted plane tickets.

"You're a huge fan of the show," he says, turning back toward me, fingers gripped on the edge of the dusty dresser.

"Sure. So is everyone that auditions. It wouldn't be one of the longest running TV game shows without having legions of superfans." Rationality has never been my strong suit, so I'm surprised at how reasonable I'm being. "Besides, we don't know each other. They only cast pairs with interesting histories. I don't think meeting in a hotel lobby and almost fucking counts as *interesting*."

"We have to do something!" he says, throwing his hands up in the air in apparent exasperation. "I can't tell my mom I lost this job, which means I can't be home during the day when I'm supposed to be working which means…which means…" He groans loudly and drops his head into his hands. I can tell by his motionless, sculpted shoulders that he's not crying, but his misery is an overpowering fog creeping through the room.

The bed I'm sitting on becomes a boat, one with holes in the siding, filling and sinking and, just like Leo, I don't have a flare to call for help. If *Madcap Market* is a half-inflated life raft floating by for both of us, shouldn't we at least try to take it to safety?

It's that question that prompts me to say in a tentative voice, "We could pretend to date."

Leo's head rises slowly, one eyebrow quirked. "Go on."

"Strangers who almost slept together won't get us on the show, but if we were a couple…" I say, the thought still forming fully. "I just think we'd have a better shot." That's why I wanted to audition with Buckley. I knew our relationship status would gain us brownie points.

A smile crests across his face. "Does that mean you're in?"

Despite the ridiculousness of my uncharacteristic snap decisions, I decide I have to see this pipe dream of mine through and this devastatingly sexy no-longer-faux-concierge might be my only shot. This, like everything else related to this trip, could go up in flames so easily, but Leo's kindness and honesty have wedged open my trust. I want to help him.

Caution? Meet Wind.

"Yeah, I'm in," I say, anxious.

We shake on it.

Eight

Leo's shocked expression tells me he was not prepared for the sheer level of intense love I possess for a grocery-themed game show.

"How many episodes of this are we going to watch exactly?" he asks. We have his laptop plugged into the TV through an HDMI cable. I've been giving him a crash course on the series, streaming and dissecting all my favorite episodes so he understands the tone, structure, and style. Pointing out which prepared package tapes make for the most compelling contestants. We'll need those to craft our cover story, which is threading together loosely at best.

"No! You asked *me* out," Leo adamantly argued.

"Is it so unbelievable that you'd have made a move on me first?" It was a hit to my ego to say the least.

"Look, we're already nerding up my reputation by saying we met in a *Madcap Market* fan forum—which feels a little pandering, by the way—so this is the least you could do me."

I sighed but relented, inking as much detail as possible onto a napkin from the takeout we ordered. When finished, I made us both sign it. It won't hold up in court but having a physical manifestation of this agreement is pertinent. We have equal amounts to gain and lose.

"In our story, you're a big fan. We've only watched four episodes so far," I say. I'm browsing the streaming library for a specific episode—one Mom really loved.

"They're an hour each." Leo groans for emphasis.

I arch an eyebrow. "Do you have anything better to be doing and anywhere better to be?" He zips his lips at that, defeated. I would feel bad about the low blow, but we've been laughing over his hatred of the concierge position for the last few hours between episodes, so I know he won't take it personally. I hit Play again on the computer. "It's all about strategy. The better you know the game, the easier it will be plotting our plan of attack."

"You sound like we're going to war."

"Have you been watching? It's a battle just to make it to the finale. Did you not pay attention to the episode where they made them joust with stale baguettes while standing atop a tower of Campbell's Soup cans?"

"If only Andy Warhol had been alive to see that. His art wouldn't have been as shocking." Leo's sarcasm is playful and enjoyable. Buckley never had much of a funny bone, which isn't to say he was humorless. It was more that he gave every aspect of life very serious consideration with little room for mindlessness.

After Mom died, I needed mindlessness. I needed escape.

I needed someone who understood that. For the first time, I consider that our breakup was for the best. Maybe our paths were carved out too differently. Maybe I needed to venture off mine for a while, get lost, see what I find.

Turns out, I've found a former-faux-concierge who's opposed to binge-watching. Even so, I lean over and notice he's been taking notes on the hotel stationery pad. He's got neat, organized handwriting. It's endearing and makes my anxiety morph into excitement.

I wonder momentarily if this is the kind of adventure Dad had in mind during our call earlier today.

"There's just one more episode I really want us to watch." It featured a mother and son duo and while it's never said explicitly, it's alluded to that the son is queer and the mom couldn't be more accepting. Annoyingly, I'm suffering brain fog and can't quite remember which season that was, as if I haven't seen each of these episodes a couple times.

Leo must pick up on my tone because he repositions himself in the chair beside the bed, reverting his attention. "It's interesting. You know these episodes like some people know quotes from *The Office* or *Friends*. What is it about *Madcap Market*?"

I know it's not an intrusive question, but it plucks at the raw spot where Buckley had wounded me that fateful night in Manhattan. "I don't know." It comes out tart, which shuts Leo up. I don't mean to be curt, but I can't unpack my trauma for him right now. We only have so much time to come up with a clean backstory for our audition that will secure us a spot and, hopefully, one hundred thousand dollars.

"Fine. Geesh. Don't tell me." He taps one end of the pen impatiently against the bedside table while I locate the episode.

Finally, Pat Crumsky's face—tan skin, bright eyes, salt-and-pepper pompadour hair—takes over the screen. The theme music, which has always been funky and retro, blasts from the speakers as cartoon cans roll, spin, and stack into letters. I sit on the edge of the bed, eyes unable to move or blink for the full forty-seven minutes. Pure rapture.

The mom, Carol, and the son, Logan, compete in matching pink sweatshirts with rainbow ascots tied around their necks. "We'll have to come up with a sweatshirt color," I tell Leo, not even blinking or missing a second of the episode.

"Eggplant purple."

"Why?"

"Because we're going to be Team Eggplant."

I pause the show. "Absolutely not."

"Come on. It's funny."

"It's an easy joke."

He points at the screen. "This show is pure camp. No questions."

I consider this and relent. "Fine." I turn back to the TV. "But only because I look excellent in purple."

Back in the episode, Carol bests the competition in the trivia round, Logan racks up the lowest receipt total, and in the grand finale, the two of them race through the store like seasoned pros after chugging the sponsored energy drinks (it was the early 2000s—nobody knew your heart could explode yet!). Only, their final clue in the scavenger hunt is impossible—*Need a hand with that meat?* They were vegetarians who hadn't done their homework. It was Hamburger Helper.

No matter how many times I yelled that at the TV, they couldn't hear me.

"See," Leo shouts, comically incredulous. *"Need a hand with that meat?* This show loves a saucy innuendo. Or should I say *sauce*-y."

"You should say neither. Now, shhh." I wave him away. Yes, it's ridiculous and intentional and probably cringey, but I don't care. It's deliciously entertaining and mind-numbing.

Even though I've seen this before, even though I know how it ends, my heart thumps rigorously for this mother and son team. In their package video, they talk about how Carol plans to surprise Logan by using the money to pay for him to go to his dream college and get a degree in theater.

Back then, it resonated with me because in that taped address to the camera, I knew Carol loved her son unconditionally and I, like her, could see so clearly how he would thrive in a college setting, where his queerness could blossom. I worried if Mom would feel the same, if her acceptance would come as easily.

Now it resonates differently because, little did I know, Mom had been setting aside money for years to put me through college until the cancer came and that money needed to be used for treatment and I begged the government to take pity on me with student loans which they did, and then said LOL JK when repayments kicked in.

"The people on this show are so funny," says Leo, standing up and stretching. "They went home with seventy-five thousand dollars. That's more dough than most people will see in a lifetime."

"I think when you set your heart on something and you get within inches of achieving it, the fallout is difficult." I shove away annoying thoughts of Buckley and the domestic future I foresaw for us. "Imagine having all that adrenaline surging through you, hearing the right answer, and knowing you were two aisles over when the clock ran out."

"I guess, but they still beat the other contestants. They still won." Leo's not getting it. "Their smiles were so fake there at the end."

"I'm sure that dawned on them, when the cameras stopped rolling, how much money it really was, but that mom had a plan for that one hundred grand. Twenty-five thousand less is a significant difference." My mind is overrun with loan payments and pauses and income-based plans. How my bank account is probably tired of being taken from but never repleted. "I'm not saying I would feel the same way. I'm saying I can understand why they might react like that."

Leo's pouty lips become poutier. "I would be thrilled with half that. Anyway, at least the queer guy won. I was rooting for him." He thrusts a fist in the air.

"I've seen this one a bunch of times," I tell him, reminiscing. "We had it saved on our DVR at home for a while. I know representation matters is kind of a cliché thing to say nowadays, but I really think it does. Logan was the first person I saw on TV that I thought, 'Hey, he's like me.' I had no idea what I even meant by that at the time. I think that's why *Madcap Market* did for me what narrative TV couldn't. I knew Logan was a real person living a real life."

Saying this gives me pause. If Leo and I go through with the lie, am I going against what I love about the show? Real people sharing their real lives competing for real money? I shelve that existential crisis for now and say, "This show means a lot to me because it was my mom's and my thing. For a long time. I also think this episode being one of our frequent rewatches was my mom's way of hinting at me that she knew I was gay and that she'd be okay with it if I came out." I didn't realize that at the time, but it's clear now.

Leo sobers, meets my eyes with friendly warmth. "Was she okay with it? You know, when you finally told her?"

I nod. "More than okay. Like, baked-a-rainbow-cake-to-celebrate okay. It was my fifteenth birthday. She'd somehow overheard me on the phone with one of my friends who already knew, discussing how I'd tell them. That night, before dessert, I blurted it out, they both reacted fine if somewhat lukewarm as if they already knew, and then I cut into the cake and noticed all the colorful layers. That's when we all started crying. Happy crying."

"That's intense, but very sweet. Was it a good rainbow cake?"

"Oh, yeah. My mom was an amazing baker." Grief lunges up into my throat. "She was amazing at everything, really." It pains me that I didn't inherit that from her. I'm not automatically skilled at everything I set my mind to. Honestly, there's very little I excel at, and because she's not here, the voice in my head is allowed to manipulate me into thinking she wouldn't be proud of me.

But if I win *Madcap Market*, I know with one-hundred-percent certainty that she'll be smiling down on me. That's enough of a reason to go through with this harebrained scheme. The money to pay off my loans and be independent are the icing on the rainbow cake.

When I look over at Leo, he's writing on his notepad again. "What are you jotting down?"

"Stuff about your mom." He pauses, looks at me with deer-in-the-headlights eyes. "That sounded wrong. I just don't have the best memory, and if we're going to fake date then I need to study up on Holden James."

A warmth stretches inside my chest. The fact that he not only suggested this, but he's taking it seriously and listening to me and looking like that. His relaxed, sprawled-out posture and earnestness are almost too much to handle, but then he asks, "What else should I know?"

"What else do you want to know?" Buckley never really asked me questions. I retreated inward after Mom passed. College was the place where I was not only supposed to come out of my shell, but shed that shell entirely. Chuck it into the wind. Instead, I built a second shell on top of the original—one made of iron—to keep out any potential upset.

On the plane here, I was certain I was bulletproof. Leo, in two short days, has proven that wrong as he continues to lob shots in my direction, causing tiny cracks in the armor that spill light inside.

"Maybe let's start at the beginning. Tell me about what young Holden was like."

"Neurotic," I say without thinking.

"So nothing's changed, then. Got it." Leo pretends to write that down.

I throw a discarded sock at him. His or mine? Who's to say at this point? We've spent all day holed up in this room, ordering food, watching TV, strategizing, and growing more comfortable with one another, as if we've known each other for ages. "I only mean that I was an intense kid. I was an only child with two working parents. I had to be creative and resourceful, which also meant I had to grow up quickly so I could take care of myself when my grandparents couldn't babysit. I made a lot of toaster oven chicken nuggets."

"Dinosaur-shaped?"

"Of course."

We share a smile that goes on for a beat too long, but I like it. I like it a lot. And now I'm craving chicken nuggets.

"I'm guessing you grew up even quicker when your mom died." Leo's words are careful. I appreciate that. He makes it known, just through his tone, that he'll drop the topic immediately if I ask. But having shared this show with him now, I'm open to the idea of unloading some of the emotional groceries Buckley never had room for in the pantry of our relationship.

I nod. "My dad is a ray-of-sunshine person. Always optimistic and a little too lenient. I had to play the storm cloud for a while—yelling at the phone company when they refused to close Mom's line and playing defense between my dad and my grandma when they fought over who would get to keep the ashes. It was taxing, especially when I was trying to make it to graduation in one piece. The only saving grace was being excused from finals and already having committed to a college."

"Nobody suggested you take a year off or go to community college for a bit?"

"No, I wanted things to remain as normal as possible. My mom was so excited when I got into that school, so I was going." I recall the restlessness inside me that made every outing without Mom somehow seem like a betrayal of her memory, even if I refused to lock myself away in my room and rip my way through a box of tissues. "Life got so hectic. I don't think the grief really caught up to me until a few years into college."

It was chicken parm night in the dining hall. Mom used to love cooking chicken parm for Dad and me on the nights we were all home for family dinner. The missing-her I had tucked inside a secret chamber of my heart escaped, and suddenly I was crying in a corner at a table all by myself.

Until Buckley passed by, noticed me, and said, "I relate. The food here is pretty bad."

I surprised myself by laughing, then surprised myself even more by asking him to sit.

My universe shifted then. I threw myself headfirst into a whirlwind relationship with that Buckley.

Where did that Buckley go? The one who talked to me for hours about cardboard-flavored pizza and torturous lectures until I forgot I had even cried at all. Surely, he didn't do a one-eighty in that restaurant in Manhattan. I must've lost that version of Buckley long before.

Great. Yet another loss to add to my list.

"You know what," I say to Leo, noticing this room is feeling claustrophobic thanks to that unwelcome memory. "Let's save the biography for later. Any chance you'd be up for a field trip?"

Nine

Leo drives us to the nearest grocery store for a crash course.

His car is a Honda Civic in an orange color that reminds me of bruised tangerines in a discount farmer's market. The inside is a mess of receipts and ripped bags. Every time I move my feet, I'm greeted with another crunch. I start a game of: Is it In-N-Out or Chipotle?

He's playing Rina Sawayama at a low roar, but singing along at full volume. His voice can only be described as couch upholstery being ripped apart at warp speed, yet he's so committed that I can't help but be charmed by it. The smorgasbord of sounds in this car is overwhelming, but it's a nice break from my own swirling thoughts about how we're going to make this work when all I know about him is his full name, his unemployment status, and that he's in desperate need of a car wash.

"You like Taylor Swift and Rina Sawayama." I file this

in my things-to-know-about-Leo bank. "I take it you're a pop music fan?"

"Guilty as charged." He turns the music down a tad more so I can hear him better. "Unlike you with TV, music was the way I first connected with being gay. I realized I never connected with 'boy music' if that makes sense. I loved a diva. I loved a lavish costume. I loved Lady Gaga spewing blood from her corset while dangling from the ceiling, singing 'Paparazzi' on the MTV Video Music Awards."

"A cultural reset."

"Exactly," he says, smiling over at me, making me go all gooey inside. He's got a stellar, disarming smile that's almost as beguiling as his smirk. "Female pop singers make me feel powerful. Just like video games make me feel invincible. I like disappearing into a song or a game and imagining I'm someone else. I can blast or dance away my real problems."

For a moment, I wonder if he's treating our *Madcap Market* plan as a self-insert video game situation. Rocked by the frustration of getting fired, is he pretending this Leo—the one driving a little far over the speed limit for comfort— is a pixelated character on a screen where someone else is bashing the controller?

"I can understand that. Real life can be exhausting." After I say that, it dawns on me how alert and awake I am. A month of restless nights has suddenly been cured by jet lag and Leo's nearness.

As he monologues about his favorite artists and the music videos he played a million times on YouTube just to learn the dance moves—"Me Against the Music" with Britney

Spears and Madonna being his number one, much to his dad's dismay—I listen intently, watching his animated face as it shifts from wistful to excited and back again. From the moment I laid eyes on him, his sexiness was never in question, but his adorability comes into sharp focus, causing my lust for him to tip into far mushier territory.

"I'm an ace at playing pretend, which is why fake dating will be a cinch." The jolt of the car flipping into Park kills the ignition on my emotions as well. This isn't the getting-to-know-you part of a real connection. It's a business transaction. All about a dollar sign and a promise to my dead mom. That's all.

Obviously, we can still fuck, but fuck without feelings. After the earlier reminder of who Buckley was when we met versus who I sat across from four weeks ago, I can't overextend myself like that again.

The chain grocery store we've arrived at is mostly empty aside from the late-afternoon errand runners. Fluorescent strip lights buzz, casting the whole floor in an overexposed, yellow-tinted haze. Even still, Leo looks exceptionally good—white button-up balled up in the back of the car; the only thing left a white ribbed tank top he was wearing underneath. It clings like a second skin, showcasing elegant contours I'm certain he's worked hard for.

I avert my eyes and grab a shopping cart with a wonky wheel that keeps veering left as I try to go right, nearly knocking over an entire display of cookies.

"Give it to me," Leo says. With a bit of elbow grease and bulging biceps, he course corrects the cart, making veins snake across his tan skin. I wish he would stop getting hotter by the second, so my internal fans could cool down. "Where to first?" he asks.

"Let's start with the snack aisles." Because, at the very least, there's nothing erotic about bland crackers.

We make our way past the registers where bored-looking employees eye us wearily as they pass the time until their shift ends. Air-conditioning is blasting down causing a shiver to race through me, forcing me to wonder how Leo can stand to be here in only that torso-hugging tank.

To keep my mind off Leo's distracting physique and our abandoned plans for afternoon sex, I begin picking up various boxes of cookies and bags of candy as a test, pointing to brand mascots and covering up price tags to see if Leo can correctly answer the on-the-fly trivia questions—How much does this cost? What's this guy's name? It's good to find his baseline knowledge of grocery goods, see where we need to improve and what kind of homework I should send him away to do when we're apart, which turns out to be a lot.

He calls the Keebler elf, Buddy the Elf, the Planters mascot "that dapper Peanut Guy" and the Cheetos mascot "Charlie? No, wait. Carl." In the candy aisle, when I ask Leo how many licks it takes to get to the center of a Tootsie Pop, he responds, "With my dexterous tongue or with a normal person's?" After a wink, he guesses five, which extinguishes any arousal that may have sprung up from his tantalizing, joking question.

Unfortunately, we fare no better in the cereal aisle.

"The tiger's name is?" I ask, breath hitched with hopefulness, pointing to a grinning feline giving us a thumbs-up.

"Uh," Leo says, thinking lines running across his fore-head. "I want to say... Tyler?"

I make a buzzer sound. "Tony."

"I was close."

Exasperated, my eyes land on a box one shelf up. "What about these guys? You gotta know these guys." I Vanna White my hands around the three cherubic elves pouring milk into a bowl of Rice Krispies.

"Snap, Crackle, and Pop..." I'm about to congratulate him on a job well done when he continues, "*pers*."

"Huh?"

"Pop...pers. *Poppers*." He cracks himself up as I roll away in a huff. "Oh, come on. It's a joke. It's funny!"

"You're not taking this seriously anymore," I whine over my shoulder, cart wheeling willfully in the wrong direction as if it has a mind of its own.

His laughter dies down. "No, I am. I promise. Their names were on their hats on the box. They could've been Huey, Dewey, and Louie for all I knew. If I had known there was going to be a test, I would've studied."

I've only known him for two days, and I already know that's not true, so I arch an eyebrow at him.

"Okay, I would've made an attempt at the very least. It's not my fault I'm bad at this." He sounds genuinely dejected, which tempers me.

"No. It's fine." I try to bolster my tone, so he isn't dis-couraged. I had just hoped this would be easier. "You have a body like that." I circle the air beside his mountainous bi-ceps, gracing him with a compliment that will stroke his ego. "Naturally you don't know about snack foods. Let's try the produce section instead."

I probably shouldn't be manhandling avocados and grapefruits, but since we're mostly alone over here, I don't see the harm.

He nails limes, Granny Smith apples, and nearly ends his streak with kumquats but saves it at the last minute, cheering victoriously—doing that dance from the other night when he won Monopoly. In the light of day, he's got that undeniable B-boy energy. I could totally see him being a background dancer for a singer at some point.

"Did you ever take dance classes as a kid?"

"I did. When I was in middle school, I joined a step team. I was one of the only guys since most of my friends were girls. Shana, one of my closest friends, was taking a hip-hop class at a local rec center and brought me on bring-a-friend day. The whole thing felt like being in a music video. When I got home, I begged my mom to enroll me, so she saved up her tips and got me a spot."

"That's cute." I picture Leo up on a stage in a school basement wearing shiny pants and platform sneakers, kick cross stepping to the beat of a Jason Derulo song.

Across the way, I grab a cucumber from the collection and hold it up. "All right. Next question, what can cucumbers become?"

"Slap a condom on it and it can become a pretty efficient dildo." He nudges me with an elbow.

Thank God no one is around to hear that. My cheeks flame up to inferno levels while briefly imagining Leo plus sex toys. I set the cucumber down, flustered. "Leo! Please don't say anything like that at our audition or, God willing, on live TV. It's a family show!"

"Weren't you just saying we needed more accurate queer representation?" He smirks the smirkiest smirk. "What's more relatable than using produce for questionable self-exploration?" He's grabbed the cucumber now and he's waving it at me like it's a sword.

"I did no such thing." I'm embarrassed yet electrified, jostled out of my comfort zone. Leo seems exceptionally no-filter, which is equal parts unsettling and refreshing.

"Didn't make the boy Sims kiss. Didn't steal vegetables for self-pleasure. From the way you were grinding into me this morning, I hadn't pegged you for a prude." He knocks his hip into mine, sending me into the refrigerated display case which has begun its water spray. My arm is wet when I pull it away.

I shake myself dry. "Cucumber is a fruit."

"Takes one to know one," Leo jokes with a cheeky wink.

Ignoring that: "There are seeds on the inside!"

"I know all about seed on the inside."

"I'm not a prude for not defiling myself with produce!" I can't believe I'm having this conversation with someone I barely know in a grocery store I've never been in on the opposite side of the country from my home. This whole trip is outrageous and unexpected.

Not in a bad way, though.

Leo must notice that my defenses are building back up because he lowers his voice, retracts the phallic fruit. "I'm just goofing around. I tend to make jokes when I don't know what else to do. I don't come to stores like this often." His gaze floats away.

"Grocery stores?" I ask, confused.

"*Chain* grocery stores." He scrubs a hand on the back of his neck revealing that small patch of dark armpit hair that drove me wild this morning. The sight. The scent. I...

"My mom and I would go to Koreatown every other weekend to shop for ourselves. My dad was Irish, but my mom made sure I learned about my Korean side through food, which meant long walks to my mom's favorite market to pick up ingredients for hoeddeok or bibimbop."

"That sounds nice." I can tell there's more to the story when it comes to his parents' relationship, and it's clear how much he cares about his mom, given this and what he told me last night over Monopoly, which endears him to me. I like that family is important to both of us.

He shrugs. "She worked a lot. Still does. You and your mom had *Madcap Market*. My mom and I had the Korean market." Leo's expression lands between dreamy and nostalgic. "I got to know the layout really well and most of the employees would sneak me pieces of sour candy when my mom wasn't looking. I always loved being able to practice my Korean there, too. My mom and I both work most weekends now—well, not me anymore because, you know—but I still go out there to shop for her when she can't because it's habit, which is all a long-winded way of saying I don't know all the brands or logos or mascots you do unless they stock them in the vending machines at the hotels because I didn't grow up around them."

"That makes sense." I think about how all of these products imprinted on my brain when Mom would wheel me down the aisle of the Shoprite by our house, humming a Cher song to herself. I'd wave to the Jolly Green Giant in the freezer aisles. Salute Mr. Clean as we picked up toilet cleaner.

When I wasn't looking, Mom would give Buzz the bee on the Honey Nut Cheerios box a funny voice. "Hello, Holden!" he'd say. "Hope you have a great day!" My eyes would widen and I'd cry, "Mom! Mom! Did you hear that? Did you hear that?" And she'd nod her head and smile, eyebrows raised with secretive delight.

"Sorry." I pull myself from the sudden, vivid memory. "That was completely insensitive of me."

"I'm not trying to make you feel bad. Why would you know that about me? It would've been just as insensitive if you had assumed." He stops and leans effortlessly on the cart, which is so adeptly in his control that it doesn't even shift at his weight. Amazing. "I'm just saying this isn't the part I'm going to excel at. This is."

He drops the cucumber in the cart and takes off running with it, down an empty aisle, makes a sick U-turn—wheels slightly skidding—then catapults back, riding on the beam. He flies by in a whir with a wave. If there were Olympics for shopping cart riding, Leo would take home the gold.

When he returns to where I'm standing, not even slightly winded, he smiles. "You be the brains. I'll be the brawn."

"Okay. That's fair. But we're each going to have to be a

little bit of both. That's how the show works. Teams have to do the challenge fifty-fifty."

His eyes go toward the ceiling. "Good point. You have my permission to randomly quiz me from now until the audition and, fingers crossed, beyond, if you agree to work out with me tomorrow. We'll whip you into shape." He flexes, and I hold back an audible swoon.

"Excuse me. What's wrong with this shape?" I give him a three-sixty spin. "I'll have you know that this shape is courtesy of Cardio Dance Fit."

"Okay," Leo says, a smile stretching across his face. "What I had in mind was a bit top-heavier, if you know what I mean."

"You want me to lift weights?" I ask. "With these spaghetti arms?" I flap them for emphasis.

"Didn't you just say teams are fifty-fifty?" I both hate and love that he's using my words against me. "Those giant hams aren't going to heave themselves."

"Fine." I crack a crooked, playful smile. "Let's get out of here." We start toward the exit so we can put the cart away when I notice the errant cucumber is still rolling around in there. "We should probably put that back."

"Oh, no," Leo says. "I'm buying that."

"Why?"

He quirks a brow at me. "I think it might just come in handy at some point..."

The furious heat rises to my cheeks once again as he saunters in front giving me a full view of his perky ass in those dress slacks on the way to the self-checkout kiosk.

Ten

When we pull back up to the hotel, I invite Leo up to my room to no avail.

"Sorry," he says, playing it cool in the driver's seat, one hand slung over the wheel. "My mom is expecting me for dinner, and since I'm not going to tell her about the lost job just yet, I don't need her grilling me on why I'm late."

"I understand," I say, moderately disappointed, but we go our separate ways with plans to meet early tomorrow morning for what Leo calls "a special surprise."

Here's hoping that surprise involves no pants.

I get stopped crossing the lobby while holding a single, bagged cucumber. I probably look like a freak. A very red, very embarrassed freak.

The dark-skinned woman behind the counter wearing blue eyeshadow and a name tag that reads Annabelle, waves me over to the desk. "Are you Mr. James?"

"That's me. Yes." I surreptitiously try to hide the cucumber behind my back, which seems to only draw more attention to it.

Annabelle hits me with a suspicious look before proceeding. "This came for you while you were out." After rummaging around in a nearby room, she wheels my blue suitcase out from behind the desk; the sparkly luggage tag catches the light. A relieved breath saws out of me.

"Oh, my God. Wow. Thank you. I had almost figured it was gone forever." Though, in truth, Leo had nearly made me forget all about it.

"Well," Annabelle says, returning to her post. "Seems like it's your lucky day."

I think about Leo again. About watching *Madcap Market* together and our grocery store outing. Out of all the faux concierges that could've been here the day I arrived from New York, it seems fated that it was Leo. Perhaps I am coming into some luck after all. I just needed to leave my comfort zone and my zip code to do it.

"Thanks again," I say to Annabelle as I start toward the elevators.

"Oh, and Mr. James." I turn back to catch her sporting a new, unnervingly professional expression. "If you could keep the Taylor Swift to a dull roar this evening, the guests and I would greatly appreciate it."

My mood has lifted to insurmountable heights, so even this light dig can't drag me down. "You got it." I flash her a kind smile before going up to my room.

The room has been cleaned since I left—the carpet vacuumed, the bed made, and Leo's and my trash disposed of.

Leo's mountain of unopened snacks is still piled high on the bedside table next to where he slept last night. So much has happened in the past forty-eight hours that my head should be spinning. Instead, my heart is sort of fluttering like it's grown wings and become a creature inside my rib cage that's ready to break free.

I hoist the suitcase onto the lopsided stand and sort through the pockets. Everything seems to be where I left it. Nothing lost or stolen. Since Leo insinuated we'd have an extra early morning, I break out the rest of my athleisure pieces—Fab Fitness Flair finally coming in clutch for *something*—and mix and match to find the right outfit.

For the next hour or so, it's like high school all over again, getting ready for a homecoming dance or a big presentation, anticipation fizzling as I make my decision. Which shirt is going to make my chest look broad, and which pair of pants is going to make my ass look the best? At that thought, I pull my collection of fun underwear out of a pocket in the front of the bag. I lay out a collection of jockstraps and thongs I packed with the intentions of being a little slutty while visiting Sin City.

Oh, wait. That's Vegas.

No matter. Sin isn't city specific, and I plan to absolutely debauch Leo.

For my first option, I pull on a lime-green jockstrap, a super thin pair of running tights, and a heather-gray, racerback tank top. Even in the stark bathroom light, I check out my reflection and find that I'm feeling myself. Maybe it's the change of setting. Maybe it's my new fake boyfriend. Either way, I look good and feel even better.

I snap a picture of each of my outfit choices, then get the idea to send them to Leo. Which one should I wear for our outing tomorrow? I text him.

Leo responds almost instantaneously as if he were waiting by the phone for my text after we exchanged numbers earlier today. Is he harboring that first-crush bubbliness I'm suddenly floating away with?

How can I make an assessment when I haven't seen the outfit from every angle? ☺

I quarter turn, pop my heel, and lift the back hem of my tank, giving a better view of my assets. How's this?

Much better. 😈

A rush of validation tap-dances down my spine. Since the breakup, I haven't been in touch with my sexual or sensual selves. I stuffed those relics into boxes when I moved in with Dad. Now I'm unpacking them like bodysuits from my newly returned suitcase, trying them on once more, and realizing they fit like gloves. I missed them, and I want to wear them proudly for Leo to see.

A second text pops in from Leo: Is that the waistband of a jockstrap I see?

Maaaaaaaaaaaybe. ☺ Our shirked rendezvous this afternoon becomes the only thing on my mind.

Why don't you come back here and find out? Let's finish what we started this morning, I send.

I wish I could, but I don't live that close. ☹

Boo.

His typing bubble appears, disappears, and then: But that doesn't mean we can't have fun this way...

My heart thumps at the enticing thought as I tug down the waistband of the tights exposing the backless underwear I'm wearing. Adjusting for lighting, I get the perfect shot and send it. You mean this way???

A minute goes by and I'm afraid I've overstepped. But then, I'm graced with a picture in return. It's shirtless Leo sprawled out on a queen-sized bed, one hand behind his head giving me full permission to ogle that immaculate biceps. Lower is where it really gets good, though. He's wearing nothing but a tiny pair of silky thin black shorts. His erection rockets up underneath them, pointing toward his belly button. I'm salivating.

That's exactly what I meant. Next, he adds: Show me more.

I waste no time stripping down and going back into the bedroom, overcome by a rush of headiness and desire. Leaning onto my elbows, I arch my back so I can frame the front-facing camera in a way that it shows half my face and half my exposed ass up in the air. Is this the "more" you had in mind?

I'm surprised when instead of a text, I get a voice memo. When I play it, it's Leo groaning a single word, "Fuck." That one word unlocks me. That one growly, gravelly, hedonistic word makes the pouch of my jockstrap full and constrictive. I play it again. "Fuck." And again. "Fuck." Until I'm grinding my bulge into the mattress, so damn eager for touch.

Leo's touch especially. Witnessing those strong hands expertly maneuver a shopping cart through a grocery store is somehow fueling my fantasy. What is happening to me?

I'm about to send something back when I get a photo. Leo has lost the shorts. They're bunched up at the end of his bed around his large bare feet, and his erection is on full display. My mouth waters more, remembering the taste and warmth of him from this morning. The slick saltiness that could become my favorite flavor if I got another ounce of it.

I scoot over on the bed so my ass is in line with the mirror over the dresser. Maneuvering, I'm able to take an over-the-shoulder picture that leaves nothing to the imagination. I'm frisky, fearless, and shaking off any inhibition as I send back a voice message: "I want you to rail me like you promised."

Next thing I know, my phone is ringing.

FaceTime from Leo Min.

I accept, and Leo's handsome face takes up my whole screen. His hot chocolate eyes are rolling back in his head and he's moaning. "You don't know how badly I want that right now," Leo whisper-groans. He's got wireless earbuds in so I can hear him loud and clear, and it's like he's right in the room with me. He's back in this bed, hard and ready for me. "I want that final installment of our repayment plan."

With my phone up against a pillow, I close my eyes and continue writhing into the bed, making the springs squeak but I couldn't care less if anyone hears. "Tell me what the final repayment is."

"This." He flips the camera so I can watch him touching himself, thrusting his erection into his wet fist, slippery head poking out the top every other second. I imagine that he's inside me. I reach a hand back and press a finger to my hole. "I want to give you this." I like the dominant tone he takes with me. It makes my mind go blank and allows me to access a primal itch that he scratches skillfully with the scrape of his voice. "But I don't think you're quite ready for it."

"I'm not?" I ask, opening my eyes and noticing that he's pulled the phone away. I have a clear shot of his body from the side. Part of his face. All of his torso. His throbbing penis and that dark patch of trimmed pubic hair right above.

He shakes his head wearing a devilish grin. "What did you do with that cucumber?"

Confused, I say, "It's in the mini fridge. Why?"

"Because I want you to use it on yourself."

Embarrassment burrows through me. "Uh, I don't know about that." While Buckley and I were open, the sex we had together and with others was mostly vanilla. We never much got into toys, especially not ones you could theoretically slice up for a salad. Oh, God.

"Come on," he says, still jerking himself. "Reach into the bedside table. I left some things there that will be of use."

When I yank it open, I find a few blue condoms and a couple single packets of lube.

"Unfortunately, we didn't get to use them earlier. I think you should take advantage of them now." His eyebrows go up, as if he's challenging me. As if he's waiting to see if I'll talk back, fight the urge, stop this altogether.

The thing is, I barely know him, but I know him enough that he won't push. If I say stop, he'll stop.

I'm shocked to realize that I don't want him to stop. I want to keep doing what he's telling me to do because it's making my balls tighten and breath pick up. So what if it's not what I'm used to? I didn't come all the way out here to follow routine. I came out here to shuck some of what's been holding me back. Leo's unabashed confidence has set the scene so well. I give myself over to the pleasure.

"Okay," I say confidently, moving to the mini fridge and finding what I'm looking for. I wash it in the sink and then return to the bed with a fresh towel.

"Very good." Leo's slowed his stroke. I can tell he's edging, moving close to the brink of orgasm and then backing off to prolong this, which I appreciate. "Suck it."

The ridiculousness melts away as I place the makeshift toy in my mouth, never once breaking eye contact with Leo through the screen. It feels wrong in all the right ways, a pulsating need cropping up low in my gut.

"Mmm. You've got good technique." His eyes sparkle.

I stop to slick my finger, then reach around myself to prepare, gently inserting the finger inside me, moaning right away from the exploration. I'm rediscovering my body. Reminding myself that pleasure isn't just a luxury, it's a right. And I plan on exercising it more and more.

"Another finger," Leo commands, and I oblige, enjoying it.

Eventually, I'm ready for the big show, so I tear into the condom with my teeth and roll it down the thinner end. "That's it. Ease it on nice and slow. Don't rush."

Leo's moved his hand away from his penis, relocating it to his nipple. Clearly, he's enjoying the show too much. I like that this is a performance without it being performative. Despite the cam show setup—my phone propped up on the bedside table—this is as much about my pleasure as it is about his. Confidence is a cloud of fairy dust around me.

I love that I can bring out this playful side of Leo who's fully present in this hot-as-hell moment.

After applying a healthy amount of lube, I sit up on my knees and gently, gradually lower myself onto the end of the DIY dildo. My senses level up. It's like my whole body is experiencing everything on double-power mode. I adjust. I open. I take it deeper.

"Take your time," Leo instructs, resuming his own enjoyment with his free hand, still tweaking the nipple closest to the camera. "Close your eyes and think about what it would be like straddling my hips, taking this." He waves his springy cock, and I groan on command because at that moment, the toy hits my prostate, sending sparks upward.

"Fuck," I whimper as I start a slow and steady rock that hits and hits and hits my spot.

A few minutes later, Leo tells me to get on my back. Without hesitation, my legs are in the air and my act is on full display. My penis strains against the cotton of my jockstrap some more so I finally pull the pouch aside and let it out, allowing it some relief. It only takes a couple strokes for me to sense a buildup from underneath. To feel my yearning become stronger, my desire to grow deeper. My head flops back in bliss.

I'm practically planting roots on this bed, unable to stop tilting toward the sun. "I'm... I'm..." I utter, barely able to get out the other word. *"Close."*

"Stop." I feel the word before I hear it. My senses uncloud.

"Huh?" I ask, still following orders but frazzled.

"I said stop."

"Wh-why?" I ask, aching to grip my shaft again as it bobs between my legs.

"Because—" he adjusts the camera so it's only his face again "—I want you to save it. For me."

The way he says *for me* makes my entire body shudder as if I had orgasmed. As if he could wring me dry with his words alone. It's been so long, and I'm so gone for him. I let my erection dip as I nod in understanding.

"Good," he says with an earnest smile. "Now, clean yourself up and get some rest. You've got an early morning workout to be prepared for."

"Don't work me too hard before you've gotten a chance to *work me hard*," I tease.

"Don't worry," he says with a laugh. It's a throaty thing. Super pleasing. "I know what I'm doing." Oh, boy. Does he ever. "And don't think I won't notice tomorrow if you disobey my order once we hang up."

Unable to wrap my head around how into this I am, I say, "I can be disciplined when I need to be."

"Good. I'm holding you to that. Good night, Fake Boy-friend," he says sincerely.

"Good night, Fake Boyfriend."

"Sweet dreams," he says, and then ends the call.

And I know for certain, all of my sweet dreams are going to be populated with Leo. *Panting, sexy, sweaty Leo.*

Eleven

The sweaty Leo from my dreams last night is five strides ahead of me, and I'm the one panting while trying to keep pace.

When Leo picked me up, I dropped two to-go cups of terrible coffee from the continental breakfast in the cupholders and asked, "Where are we going?" But he wouldn't tell me.

That's how I find myself on a *hike*. I went to school in Manhattan and moved to a bougie New York suburb where walking trails were sidewalks through garden parks. I expected to fake my way through a gym workout with long breaks between sets. This is way more intense than I anticipated.

We're taking the Riverside Trail to Vista Viewpoint at Griffith Park. Leo thought burning calories on a less touristy hiking trail would force us to bond in a way no other LA activity could allow for.

Because I'm sweating so much even though it's early and the sun has not even hit its peak, I slather myself in a second layer of SPF 1000 sunscreen. Nothing says "cut!" more than a pasty boy with a sunburn so bad he could be mistaken for a lobster. We need to look pristine for our audition—fit but not unattainably so, dressy but still a tad casual, and gay but not in a way that makes the conservative, prime-time TV watchers clutch their Rosary beads. It's a fine line to walk in a matter of days, but I'm certain we can perfect it.

After parking on the street, we entered through a white gate bordered by stone walls and moved past fairways and picnic tables, coffee drinkers and joggers. The pavement was solid beneath my feet, reminding my body that it's not a waste receptacle for poisons, yet rather a living, beating instrument that needs exercise to survive.

Now the pavement has given way to mulch and the even ground has become an incline toward a speckled water tower, and my lungs feel too small to live up to the task.

"Can we slow down?" I ask, out of breath.

"What? Those cardio dance classes you teach haven't upped your stamina?" he asks.

"Grapevines don't take that much energy!"

"Do you wear the headset with the microphone like some Britney Spears wannabe?" he asks.

"Yes," I say like it should be obvious. "And, please, Britney wishes she had moves like me." In a display of utter theatrics, I jump out, cross my legs, and do a spin.

"I think the *Madcap Market* casting directors will be *really* impressed by that." Leo laughs at me good-naturedly.

"Shut up!"

"Do you think we should choreograph a school talent show dance for them? We'll do it to the theme song." He starts humming it from memory, missing notes, but it doesn't matter because he's pumping his chest and rocking side to side. I can't shake the idea that he belongs onstage. At least if we get cast on *Madcap Market*, he will be.

"We'd definitely stand out."

"In a good way or a bad one?" he teases.

I catch up to him and give him a playful push. Our first intentional touch of the day zaps through my nervous system at lightning speed. My body sparks awake, last night's energy bursting forth, filling my head with fantasies of what's to come. How we might shower together to wash the morning sweat off our skin—getting clean while getting dirty.

To quiet my libido, I ask a question I pondered before falling asleep last night. "Okay, give it to me straight. What's your dating deal? Are there any exes we need to get rid of? Any recent hookups who need to be paid hush money not to kill our plan?"

"Okay, calm yourself, Assassins Creed," he huffs. "We're in the clear."

"Because your exes would believe you started an online relationship with me on a *Madcap Market* fan forum?" I know looks can be deceiving and you aren't supposed to judge a book by its cover, but Leo looks like he could be on the cover of a romance novel—all ripped and smooth and oiled. I want to know what's hidden in his pages.

He's quiet for a while. A too-long while. "I don't have any exes."

"You mean no recent exes?"

He shakes his head. "No, I mean no exes at all."

"So, I take it you're not the relationship type, then?" I ask, plugging his puzzle pieces together. He's stalwart. "Hello? I need to know these things if we're going to sell our story. I need to come up with a logical reason you'd abandon your single ways for me!"

"It's not that I'm not the relationship type," he says. "I've dated. I've just never been someone's boyfriend or partner or whatever."

My stride stops. Confusion pounds around in my brain. "But...but...you look like *that*." His sun-dappled skin with its appealing sheen of sweat across it is mind-blowingly perfect. Who wouldn't want to lock him down?

"I didn't always," he says, not bothering to stop for my stupefaction. He trudges on, muscular calves flexing with each set of his foot upon the ground. I never knew calves could be so beautiful.

"Okay, but...but...you're charming and funny and kind." I might be overly complimentary to someone I've known for less than seventy-two hours, but guys who frequent the gym, have good relationships with their moms, and provide pizza and company when you're spiraling are not just Fake Boyfriend Material. They're Boyfriend Material, full stop. "You deserve a relationship."

That's a funny thought to be having when we're playacting one for a prize.

Leo throws me a wayward smile over his shoulder. "I appreciate that, but I don't think relationships are deserved—they're earned." The set of his jaw grows more stone-like.

He has a fair point. "What about fake relationships?" The question lingers in the fresh air.

"You went through a breakup. I got fired. We earned this." As he speaks, he gestures ahead of him, to a wonderful view of downtown Los Angeles that shimmers with possibility, hope for a future brighter than today.

When we begin to walk again, I nudge Leo's side. "Just know that I'm taking this fake boyfriend thing very seriously. I'm going to fake rock your world."

"Love the enthusiasm, but let's stop saying the word *fake* even when we're alone to avoid getting tripped up." He waves and smiles at a woman jogging by in bright pink Adidas running shoes. "Also, I hope you plan to *really* rock my world when we get back to the hotel."

While I'm more than ready to fuck Leo sideways, I start thinking about the hotel, how Leo got fired, and how that might not be the place he wants to be right now. "Are you good with going back to my room? I mean, after everything that happened yesterday, I wouldn't blame you if you needed some time away from the hotel."

He scoffs. "I'm a big boy, Holden."

"Yeah, you showed me as much last night," I joke, but unconsciously bite my lip. My sex drive is a car with the gas pedal zip-tied down. "I just mean, seriously, how are you holding up?"

His shoulders slump, but only slightly, making his A-plus

posture more of an A-minus. "I'm not over-the-moon about it if that's what you're asking, but it's not my first rodeo so I know how to handle myself."

"Care to elaborate?"

He throws up his hands, visibly at a loss. "I crave new-ness. If I get stuck in a routine for too long, I feel trapped. I worked fast food in high school before I started experiment-ing with the spice combinations which was *against corporate policy*. Right out of high school, I worked as a barista at a hipster coffee shop, but I couldn't stand the snooty music playlist my coworkers looped on the daily, so I quit."

"There's only so much alt-rock one person can stand," I say in his defense.

"Exactly." He shrugs again but bigger this time. "Noth-ing fits. Nothing feels fulfilling. I guess I never considered that when I was in school. We'd have college fairs and ca-reer days and nobody ever talked about how we might end up doing a mundane task for forty hours a week just to live, which I know is a privileged thing to say. I'll be okay for a bit. It's just…"

"What?"

"I watched my mom work herself to the bone at jobs she hated to provide for me after her divorce. I…" His thought hovers between us. It's clear he's having a hard time form-ing a coherent sentence as we embark up another crest, this time leading to a patch of pavement where some people sit on blankets. "I never wanted to grind myself down like that. But I never zeroed in on a passion, so I guess I'm just one of those unfortunate people who never finds their calling. I gotta be cool with that."

His playful, poking personality goes into remission as he slows his pace to take in the view. I give his admission the space it deserves. This is the first glimmer of truth he's shown me, and I respect that. "Leo," I say softly when we've reached the edge of the lookout, Los Angeles a postcard-perfect panorama. "You're young. You have a lot of time to discover that stuff."

"Doesn't feel that way," he says with a rankled expression.

Part of me wants to reassure him that I'm right. If only I could proffer an example. Aren't I in the same situation he is? My jobs are dead ends. My spirits are low. My living arrangement is not long-term tenable. How can I offer assurance when I'm as unsure and uninsured as he is?

"We have a lot in common," I offer instead. Because it's the truth and it ties me to him, an invisible lasso swung round and pulled in. Somehow, it doesn't feel as restrictive when there's two of us trapped inside the scratchy rope.

Leo's face breaks open, brightening up a bit like the sun peeking out from behind a cloud. "Can't tell if that's a good thing or a bad thing right now."

"Valid."

"Look." He points to a white building with a gray domed roof. Beneath it, red seats speckle the landscape—the Greek Theatre, I believe. "The view is worth the sweat, right?"

I nod, scanning the horizon, but then my eyes swerve to land on his profile. Strong jaw. Killer eyelashes. A long neck that descends into bitable collarbones. I dream about the marks I'd love to leave there if he lets me.

From the zipper pocket in my shorts, I grab my phone. While Leo's still swept in the morning magic of Los Angeles as it bursts back to life, I snap a candid photo of him.

Right as I'm about to take another, he says, "I saw that."

I flush hot. "We need photos of us together for the audition!" I argue. "Really thought I was being sneaky, though."

"Good thing you're not a paparazzo."

I let out a pfft. "I'd be flat broke. I can barely take good selfies."

He angles into me. I track a single bead of sweat as it snakes down his neck and disappears between his defined pec muscles. Ungodly hot yet godlike. Damn. "I don't know. Last night, I think you made a strong case for the contrary."

I had almost forgotten about that influx of confidence, the dizzying mental fog and hunger I felt for him, for my own body and all it can sense and achieve. I could've bathed in that feeling. I want it. Again. Now.

"Don't worry," he says, quieter, probably taking my silence as a bad sign. "I deleted the photos and videos you sent me. I didn't know where we stood on saving, and I didn't want you to think I was some kind of collector or creep."

"I wouldn't have thought that, but thank you. That's very considerate of you." I know it's a simple courtesy, but frankly most guys wouldn't think to do that, let alone tell me they did. Leo's damn considerate and respectful which is almost as arousing as his kindness. "Guess I'll just have to send them again… Or, take more for you."

I step closer to him so that the toes of our mesh, dirt-stained sneakers are touching. Physically, it barely registers. Emotionally, I'm overloaded. Everything from his rugged scent to his barely there stubble sends shock waves through me.

"You could always just…" He nudges his toe closer. "Show me in person."

My heart jackhammers at the inside walls of my rib cage. I barely squeak out, "Happily."

He raises an eyebrow at me. "Should we get out of here, then?"

My whisper is a barely audible scrape. "I thought this was just the workout warm-up."

"Yeah," he says, self-confidence cascading out of his mouth. "The warm-up before I work *you* out."

My legs go weak, two melting candles on a windowsill. "Take me back."

"Can't wait anymore, can you?" There's that dominant tone again, a deep bass that strokes my desire for him. If there weren't so many people around, I'd pull him into a secluded path sheathed with shrubbery and service him. That's how hot the iron poker is prodding at me. I don't care how torn up my knees would get. They'd be welcome wounds.

I shake my head. Again and again until he understands how badly I need this.

"Let's go," I say.

He tugs me back by the edge of my tank top. "Not so fast." He takes his own phone out from the armband he's been wearing, positions us just so, and instructs, "Say cheese."

There, the front-facing camera captures Leo and me, side by side, the Griffith Observatory hovering over my right ear. Our faces are alight with genuine smiles. We take one normal. One silly. And on the third, he surprises me by taking his inside hand, cupping my chin, and gently guiding it up to meet his.

The third photo turns out the best: the two of us, drenched in sweat and sunlight, kissing our faces off.

Twelve

As soon as the elevator doors in the hotel close, I'm on Leo and he's on me.

My hands wander up underneath his sweat-soaked shirt. Rigid, gliding muscles tense under my fingertips. His hands tiptoe lower, exploring beneath the waistband of my leggings, before his palms rest on my exposed ass cheeks. An ecstatic sigh corkscrews out of me.

"Same jock or different one?" Leo growls the question into my mouth. A heady rush like he's shotgunning me, a high I've never felt before.

"You'll find out shortly."

The ding of the elevator is an unwelcome disruption. I want to smash the stop button, hot-box the space with our bodies. I'd like to have him ravish me against the mirrored wall so I can watch our tension as it sparks, but Leo must read my mind because he whispers, "Camera."

My eyes wander up to the small red light in the corner.

I groan a different kind of groan as I follow him out onto my floor. The mood morphs, but doesn't stop.

Leo walks backward, never dropping my hand. He yanks me close, presses my body to his. We waddle like a pair of cuddling penguins toward my room.

We're caught up in the rush of a swollen kiss when Leo jolts and stumbles forward into me. The sound of items hitting the carpet ring out behind him.

I open my eyes to see a housekeeping cart sticking partially out of the ajar door to my room. Rolls of toilet paper are unraveling across the floor like an April Fools' prank. A short woman with a round face and jet-black hair pops out from the bathroom.

Damn.

"Leo?" the woman says.

"Umma?" I swear I notice Leo step farther in front of me, blocking me from the woman's sight lines.

The woman sounds perplexed as she asks him a question in Korean. Leo's body remains a sturdy wall between me and this situation.

It clicks. Umma must mean mom in Korean. Leo may have gotten fired from Traveltineraries, but Mrs. Min, his mom, still is a permanent housekeeper here at this hotel, and we arrived just as she was cleaning my room.

Double damn.

"I'm off from work today," Leo switches to English and lies through his teeth. I forgot that not only are we faking our relationship for the show, but he's keeping his employment status from his mom. If we get cast, what's he going to tell her then?

At least with Dad, he'll watch *Madcap Market* live and I can answer his million questions after. Leo lives with his mom. He can't dodge her curiosity forever.

And now I'm undeniably nervous about this introduction I didn't prepare for. *Neither of us* prepared for. Tongue-wrestling in front of her isn't the best first impression.

There's stark silence from his mom's side and then: "Who is your friend?"

Hesitantly, I poke my head out. "Hi there." My wave makes the situation more awkward.

"This is Holden," Leo says quickly before I can get any other words out.

"Holden who?" I get the impression that Leo and his mom share a lot. How can you not when you've lived together alone for so long? Obviously, he's never mentioned me before which reads like a major red flag to her. On the hike, I was worried about Leo's exes, but maybe I should be more worried about Leo's mom blowing up our spot.

"Holden James," Leo says as if this offers any further explanation. "He's, uh, staying here. In this room. That you're cleaning."

She eyes us both. "I'm done cleaning. Well, almost." She shuffles toward the runaway toilet paper rolls, sighing the whole way, winding them back up. There's a quizzical set to her eyebrows when she returns. "Where did you two meet?" Somehow, it's like a I stumbled into a job interview.

I answer for a stammering Leo. "On an online forum for

a game show we both like." He shoots me with a look of surprise. It was the best I could come up with, and at the very least, it's good practice for when we tell the casting directors at *Madcap Market*. As queer men, we have undeniable practice in withholding secrets until we're ready to share.

"You watch game shows?" She steps closer to her son. I notice a name tag on her chest. It reads: Sun Young. When I look up to meet her eyes, it's abundantly clear she's not buying any of this, and from the flush on Leo's cheeks and the puffiness of his lips, she knows our true afternoon intentions, which is a new level of mortifying.

"Yeah, a bunch. When I get home from work. In my room. They're relaxing." Leo's shaky voice isn't exactly convincing. I'm going to need to coach him before Monday. He needs practice, needs to utilize that bedroom confidence he possesses. God, do we have our work cut out for us.

But right now, my only care is Leo's unease. We talked about my coming out, but not his. While agreeing to our scheme meant he was publicly out, that doesn't mean his mom is accepting as mine is.

Was.

"I thought you were always playing those video games on your computer." That makes sense to me. I picture Leo hunched over in a gaming chair, headset on, talking shit with his *Minecraft* buddies. Maybe he even live streams his adventures. While it's not my cup of tea, I could get behind spending lazy, rainy Sunday afternoons having Leo teach me about his favorite games, maybe even creating characters of my own to play side by side. Monitors and rolling chairs and quests and slow, sensual sex when our eyes grow too fatigued to look at screens any longer.

Wait, what am I talking about? There's no future beyond *Madcap Market*. *Focus, Holden*.

"Sometimes I'm playing video games," Leo answers. "Sometimes I'm watching *Madcap Market*."

The veil of befuddlement doesn't lift from Sun Young's face, which leads me to believe she's unfamiliar with it. I wonder what she'd think about her son going on a televised competition show. "Interesting. What are you doing up here?"

Judging by her expression, she absolutely knows what we were doing up here, but Leo speaks anyway, dispelling most of the uncomfortable tension. "We just got back from a hike. Holden was going to shower and change before we go out again."

His cover story feels scattershot at best, but Sun Young seems pleased enough to drop the subject, gathering her cleaning supplies and pushing her cart toward the hallway, nearly knocking me over in the process. She nods at me as she passes. "Don't forget that it's your turn to cook dinner tonight. I don't want that pickled cabbage going to waste."

Leo glances at me first. "I won't forget, Umma. I'll be home in enough time to make the bossam. I promise."

"Good. You are welcome to join us," Mrs. Min says to me before moving on to the next room.

"Oh, thank you." I'm oddly touched by the invitation, even if it sounded offhanded and not entirely welcoming.

That interaction was an ice-cold bucket of water dropped

on our afternoon. Even though the door is closed and Leo's mom is gone, her presence lingers. We can hear the vacuum start up in the next room. How can we baptize those sheets when Leo's mom has just changed them?

"Sorry, uh, about that." Leo ventures farther into the room, a frantic energy bouncing off him, even as he sits in the chair at the table he's become so familiar with.

I shut the door. "Don't be sorry. It's not your fault."

"I know, but..."

I laugh a little. "I think we can both restrain ourselves for a bit longer."

"It's not just that." He slides a hand down his sweaty face. I want to understand what's plaguing him right now, but his face snaps back from sad to frustrated too rapidly. "Whatever, please don't feel obligated to come to dinner. She will ask you a trillion personal questions if you do."

I consider this. "Maybe I should, then." Leo's eyes widen. "Come on, if we can convince your mom that we're internet friends turned boyfriends, then there's no way a team of casting professionals won't buy it. It'll be a good barometer. It's not like your performance just now was very strong."

"Sorry I'm not an actor." He rolls his eyes.

"You should be sorry. You have a face for the screen." He blushes at that, exactly as I hoped he would. "Anyway, we can spend all day today preparing, so that by tonight we're absolute pros. She'll think we're wild for each other."

He hems and haws, even if I do detect newfound delight behind his eyes. "Okay, sure, but I don't have that much time. Bossam is kind of a labor-intensive dish to make. The pork belly can take a while to cook depending on the thickness of the cut."

I shrug. "We'll multitask. I'll help. Consider me your sous-chef."

"Have you cooked before?"

"Not much, but you can trust me not to burn your apartment building down." I smile innocently at him. "What do you say?"

He stands. "I say be prepared to take orders because I'm notoriously bossy in the kitchen."

"Good," I purr back. "That's just how I like it."

Cooking with Leo is a lot like what I imagine finally bottoming for him will be like.

Leo dominates with agile hands, firm instructions, and occasionally positions my body to get a better angle on my task.

Dutifully, I take the orders as we work toward our desired results, adding ingredients and spices one by one to a bright orange Dutch oven that sits on the stove top in the kitchen of their two-bedroom apartment.

The place Leo shares with his mom is small, yet the furniture is arranged for maximum openness. A cherrywood table with drop-leaf sides. A love seat and a recliner in matching maroon fabrics. A TV mounted to the wall (probably Leo's doing) with no clunky furniture beneath.

Between the island and the stove, there isn't much room for two adult bodies who are peeling and slicing radishes, which means we continuously bump elbows, brush arms.

Sometimes, I sense Leo lean into a brush, and the temptation to kiss him nearly kills me.

But I don't kiss him. I focus so I don't lose a finger.

Even as, over a cutting board, he wraps his arms around mine and the sharp knife in my grip becomes an extension of both of our arms, binding us in an intimate way.

"We met on the forum as friends. You always had feelings for me but I was dating someone. When you found out we'd broken up, you invited me out here anyway and, on a whim, we decided to audition for *Madcap Market*." I'm going over our agreed upon spiel again, so we master it.

"How long were we talking for?" he asks, adding Korean chili flakes to the radishes. He taps them out with such precision.

"Maybe four, five months? Time flies when you're talking about your favorite show."

"That's good." Leo sets the shaker down. "I might use that."

Leo lets me mix in the green onions and sesame oil before we set our creation in the refrigerator to chill. As he checks on the simmering pork, he says, "I think we can get away with the rest by saying it was love at first sight."

"Huh?" My heart wriggles into my throat. "Love? Who said anything about love?"

His eyes crinkle. "Well, how else are they going to buy the fact that you checked in on a Thursday and we're dating on a Monday. Love has happened in less time. Ever heard of Romeo and Juliet?"

"Nope, are they friends of yours?" I joke, starting on the

garlic slices which will be used as a garnish. "Fine. We're in love." I get hit with a quick flash of Buckley sitting in our old living room watching TV, flipping channels until he lands on my face. He'll stop just long enough on the new episode of *Madcap Market* to hear Leo say we're in love. Will his stomach sink slow like a penny to the bottom of a fountain or quick like an anchor dropped off the side of a boat? Either way, fake or not, karma will collect that day, and I'll be the one smiling about it.

Smiling doubly because good-in-the-kitchen Leo will be beside me. Just like now. Making every moment more electric than the last.

"And let's say we have plans for me to come visit you in New York next. I'll meet your dad and see where you grew up and you'll take me to my first Broadway show." He sounds excited by the prospect, even if we are weaving a false reality. Even if, at the end of this, we'll probably just split our winnings and go our separate ways. A handshake to seal this experience off. It's not like you can build a life in one week.

"I wouldn't have pegged you for the show tune type."

"I'm not, but I'm big into those flashy jukebox musicals. Give me a diva belting a pop hit in a shiny costume, and I'm there." The playlist we've been listening to since we started cooking included a lot of Carly Rae Jepsen, Katy Perry, and Beyoncé.

"We should go to *Moulin Rouge*, then. You'd love it. The cast recording is awesome. I wanted to go with my ex, but he said it was all style and no substance." At the time, I took it solely as an insult to the show, but in hindsight, I wonder if he was judging my tastes as well, turning his nose up at the prospect of spending a hundred dollars on escapism.

In a way, being with Leo feels like escapism, except… tangible.

"Look, no offense, but your ex sounds like a massive jerk. Everything you've told me about the guy sounds like a high-flying red flag."

"No. I'm making it out to be worse than it was." I arrange three small glass bowls on the countertop. "He just didn't want to spend money on things he knew he wouldn't enjoy. Then again, he knew I wouldn't enjoy his work holiday mixer at some virtual golf establishment, but I went anyway with a smile on my face."

"That sounds, uh, not exactly fun, but at least intriguing."

"It was neither fun nor intriguing," I admit, setting the table. The clock tells me Mrs. Min will be back soon. "To make matters worse, he didn't even introduce me. Instead, he called me over, 'H! H, come here!' He was three drinks down the rabbit hole at this point. I stood there, cocktail sweating in my hand, forehead slick, too, wondering what he'd told them about me. Everyone in the room appeared straight-presenting, and he was weird about introductions back in college."

"He was out, though?" Leo asks.

"Oh, yeah. He was out, but I guess not to his coworkers because this woman Helena with short curly hair wearing a poinsettia-patterned shirt asked how long we'd been *roommates*."

"Christ, that's fucked-up."

I shrug. "I excused myself for a drink refill, but really, I dipped into the bathroom. In a stall with a TV screen built into the door playing some old golf game, dozens of men in polos, I sobbed into a roll of single-ply toilet paper."

Leo stops what he's doing, eyes softening. "I'm sorry you went through that."

"Hey, it's fine. We're over now. It's cool," I say, even though I'm boiling with the memories. "Maybe he had homophobic coworkers. I'm sure he had his reasons."

Leo crosses to the table, unspeaking. For a moment, I think he might not say anything at all. It's not until he flips up the end of the table I'm going to be sitting at that he finally looks toward me. "I think anyone who ditches out on you is an idiot."

My excuses peel away like price tag stickers, and the compliment cozies up inside my heart. I smile, I nod, but I don't say anything because the front door is opening. Mrs. Min comes inside and sniffs the air.

"Smells delicious." She sets her bags beside the doorway.

"Wash up, Umma. Dinner's almost ready." As if to punctuate his point, the timer for the pork goes off.

Thirteen

The pork may be cooked to perfection, but Mrs. Min drops me and Leo in the Dutch oven—heat turned all the way up—the moment we set our napkins on our laps to eat.

From there, her line of questioning is pointed, and the sweat beads at my hairline immediately. We trained for this, so how do I still feel woefully unprepared to answer her? Even the softball questions are lobbed from a haywire machine in a batting cage, each shot rattling the chain-link fence we tried to build up around us.

I try to focus on the tasty meal we cooked. I wasn't too familiar with Korean cuisine prior, but now I'm certain I'm going to need Leo to share more recipes with me before I go. When I get my own place back in New York, I think about how I'm going to teach myself to cook. Meals for one may sound sad and solitary to some, but each bite of this dish is made more delicious because it came from my hands. I want to bottle that pride and hold tight to it.

"How long have you two known each other?" Mrs. Min asks.

"About five months." Leo takes a bite of cabbage wrap so he doesn't have to elaborate, which he's been doing this whole time. Skillful. The last thing we need is to contradict ourselves. I wish there were a stenographer in the corner typing all this out, keeping a running record of our masterful lies for posterity and to study later.

Mrs. Min's knife scrapes the bottom of her plate, making me jump. "Weren't you seeing that guy from the hotel in South Park, near that music museum you liked, five months ago?" Her eyes never lift from her meal. It's apparent she thinks she's trapped him in a lie because she evidently knows his tells.

Strangely, I have no way to swoop in and save this one for him. Leo said on our hike that he had a dating history yet had never had an official partner. Are he and his mom that close that he'd talk about someone he was seeing casually? It seems suspicious, and I'm lightly jealous.

"I was." Leo's plate is clean and his glass is empty. His eyes grow panicked without a stall tactic. "Holden and I were just friends then. You knew about Carter, right?"

Carter. I don't think I've ever even met a Carter. "Yeah, of course I knew about Carter."

"He was a nice man. Very polite." I can tell by her tone that this isn't a slight to me, but her spoon has become a trowel because she's digging for answers. It's both concerning and sweet. She cares about Leo enough to want to be abreast with what's going on in his life. Right now, though, I wish her curiosity would satiate itself for the sake of my sweat glands.

"Umma, I told you, Carter won't be coming around anymore." Leo's firm on this.

"You bring home a nice half-Korean man who is very respectful and then, poof, he never shows up again. You never told me why. Naturally I'm going to bring it up." She murmurs something in Korean.

He shoots her a withering look. "Umma, we have company. Please."

"You said he's just a friend..." Her eyebrows are raised in challenge.

"I said he *was* just a friend," Leo corrects. "Now we're together." He grasps my hand which has been fisted on the table beside him. It unravels and our fingers link together. The touch of his palm is welcome and convincing. Even my own brain is tricked into thinking he's sending me a supportive message with his gesture.

It's not difficult at all to muster up a gooey, loving smile for Leo—after the board game and the grocery store and the hike and the cooking, I can see all the little ways he'd make someone an ideal partner.

Not me, of course, because this is fake.

There will be flirting and cooking and sex (please, God, let there be more sex), but there won't be feelings that can be dashed to pieces. There won't be ties or tethers or year-long leases or shared kitchen appliances.

At the end of this, there will be no broken hearts. There will be a massive check and a mutual parting. So, I put on a smile and perfect the role I'm performing in this mini play I've stepped into.

"As soon as we saw each other at the hotel, things sort of…clicked." The words don't feel like lies in my mouth. Despite our banter, there was an undeniable chemistry between us when I hassled him that day. Tense, but effortless.

"When you know, you know." Leo's uneasiness is nowhere to be found. His voice is unwavering and his eye contact goes unbroken. Those brown eyes entrap me.

"Who wants some fruit?" Mrs. Min says, breaking the moment.

Once she's left the room, with the island and a small, slatted accordion window between us, I turn to Leo and ask in a whisper, "Who's Carter?"

"No one." Leo hasn't let go of my hand. Surprisingly, I don't want him to.

"Didn't sound like no one." I probably shouldn't press, but it's important I know. If this Carter was in Leo's life enough for his mom to comment on his absence, then I should be aware. I can't curb my own curiosity either.

"He was one of the managers at one of the hotels I shuffled through. It was nothing serious."

"Serious enough that your mom knew about him."

He sighs, sags a tad. "Only because…never mind. It's really not important."

"Isn't it? I asked you if you were seeing anyone recently we had to be concerned about."

"We don't have to be concerned because he won't say anything."

"How do you know?"

"I just do?" His words sound flimsy, anxious.

"But—"

Mrs. Min is back with a tray.

"Holden, tell me more about your family." Mrs. Min says this as she passes me a bowl.

I thank her before saying, "I grew up in New York. I'm an only child. My dad's in furniture sales and he makes his own woodwork pieces, too."

"That's very noble. Does he sell them?"

"Yeah, just not at the store he manages." I fiddle with the handle of my spoon. "He has an online shop. I used to help him package and send orders when I was younger but he's doing it less these days, focusing more on the for-sure money he gets from his salary."

"I understand, and what about your mother? What does she do?"

The air goes stale; my chest constricts. Even after all this time, being asked about Mom makes me seize up.

"She's no longer with us, Umma," Leo answers for me, a kindness I desperately needed.

"Oh, I am so sorry."

I shake my head. "Don't be. You didn't know."

"How did she…".

"Umma."

"It's okay." I squeeze Leo's hand, which still hasn't left mine. Such a steady, comforting gesture. Does he realize?

Is it intentional? "She had breast cancer, which she beat, but then she got a blood clot in her lower leg. Everything happened really quickly. She drove me to school that morning on her way to work—she was a kindergarten teacher. I remember I had been arguing with her, begging her to let me drive myself like all the other seniors, but we were a three-person family with only two cars. That was the last time I saw her."

"Were you close?" Mrs. Min asks.

"Umma." Leo's voice has more warning to it.

She glares at her son. "It's good to discuss these matters. Death is not dirty. It is a blessing. It is the end of suffering."

I nod, allowing Mrs. Min's words to resonate fully. "She had been suffering. The cancer really took its toll on her, but we remained close. Our special thing was watching *Madcap Market* together. It was a good distraction from life."

There's a noticeable shift in Leo's visage like he's unlocked the answer to a question he's been holding back. I get confirmation of that when he phrases the question like a statement for the benefit of his mom. "That's why we're auditioning for the show together on Monday."

Mrs. Min chokes on her fruit. "Auditioning for a TV game show?"

"When we thought she wasn't going to make it during the cancer scare, I told her I'd win the show one day for her since we wouldn't be able to do it together. Leo has thoughtfully offered to be my partner." *In more ways than one*, though I don't say that part out loud.

Understanding washes over Mrs. Min's face, the wrinkle lines smoothing out into a gentle kindness. "In that case, I wish you both luck." I pause to consider whether she means in our new relationship—which I can tell she's finally deemed real—or at the audition.

"Now," she adds, eyes lighting up, "do you want to see Leo's baby pictures?"

Leo's groans don't sway my answer. We sit in the living room for an hour or more, flipping through pages of Leo as a child. Leo in the bathtub with a sudsy mohawk of black hair. Leo in his very first karate class looking miserable, brow furrowed, hair in a bowl cut. Mrs. Min flips fast past the pages with Leo and a tall, stocky white man with blond hair whom I can only assume is Leo's dad.

In all of them, he has a cigarette dangling from the corner of his unsmiling mouth. There are always inches of distance between the pair. There are none of them as a full family. Mrs. Min is barely in any of these pictures at all, actually.

"I don't see a lot of you in here," I say, but then regret it, considering it might be a sore spot.

Mrs. Min shrugs her shoulders, adjusts the blanket on her lap.

"She doesn't like getting her picture taken," Leo says from a recliner beside the couch. He hasn't been looking—probably because he's seen these photos a million times but also probably because some of these photos bring back painful memories. I know the way a snapshot can send you down a rickety road in your mind, only to be lost in the tangle of branches and thorns.

"Your father also never bothered to pick up a camera," Mrs. Min retorts.

By the second album, Leo's father has disappeared from the pictures entirely. I can't quite tell how old Leo is in these, but if I had to guess, I'd say he's in middle school. And from the steep drop-off in his appearances, I'd say whatever happened, it happened swiftly. Leo's dad was there one day and gone the next.

It also marked Leo's transition from yellow belt to hip-hop sneakers. I wonder if Leo's dad leaving let Leo be more himself.

I want to ask, but I don't have Mrs. Min's directness or Leo's courage. I know it will only come out wrong, and I don't want to ruin the evening. It's been so nice so far.

Coming to LA, I thought I'd be out at clubs and touring movie studios, but this quiet evening with these two is relaxing. I've spent the better part of this trip trying to fashion it into everything I envisioned, when I'm starting to realize that even the best laid plans can pivot without notice.

I thought Mom would see me graduate college. I thought Buckley was my forever guy. I thought Alexia would prove her true friendship and compete with me on *Madcap Market*. Maybe the universe is trying to tell me that clinging to my own ideas for the future has only closed me off to the myriad of surprises the world has to offer.

This trip. This man. This meal. This night.

It all might be the perfect combination to help me change my outlook.

"Would you like to see one of Leo's old recital videos?" Mrs. Min asks, closing the second book.

I cut Leo off before he can protest. "Oh, do I ever!"

Fourteen

"Last chance to back out," I say to Leo as we stand on the television studio back lot. Racks of costumes roll by and people in headsets scurry across our path, yelling indistinguishable words to unseen others. The street is alive with stress and excitement, and even though I almost get run over by a speeding golf cart, I couldn't care less because there's a large sign that says MADCAP MARKET AUDITIONS THIS WAY in front of me. Once we follow that arrow, we're in this. There's no reneging the lie, no going back.

He nudges me with his elbow. "There's no way I'm backing out. Let's do this."

After we check in at the first table and fill out our casting forms on tablets, we're brought into a massive holding room swarming with hopefuls. Everyone is talking animatedly to one another. Leo and I find a mostly empty corner to catch our breath. The temperature rises the longer the room fills

up. The heat and my nerves are the perfect tag team for pit
stains. Perhaps I should've worn a darker color.

"Y'all excited?" asks a blonde, white woman beside us
with twin braids snaking down her back. She's got a slight
twang to her voice as she bounces on the balls of her feet
with excitement. "I'm Jessica and this is my cousin, Darla."
Darla seems to be more interested in the game on her phone
than her surroundings. "What number audition is this for
you both?"

"This is our first time out here," I tell her.

"Ah, we got a couple of virgins over here." She smacks
Darla in the arm. Darla doesn't even flinch. I wish I could
be as unaffected as Darla. "This is our sixth time here."

"Seventh," Darla corrects, finally acknowledging us, voice
barely audible over the roar of the noisy crowd. There have
to be a couple hundred people in here minimum.

"Seventh. Right. Sorry." Jessica recalibrates. "You lose
track after a while."

"Is it common to audition more than once?" Leo asks.

"Absolutely. The casting directors are super picky." Jessica stresses the word *super*. She's got the exact kind of personality they feature on this show—overly bubbly. We're
going to need to lean into the theatrics to compete with
her. "Wouldn't be one of TV's longest running game shows
without the right combination of contestants on every episode. A new crop of locals come to the weekly open calls
over and over. Sometimes they cut you based on your outfit.
Sometimes they cut you based on your partner. Sometimes
they already chose another cousin duo for the upcoming

taping, which was our luck last time. We got so close and then got the boot. Still salty over that."

My anxiety doubles. Nowhere in my research did it say any of this. Though, in fairness, I was too excited to think straight when I realized I had the money to seize this opportunity finally. "Sorry to hear that."

"Oh, it's all right," Jessica says. "Just don't be discouraged if you don't get it this time. We've met a ton of people over the weeks who eventually get it. They make you wait a week or two, but you can always come back."

"Um, well, I'm from New York." I swallow a wad of panic spit that has taken up residence in my throat. "So, I kind of can't just come back."

Jessica's face falls. I swear I notice a slight smirk on Darla's lips as if she's just eliminated us as potential competition for her today. "Sorry, I didn't realize. Since they don't fly anyone out for the show and still do open calls the old-fashioned way, I just assume everyone's local."

A casting director comes out with a megaphone and a clipboard. She calls the room to attention and announces the first group of potential contestants—including Jessica and Darla—to follow her into the next room for the first round of the audition.

"Nice meeting you both. Good luck!" Jessica says. Darla doesn't even look back.

When the first group fully filters out, Leo turns to me. "This might be harder than we thought."

"Yeah." I rub the back of my neck. "You're right."

Luckily, by the time our group is called, we fly through

the first round, which was standing in a single file line in a room as an assistant walked by us and looked us over. Leo and I make a handsome pair, are sure not to slouch, and introduce ourselves with so much enthusiasm you could've sworn we were Disney World employees, so we immediately get tapped to wait out in the hall for the next round.

Our conviction builds with each round we breeze through. In the easy trivia round, I get all of mine right. Leo gets half of his right, which is a major step up and lets me know he's been taking his studying seriously. When he gives me two thumbs-ups as our names are called to advance, I want to pin a gold star to his shirt and congratulate him with a kiss. The kind of kiss that would probably get us kicked out of here.

The third round is a bouncy castle. Yes, the kind that get rented for children's birthday parties. Only one person in the pair has to partake, so Leo steps up, doing exactly as we planned—peeling off his wholesome cardigan to give the casting associates a front-row seat to the gun show still blazing beneath the tight sleeves of his polo.

It has the desired effect as Leo easily weaves his way through the tipping bags and over the hill, besting the competition by a mile at least. Even though we don't get any extra points for being the first to finish, Leo—wearing the giddiest, cutest smile—bounces onto his butt with flair and comes sliding down to meet the waiting casting assistant holding a sweat towel and a bottle of water.

It's only when Leo comes back to me that I realize my nerves have skittered away, replaced by...fun? We put so much pressure on this that I forgot one of the tenets of *Mad-cap Market* is the pure joy of the game. It's been so long since I've loosened up like this.

Once the crowd has been whittled down, we brave a final interview with the head of casting. Minutes pass like hours.

We're called into the small room where bright lights are set up and squared off to a pair of uncomfortable-looking fabric chairs. There's a large black camera on a tripod set up to the side of a long table where an older white man and an older white woman sit, shuffling through papers, whispering to one another.

"Right this way," a brown-skinned casting associate wearing twee glasses says, ushering us over to sit. I squirm, attempting and failing to relax. Then, Leo's hand lands on my thigh, a possessive touch that grabs the attention of the chatty casting directors. The camera starts rolling.

The woman's smile beams even from behind the lights. "Leo Min and Holden James, thank you for coming in. Leo, you're from town, but Holden, it says here your address is out in New York. What brings you to Los Angeles?"

Assurance blooming, I place my hand on top of Leo's and squeeze. "This guy."

He may not be the reason I flew out here, but miraculously, he is the reason I've stayed and enjoyed it. That counts for something, and makes the words sound more truthful.

The man jumps in: "Says here you two met on a fan forum. Our show brought about this spark?" He uses the cap end of his pen to point between us.

"The internet and your show, yes." Leo's voice is a calm

pond, zero ripples. I'm damn proud. "Nothing brings two people together more than the love of the game."

Leo's words resonate deep in my heart. *Madcap Market* brought Mom and me together during her darkest days. Now it's bringing Leo and me together, parting the storm clouds of grief and loss—of both my mom and my longest romantic relationship. This game really has given me a lot.

"And what made you decide to audition for us right after your initial meeting?" the woman asks, eyeing our paperwork. "You've written that you met only a few days ago. Is this a de facto first date?"

Aside from our thwarted attempts to fuck and our rehearsals, this is the closest we've come to a full day together. It is nearly a date and, from her expression, I can tell she likes the angle so I nod vigorously. "We thought this would be the true test of our connection—a high-pressure game show to see if it's really love at first sight."

The word *love* is dark chocolate on my tongue, a bittersweet shot of dopamine.

"I have to say, we've been on the air for so long and that's a new story for us," the man says, nodding to an older darkskinned man nearby who is wearing a turtleneck despite the heat. He must be the director.

"We'd use the prize money," Leo adds, "to make longdistance work while we figure out our relationship. Maybe even set some aside to find a together home."

A heat travels down me. This wasn't part of what we rehearsed. It's good, though. Even I get swept into the fantasy he weaves as he talks about wanting to meet my dad and about how I cooked dinner for his mom the other night. He's making us sound like we're a real couple and he has real feelings and I'm real light-headed. So much so that I don't even notice when they lob the next question at me: "What drew you to this show?"

Before I can question it, I'm gushing about Mom, telling them about her cancer and our cookie baking and the way we'd place bets on which team we thought would come out victorious. We never gambled more than loose change, but once I filled up a mason jar full, Mom would take me out for soft serve in a waffle cone.

Maybe it's the lights in my eyes, but I swear I see the white man pull a tissue from the box on the table. I wasn't pulling out the sympathy card on purpose. After talking with Mrs. Min and Leo about Mom, a dam erupted inside me. All the words I held back for years suddenly flowed, didn't feel like they were drowning me from the inside.

"Thank you for sharing that with us." The woman offers me an understanding smile before nodding to the camera-person who stops rolling. "It was lovely to meet you both. We'll be in touch *very* soon."

When we exit the studio, dusk blanketing the city, Leo's car in the distance, Leo jumps up and does a bell kick. "We fucking did that!" He bangs his fists on his chest and lets out a "Whoop!"

"We didn't get cast yet," I say as we cross the asphalt parking lot.

His eyes bug out at me. "Did you see them? They were eating it up! They were practically singing 'Holden and

Leo sitting in a tree, K-I-S-S-I-N-G!' We have to go out and celebrate."

He's so joyous. I hate to crush his high, but: "That's a little premature."

Leo unlocks his car but stops me from getting in the passenger's side by leaning against the door, placing a hand around my waist, and tugging my body into his. He sets me ablaze. "I'm an adult who just flew through a bouncy obstacle course for the chance to grocery shop like the apocalypse is coming. I deserve a nice drink."

I think about what Leo said on our hike, about relationships not being deserved but earned, and I realize that he's right. All this time, I've been so down on myself over all the miseries life has dealt me, assuming the universe owed me happiness now in return, but perhaps happiness doesn't work that way.

Happiness is something we make for ourselves.

Happiness is finding people who care.

Happiness is a former faux concierge driving you to a bar for drinks and driving you wild with his smile.

Fifteen

"The Silver Pig Café is the spot to go," Leo says.

I don't know the city well enough to offer up another suggestion, but I don't remember seeing it on any of the travel blogs. My reservations come to a head when we walk up and I see: Karaoke EVERY SINGLE NIGHT.

The sign makes my stomach drop.

"Leo, this is a karaoke bar."

Leo raises his eyebrows. "Yeah, and? This is where I come to celebrate good news."

"Again," I say to his back as he opens the door, "we haven't gotten any good news yet."

"It's coming soon. I can sense it, so let's sing about it." I got a taste of Leo's singing in the car the other day. It's good that *Madcap Market* isn't anything like *American Idol* or we'd have been cut way sooner.

We enter a nondescript office building through a green door instructing us not to bring in any outside food or drinks. It's a tiny dive with low-lit lanterns on the ceiling and purple and blue DJ lights spinning on the walls.

The tables and chairs are light wood. There are screens speckled around the perimeter of the room. One shows the lineup of waiting singers. The others show the lyrics to the current song: "Ain't No Mountain High Enough." Two women do a duet up on a stage. One is excellent. The other is trying her best.

Leo orders us two Horny Pigs (sugary cocktails, apparently) and a plate of dumplings to share. I'm starved after our long day. Once I settle into the atmosphere, take a sip of my drink, and down a dumpling in a single bite, the hectic, anxiety-filled audition process drifts away. It's just me and Leo looking at each other over a high-top table as the song shifts from "Shallow" to "All About That Bass."

"Why here? Why karaoke?" I ask with my mouth still half-full. I'm surprised by how unselfconscious I am around Leo. With Buckley, I always sensed a pressing need to be buttoned up. Pluck. Groom. Smile. Chew quietly. Tread lightly. Leo is loud, unabashed, and I want some of that to rub off on me about as much as I want him to rub up on me and, ahem, that's saying something.

The tiny straw in his cocktail becomes a toothpick dangling off the side of his mouth giving a bad boy air about him. "Because everybody's tipsy, excited to be here, and nobody cares if you're good. There's no prizes, no competition, just good, old-fashioned fun."

I glance over at the man up on the stage really working the crowd with the Meghan Trainor track. He does look like he's having fun. "That could not be me." I flush hot just thinking about how embarrassed I'd be.

"You can't come to a karaoke bar and not sing."

"You couldn't pay me enough to get up there."

"I couldn't pay you anything because I'm unemployed, remember?" he says, a self-deprecating jab. "You stand in front of a class and dance. You're going to be on live TV—"

"*Might* be going on live TV," I correct.

"Semantics." He winks, volume dropping low. "You showed off for me on FaceTime. You can't be shy."

"I—" I'm floundering for a response. While he's right, how do I tell him that this Los Angeles me is new? Back in New York, I don't think I'd have been so brash, so easily whisked away. Still with Buckley, I think this trip would've been regimented, planned by the minute with little room for deviation. I wouldn't have stumbled into a dive bar where an elderly woman is now singing "(You Make Me Feel Like) A Natural Woman" by Carole King, that's for sure. "I think it's you."

Leo's eyebrows furrow. "I don't understand."

"I think—" I dig deep for the nerve to be vulnerable about something other than Mom "—that you make me feel comfortable. There's something…" The right word is a butterfly fluttering away from my net. "Uh, comforting about being around you?"

"Is that a question or a statement?" he asks.

"A statement."

The compliment shifts his expression. His smile doesn't even slightly resemble a smirk. It's the most genuine smile

I've ever seen from him. "Thank you. That means a lot. I feel comfortable around you, too. You've got an energy that I really like."

"What kind of energy is that?" I cut the last dumpling up and offer him the bigger side.

"Don't take this the wrong way," he begins, biding his time by chewing.

"Nothing good comes after 'Don't take this the wrong way.'" I hide my face in my hands.

"It's just..." He audibly swallows, and I peek between my fingers. His Adam's apple bobs bringing attention to his long neck that had to have been made by a sculptor's hand. "You're sad. I can sense it, but that sadness has a strength to it."

My heart rate picks up as I meet his eyes. Words fail to come as I process this poetry he's just dropped on me.

He goes on when I fail to find coherence. "Most people who lost a parent so young and just ended an almost four-year relationship would be pretending to be fine. I think there's power in being sad and still getting out of bed every day, still going on a vacation to Los Angeles to maybe audition for a TV game show."

"Power or stupidity?" I ask, shirking his attempt at really deep connection. Wasn't coming here a bid at fineness? The whole plane ride I watched movies, drank diet sodas, and shut out the world, fantasized about leaving the hurt in the airport drop-off lane.

Leo grabs my hands, waits until I face him again to continue speaking. "It's power, Holden. You can't work through something if you repress it." He pauses for a second, tilting his head as if he's straining to hear someone else's conversation. Mulling something over, maybe. Then, he snaps back. "All I'm saying is, it's cool that you feel your feelings. There's no guessing with you. If you're sad, you say you're sad. If you're horny, you say you're horny. Makes getting to know you easy and fun."

I'm touched by Leo's words. He's looking at me with a fantastic openness that thrills me. I wish we could body swap just for a second, so I could see me the way he says he does. Since Mom passed, I've largely cast myself as the boy who lost his mom right before graduation. Then, I took on the role of Buckley's boyfriend. I hinged my identity on others, decided I knew how people regarded me before giving people a chance to get to know me. The me underneath the miseries.

Maybe Leo's right. Maybe all that grief and heartbreak allowed me to shed the worry that my interests are silly and my emotions are wrong. How could I ever be wrong when I made *this* right choice: agreeing to fake date Leo?

"Let's do a duet," I say brazenly, unable to properly thank him for his kind words that nearly brought tears to my eyes. I'll sing those words instead, and I know just the song to do it with.

"I'm down. What song?" I'm sure he's got many go-tos.

I borrow his smirk, play it coy for the fun of it. "Can I surprise you?"

He lounges back in his chair. "Be my guest, but I'm notoriously hard to surprise."

When I go up to the booth, a white man with a bun on the top of his head and cushiony gold headphones wrapped around the back, hands me a binder not dissimilar to the one Leo handed me on the first day I arrived with all the restaurants in it. The song selections are listed alphabetically by artist so I flip to the *L*'s and there among the track titles is the song of my heart, the one that I know will excite Leo the most.

Back at the table, Leo has ordered us a second round, which is good because I'm going to need it. I finish off my first glass, vibrating with anxious excitement. More people have arrived since I put our names on the list—which now appear on a screen hovering over Leo's head—which means more eyes on me. More people to judge me.

No. What is it Leo just said about me? I'm powerful. Powerful people can have a good time singing in front of strangers with a faux-concierge-not-quite-stranger. I keep telling myself that when our names are called, when we choose our mic stands.

All the uneasiness fades away when the song title appears on the screen and Leo's face breaks into the most infectious smile I've ever seen. It's "Rain on Me" by Lady Gaga and Ariana Grande and since I've started this, I take the first part—belting about good times and rainfall and pushing through misery.

My voice starts out timid, shaky, but when the pre-chorus kicks in I'm singing the refrain with a strong certainty that seems to pleasantly surprise Leo. He takes it up a notch when the chorus proper comes in and, without missing a beat, he breaks into the fast-paced, high-energy choreography from the music video. It's flawless and beautiful and full-bodied. He's jumping, kicking, and body rolling, completely undisturbed by our audience who, by their cheers, are eating this up.

So am I. I'm awed by his moves and his charisma. Even more wowed when, barely out of breath, he picks up Ariana's verse. Does he sound good? Absolutely not. But it doesn't matter. His whole heart is in it, so I match him.

By the time the bridge comes in, we're trading lyrics like secrets, sweaty foreheads pressed together, microphones at our mouths, cords snaked behind us. As we sing about throwing our hands up to the sky, the crowd does it without question, which prompts me to dance my ass off, following Leo's lead until the song comes to its declarative conclusion.

Under the roar of the crowd, Leo whispers into my ear. "You are full of surprises."

"On the night we met, you said surprises aren't all they're cracked up to be."

"You're the exception to the rule."

Then, he kisses me deeply for the entire crowd to see, and I'm utterly enchanted by him.

Sixteen

"My place isn't far," Leo says when we step offstage.

That's how, twenty minutes later, I find my back pressed against his paint-chipped apartment door as he fumbles to get the key in the lock while kissing me with fervor and tongue.

"Uh-oh, this doesn't bode well," I joke, breaking the kiss to look down at his shaking hand that can't seem to find the hole.

"Oh, shut up," he says on a laugh, giving me a playful shove that riles me up even more. "I know what I'm doing." Right then, the door gives way and I stumble inside backward, nearly landing on my ass, but Leo—superhuman Leo—catches me before I hit the ground.

"Really sweeping me off my feet, huh?"

He bites his lip. "I do try my best."

When he stands me upright, I catch a glimpse of his mom's shoes by the door. "Is she…"

He shakes his head. "No, she's got an overnight. I double-checked." I appreciate his preparedness.

With a nod, he takes me to a room in the apartment I hadn't seen on my last visit: his bedroom. It's smaller than it looked during our FaceTime. He's got a queen-sized bed in the center of the room, a small bedside table with a lamp, and a string of fairy lights draped over the window. When he plugs those in, the room is awash with an intimate amber glow.

The click of the door closing makes my heart trip inside my chest. I sit on the edge of the bed, run my hand along the black comforter. I worry for the first time that our sex won't live up to the lofty expectations. This has been so drawn out. Can the reality match the fantasy we've been toying with this whole time?

Leo comes to stand in front of me, wickedly smiles down at me, and I let those founded fears drift away for now. He's removed his shirt so effortlessly. He grabs my hand with a gentle force and presses my palm to his stomach. The skin is hot, and it grows hotter as he directs my palm downward to the rounded bulge tenting the front of his pants.

"I think it's time for a different kind of duet," he tells me with hooded eyes and messy hair. "Strip."

It's a knee-jerk reaction to follow orders. My shoes fly across the room, and in seconds I'm completely naked in front of him. From the bed, he drops a pillow in front of him and points down. I sink to the floor, so my face is exactly where he wants it. Where I want it, too.

Following his lead is the most natural thing.

"Take my pants off," he instructs, but when I loop my fingers into his underwear as well, he stops me. *Just* my pants."

They fall revealing a pair of black boxer briefs that push his package forward, a delicious display. I run my hands up the backs of his muscular calves I admired on our hike, feeling the sparse black hairs as my palms rove over him. Overcome, I start kissing and biting the inside of his juicy thighs.

He steps back. "Can't keep your mouth off me, can you?"

I shake my head.

"I like how eager you are, but this has been put off so long that I want to make it last." He licks his full lips, looking down at me. "Take off my underwear nice and slow. Slower...slower..." It's a whisper, a prayer. His erection springs out from beneath the waistband and I'm hit with the scent of him, clean musk that goes straight to my head. "Are you okay with this arrangement?"

There's a sweet hesitancy threaded into his question, which helps me understand him all that much better. Leo has so little control over much of his life that here, in the bedroom, he can play a role that goes against his everyday nature. I nod, all too ready to give myself over to him in this way, be the good submissive for him tonight.

"If it ever gets to be too much, just say pizza."

"Why pizza?"

"Because," he says, stepping closer to me, "ever since our Monopoly night I can't smell a slice without thinking of you, of that first kiss and you asking me to stay."

I hadn't realized that night still lingered for Leo, too. This is all about a game show and a payout, right? I'm out of time to contemplate that because Leo's next instruction comes and my mind goes blank.

"Stick out your tongue."

One inch at a time, he works my mouth open with his cock, pleasures himself while telling me to keep my hands behind my back. I do so dutifully. His need registers for me in each thrust, but there's such care there as well. He tastes like heaven and he bucks wildly.

He instructs me onto the bed, facing the headboard, knees splayed; my hips experience a blissful stretch that spurs my exhilaration further. Leo's fingers rake across my hole and goose bumps pop up across my skin. "Beautiful," he murmurs to himself. I push back into his touch like I can sense he wants me to. It's miraculous how we instinctually know the moves, like we studied the choreography ahead of time as Leo loves to do with his favorite pop princesses.

Leo's tongue lands where his fingers were. A moan rockets out of me. He explores the spot, drawing out his laps with a hunger that sends my body to the astral plane. Strong hands grab my ass cheeks, parting them with such expert efficiency that I open and open and open some more, making space for his finger which he's slicked with the lube I didn't even see him pull out from a nearby drawer.

"How's that feel, baby?"

Baby. The word sends a ripple through my spine. Instead of responding, I rock back on his finger, already aching for something larger, yearning to feel fuller. Maybe Leo can read my mind because he adds another finger, and I squeal with delight. I drop my head to the mattress, unable to handle the rush that is his third finger.

"You like that?"

"Mmm-hmm." My mind is blissfully blank, wiped of anything but beautiful sensation.

"Good." And after a minute or two of adventuring, he says, "I've got something even bigger for you. Do you want it?" He comes around to the side of the bed so I have a good view of him rolling a condom onto his penis which points right at me. An alluring threat. A provocative promise.

"Mmm-hmm."

"Use your words." Leo raises his right eyebrow. "Do you want it?"

"Yes." I gulp.

"Yes what?"

"Yes, sir." I surprise myself at how quickly and thoughtlessly that came out of my mouth. How natural and easy it was to say and mean. Panic strikes me as I glance up at Leo's face, afraid it's time to call "Pizza!" because I've pushed this too far, but instead I find Leo grinning ear to ear.

"That's it, baby. I'll give you what you want." Then, he mounts me from behind. Presses his head to my hole and teases it, tempts me. I realize, then, that I haven't even touched my own erection. I'm hard as all hell, yet I haven't paid it any mind. I'm too lost in this new, exciting headspace that I don't need to. My body is swarming with too many invigorating sensations.

And then, I feel it. The sensation of all sensations. His cock pushing inside me—slowly, infuriatingly slowly.

Doesn't he know how badly I want to stretch around him fully, feel his pelvis flush to my backside? I need that.

But I don't dare rush it. Because he said he wanted it slow. And I want what he wants. No, I need what he wants. I flip my thinking and focus instead on the delectable ache of him, the momentarily uncomfortable friction that turns to sizzling indulgence the instant I accept him.

"Your hole feels so good and tight, baby. I love being inside you. I love how your body gives way for me." I breathe into that, loosening any clenched part of me that's not completely succumbed to this. "Just a tiny bit more. Oh, there. I'm going to hold it there."

Once he's done holding, praising me, settling in, he makes good on his promise. Railing me. Fucking me. The pads of his fingers dig into my hip bones, and pleasure bursts out from each contact point as my ass slaps and pounds against him. And I gasp in ecstasy.

Gone are thoughts of home and game show competitions. There's only sweaty flesh and frantically beating hearts.

He grabs a towel from the closet and flips me over on my back, starfishing me out the way he had me do for him on FaceTime. Hanging back, he admires me momentarily. I blush. "Don't go shy on me now, baby."

"I won't, sir." I beam. "I'm yours, sir."

There's not a false note in my voice.

He sidles up onto the bed, grabs my calves and kisses my right ankle before entering me again. If I thought he felt good from behind, this is an otherworldly sensation as he presses a sensitive spot inside me repeatedly. Watching Leo above me, a light sheen on his forehead, I grow more and more aroused.

Leo notices the throb and wag and drip between my legs, and smiles as he says, "You can touch yourself while I'm inside you. I give you permission."

The tug of my hand and the rhythm of Leo's strokes match up until I'm blissed out and panting. A sprawling, mushy mess of limbs and live-wire nerve endings. Leo leans over and kisses me hard on the mouth, tongue dipping inside as his thrusts become faster.

"I don't think I'll last much longer, baby."

"Let go," I tell him. "Let go for me."

A minute later, he does. His eyes scrunch and his forehead creases and his mouth drops open as a primal sound escapes him. The pulsating inside me is so intense that it takes me two tugs and I'm shooting ropes up my stomach and across my chest.

There is spent, and then there is whatever we are once we're toweled off and curled up, condom disposed of and comforter on the floor. His heartbeat pounds against my eardrum as I close my eyes and turn it into a symphonic composition written for me.

"You did it again," Leo whispers into my hair.

"Did what?" I don't even bother opening my eyes. I'm sleepy.

"Surprised me."

Those twinkle lights bordering the windows take up inside my chest. "How?"

"Calling me sir? I didn't expect that."

My finger stops drawing lazy circles on his stomach. "Was it too much?" The scent of our sex still hangs in the air, still intoxicating. I want to bottle this up, wear it proudly like a cologne called Conquest by Holden James and Leo Min.

"It was just right. Everything I've fantasized about." Butterflies beat their wings inside my rib cage. He's helping make my *Madcap Market* fantasy come true, so this is a pittance compared to that. I'm equally satisfied, drained, and dreamily happy. "Did you like it?"

"I loved it." I snuggle farther into his chest, nuzzling my cheek against his pec. It's bizarre how safe and comfortable I feel here already. I never want to leave this spot. My breathing slows. My eyes flutter shut again. "I really, really loved it."

That night, I get my first peaceful, restful night of sleep in over a month.

Seventeen

For the second time, I wake up in Leo's arms, except there's no mistaking who it is this time, and there's no person I'd rather it be.

Last night was incredible. I let go completely and was rewarded for it. The edges of my comfort zone went hazy, expanded, and then broke off. In a small way, I'm renewed.

Sunlight sneaks in from the partially cracked blinds, creating slats of golden light across our skin. I take a deep breath before extricating myself from Leo's embrace. He stirs a bit, but doesn't wake, rolling over to face the wall and tugging the comforter up to his shoulders.

He's not the world's most beautiful sleeper—mouth half open, hair a mess—but damn if I don't stop to swoon anyway.

I pad around, naked, looking for my underwear and my phone. My briefs are still tucked into my pants which got kicked beneath the dresser, and I find my phone in the front left pocket, a notification taking up the screen. It's a missed call and a voice mail from a number I don't know.

As not to wake Leo, I tiptoe to the bathroom, lock the door, and sit on the toilet. Holding the phone to my ear, the speaker says words I've been dying to hear: "Hi. This is the *Madcap Market* casting office. Sorry we missed you. We have some news to share. Please call us back at your earliest convenience."

My fingers can't move fast enough. My foot taps impatiently against the cold tile as the call connects. "Hello, Miller Caplan Casting, this is Clarice speaking."

"Hi, Clarice. This is Holden James. I got a call from your office this morning regarding *Madcap Market*." No matter how hard I try, I can't keep my voice from cracking with excitement.

"Oh." I hear the sound of shuffling papers. "One moment please."

The next person to pick up is the casting director I met yesterday. "Holden James?"

"Yes."

There's an excruciating pause that causes me to lean forward on the wobbly toilet seat and nearly fall over. "Congratulations, you've been selected to compete on the next episode of *Madcap Market*."

There's an immediate dance party inside my heart. Everything else the woman tells me—schedules, rehearsals, etcetera—I barely comprehend, which is fine because I'm sure they'll follow up with an email. She concludes the call by asking if she should call Leo herself or if I'd like to give him the news.

"I'll give him the news. Thank you. Thank you *so* much." I'm oozing gratitude.

"Of course," she says. "We thought you and Leo had exceptional chemistry and we're rooting for you—both on the air and in your new relationship."

That second part wallops me. For a moment there, I'd forgotten we were lying our way on to the show. Probably because last night felt so perfect and real. There was genuine affection in our fucking. A surprising takeaway. Could Leo and I be something more than fake boyfriends? This experience does seem to be bringing us tremendously close together.

When I hang up, I rinse my face off with warm water and look in the mirror. In the glass, I appear well rested and happy, two things I haven't been since that fateful night in Manhattan. Leo might be a person worth keeping around once the confetti falls and the check gets handed to us.

The check! Jesus, in my existential spiraling, I haven't even told Leo the good news.

I burst out of the bathroom screaming his name only to run into Mrs. Min who's just gotten in from her shift. She jumps back, hand to her upper chest, and I fear, only for a second, that I've caused the poor woman to have a heart attack.

"Oh, God! I'm so sorry, Mrs. Min." It's at that moment that I notice I'm still only in my underwear. I grab a hoodie off the nearby coatrack, which I assume is Leo's and cover my bits.

After a deep breath, she stutters, "You scared me!"

"I didn't mean to. I didn't think you'd be home so early."

She gives me a once-over. "I see that." My exposed legs seem lurid.

"I, uh…" I begin backing toward Leo's room.

"Why were you shouting?" she asks, creating a visor over the top of her eyes to shield them, giving me the illusion of modesty at least.

"I just got some really good news."

"What's the news?" I bump right into Leo who has appeared, stark naked, in the doorway. When I notice, I hand him one arm of the blue tie-dyed sweatshirt I grabbed, which he accepts gratefully. It now flimsily drapes across both of us. This could not be more mortifying.

"Oh, Leo!" Mrs. Min says.

Leo's eyes bulge. "Umma, what are you doing home at this time?" Leo asks, panicked, both of us desperate for the fabric not to slip.

"Oh, please. It's nothing I haven't seen before," she says with an eye roll while walking past us. We shuffle so our butts aren't out as she goes. "I got off early. I did not know there was a sleepover happening here."

He apologizes to her in Korean. Their dynamic is funny to me. It's built on banter that slips between languages. Her tone is never chiding. He's an adult. She's an adult. There's a mutual respect intertwined in their playfulness. It's almost like they're friends. I wonder if Mom and I would've been like this if she were still alive.

Mrs. Min is in the kitchen now, out of eyesight, but she's still speaking to us. "What's the good news?"

"Oh, my God!" I turn into Leo. "We got it! We got cast on *Madcap Market*!"

"Holy crap! I knew it! I knew we would!" Leo and I embrace, which causes the sweatshirt to drop right as Mrs. Min is coming back around the corner.

"Oh, heavens!" she shouts, racing out of the hallway once more.

"Sorry, so sorry again, Umma!" Leo shouts back, laughing it off. I'm red-faced and pushing him into the bedroom, closing the door behind us, so there is no more indecent exposure happening here today.

Through the wood, we hear: "You can make it up to me by running to the market. I'll make pajeon since we have company and something to celebrate."

I'm relieved she wants me to stay after nearly flashing her. Also, I'm warmed that including me came naturally.

Leo asks, "Does that sound okay to you?"

I nod, weirdly almost feeling like part of the family. "Yeah, that sounds perfect."

"Put some clothes on first!" Mrs. Min yells.

We laugh, kiss, and then we get dressed.

"Leo!" a kindly bald man from behind the register near the entrance greets. He's backed by multiple shelves of pre-made comfort foods, heat lamps hanging down over them.

Leo picks up a basket and waves. "Mr. Park!" He asks him a question in Korean.

Mr. Park, eyes landing on me, opts to answer in English. "My back's been better, but I can't complain too much. It's a lovely day today." He peers out the front windows where Los Angeles glimmers with late-morning sunlight across the parking lot. "Where's Mrs. Min this fine morning?"

"Just got back from a shift. She sent me on an ingredients run."

"What's she cooking?" Mr. Park's eyes light up.

"Pajeon."

Mr. Park rubs his stomach. "Oh, you know how much I love your umma's pajeon. Save some for me?"

"Maybe," Leo says. "We'll see how much this one eats." Leo's hands find my shoulders and he playfully shakes me a little. The gesture, out in public like this, is nice. His touch does wonders for me, magically erases any unease or tension.

Mr. Park nods at me before saying, "Just got a great selection of seafood in. Don't miss out!"

Leo thanks him before striding over to the aisles. The floors are tan with intermittent blue tiles and the shelves are close together, making it a tight squeeze as we maneuver around parked shopping carts.

"My mom and Mr. Park go to church together," Leo tells me as we move past the chips and snacks. "He's not subtle about his feelings for her, but she, bless her, refuses to admit she likes him back."

"Aw, that's kind of adorable."

"It would be more adorable if it wasn't my mom, but yeah." Leo beelines toward the boxes of overgrown watermelons and a million lemons. "My dad left a long time ago, and my mom has never dated. I always thought it was because things with him were so messy. She even went so far as to pay exorbitant amounts of money to reinstate her maiden name when they divorced. She got my name changed, too. I was Leo Kenney for almost eleven years. Talk about an identity crisis. But I also thought it was because I was young. Then I turned eighteen, nineteen, and still, she never went out or met people. She's got a small group of friends from church that she volunteers with, but I don't know. Is it weird that I'm invested in my mom getting back out there?"

I crack a smile. "Not weird at all. It's sweet, actually." Underneath the rock-hard abs, Leo's a softy.

"I wish she'd give Mr. Park a chance," Leo says. "It would make me feel a lot better about wanting to move out on my own."

"She doesn't know?"

"She wouldn't take it well. It's a cultural thing. We look after our elders just as hard as they looked after us when we were young. I love her. I want to do that for her, but this morning was a prime example of why living in a tiny, two-bedroom isn't going to work for a fifty-six-year-old woman and her sexually active son!"

I laugh, recounting the morning and the mayhem. "How do you plan on making it work?"

"I was specifically saving for another unit in our building. That way I'd have a little bit of distance, but I can still cook for her and drive her to work when she needs me to. We can still be a tight-knit family. Just a tight-knit family with different front doors."

"That makes total sense." It tickles me that Leo treats family with as much respect and importance as I do. Unlike Buckley who begrudged his mom for calling often and his dad for stopping by every few weeks to see if anything needed fixing around the apartment.

Together we collect scallions, a carrot, eggs, and some vegetable oil because Leo isn't sure if they've run out. In the back of the store, we find the seafood counter. Trays with ice are set out with fish and crustaceans laid across their frozen beds. Tongs rest on top waiting to be used.

There's only one other patron browsing the selection so we sidle up beside him, which shouldn't be a problem until Leo and the man reach for the same pair of tongs and I swear all the air flies out of the market.

"Leo?" the man asks. He's tall, dark-haired, dark-eyed with a physique that rivals Leo's underneath a blue button-up and blazer.

"Carter, hi," Leo says, sounding startled. It takes me a minute to place the name, and then I hear Mrs. Min's comments from the night of our dinner, and realization rushes over me. "I didn't know you shopped here."

"I usually don't, but I had a meeting nearby and one of my coworkers said this was the spot, so I had to check it out." There is an uncomfortable tension between them, so hot it could melt the ice buckets. "You look good."

"Thanks." Leo's tone is harsh.

Looking past Leo, Carter reaches out a hand. "Hi there. I'm Carter."

"Holden," I say. His grip is firm and I wince. Why am

I so weak? Maybe we should've done that weight training instead of the Griffith Park hike. I might crumble under the weight of a frozen rack of ribs.

Leo peacocks, stepping into my side and threading our arms together. "Holden's my boyfriend."

This news is shocking, evident by the slightly open-mouthed expression Carter now wears. "Nice. Where did you two meet?"

Leo launches into the spiel, everything we spun and sold to the *Madcap Market* casting team. "We're going to be on this week's episode."

"Oh, whoa. That's…awesome. Surprised you got off of work for that. Lou at Traveltineraries is a hard-ass." Carter has no idea what kind of land mine he's just stepped on, so I reach out and squeeze Leo's arm to show my support.

Leo admits, "I'm not working for Lou anymore."

"Ah, you never did like that gig anyway." He says it with too much leftover familiarity in his voice. It annoys me, and I don't even know him.

The longer this conversation goes on, the more Leo tenses up. Whatever broke them must've really wounded Leo.

Why wouldn't he share that with me? He knows nearly every detail about me and Buckley.

Maybe he doesn't think I'm important enough to tell.

A nagging voice in the back of my mind reminds me that Leo's arm linked in mine is for show. *Madcap Market*—a show that celebrates joy and laughs—isn't going to chip away at our heartbreak for ratings. Save that for *The Bach-*

elor. "What are you doing now?" Carter asks Leo, pulling me from my swirling thoughts.

"Keeping my options open." Leo's voice is pointed. I wonder if Carter has said those exact words to him before in a different context. There's still so much about Leo that I don't know.

Carter purses his lips, runs a hand across his jaw. That's when I notice it. A wedding ring. It's black, simple, shiny.

"Well," Carter says abruptly. "It was nice to see you. Nice to meet you, Holden. I'll be sure to cheer you on from my couch later this week. Good luck." With that, he's off, leaving Leo and me in a cone of confusion.

Neither of us says anything for a long bout. We just stare at dead fish, their lifeless eyes boring through us. I can't grasp on any words, let alone the right ones, to say, so I follow Leo as he leaves behind the seafood and wanders back toward the registers.

"Aren't we—"

"You can make it without."

I zip my lips.

It's not until we're in the car on the way home, having said a quick goodbye to Mr. Park at checkout, that Leo seems to return to his usual self. After a few minutes, he pulls off to the side of the road, lowers the music and says, "Sorry I got so cagey back there."

"It's okay. If I ran into Buckley unexpectedly, I think I'd react the exact same way." I puzzle over this. "Actually, I probably would've handled it much worse. You had a lot of grace. You deserve a lot of credit for that."

"Yeah, well, he's so put together. The last thing I need is him thinking I'm a mess. I already played the crying-into-the-phone thing over him once." In Leo's eyes, I notice a kinship I hadn't seen before. It clicks that perhaps he came up to see me the night of the "All Too Well" drink-a-thon because he recognized my acute heartbreak. He brought the game and the pizza because he wished it was what someone had done for him when he and Carter collapsed. "I don't need him holding this false idea that I'm not over him."

"Are you over him or just pretending to be over him? It's okay to tell me the truth." I can't pretend the pretenses of our arrangement aren't clear, even if our sex knocked something loose inside my heart. Even if part of me could clearly imagine *more* between us.

"Like I told you on our hike, I've never been someone's boyfriend or partner. That was the truth. Carter was the closest I got to that before it blew up, so I don't know if I'd even be able to identify what 'over it' really means," he says, sadness impinging on his words.

"Do you want to tell me what happened?" I ask. "It's okay if you don't."

Leo hasn't removed his hands from the steering wheel. They remain gripped there. Knuckles red. Until he starts speaking and, word by word, the grip grows looser. "We met at one of the hotels I was working in. He flirted with me at first, but then I clocked the ring, and I backed off. Then, a week later, I get an Instagram DM from him saying he was sorry if he made things awkward but that he was in an open marriage and didn't want me to think he was doing anything wrong."

"Sounds suspicious," I say, adding my two cents.

"From what I'd glimpsed at work, he ran that hotel with such efficiency and earnestness. I had no reason not to believe him, so I continued to message him and flirt with him and when he asked me out, he assured me multiple times that it was okay, that his wife knew where he was going, but I guess I should've confirmed that." His eyebrows knit together.

I place a hand on his forearm. "Why would you do that? You trusted him. You took his word."

"That turned out to be a mistake because while it was true that he'd come out as bisexual to his wife and it was true that they'd discussed opening their relationship, what he lied about was that she had already agreed to it, so when she inevitably came to the hotel because he forgot his lunch, I went to introduce myself." His face gets overtaken with a distorted frown, like he's blaming himself for the entire situation, when a relationship consists of two people putting in the work. Not one person reading the other's mind. "I crossed a line and that night he sent me a text breaking it off and then I mysteriously was never scheduled at that hotel again, which could be a coincidence but…"

"Christ, he met your mom!" I shout. "You had every reason to believe she knew and he was invested in your relationship. Things like that make it real."

"You met my mom," Leo says. "And this isn't real." He warily gestures between us, and my heart kerplunks.

"But doesn't it sort of...feel real?" I ask, emotions stacked up high in my throat. My eyes scan over to the windshield, so I don't have to see Leo preparing to let me down easy. Because that's inevitably what's coming.

Holding on for the worst, I don't entirely react when he says, "Yeah, it sort of does feel real."

There, on the side of the road in the middle of Los Angeles with cars whizzing by at dizzying speeds, I wonder if this conversation could be the start of something more than a fake situationship.

Eighteen

"We have a rehearsal at the studio tomorrow at 10:00 a.m." I'm reading from the email sent by the production assistant only an hour ago.

We'd missed the notification as we jazzed up our dark purple *Madcap Market* crewnecks using fabric scissors, some thread, a bit of glitter, and a ton of gay willpower. I cut off the bottom hem and then watched a YouTube video on how to fashion the strip of fabric into a bow tie, which looks dapper as hell. Classic Leo, he chopped off the sleeves on his entirely so his biceps can be on full display for everyone at home. I cropped the bottom for him and made him a bow tie as well, so there's some sort of uniformity for Team Eggplant.

I'm surprised the producers didn't make us change that name, but there it is in black-and-white on the email:

Hello Team Eggplant,
Please find your show week schedule attached below.

Leo distracts me by modeling his sweatshirt like he's a bodybuilder in a big competition. I'd give him all the ribbons in the world. And kisses. And touches. And whoa, I'm overheating. I go back to rereading the email, so I don't skip over anything important.

Call times are to be followed to a T. There are a lot of moving parts to make *Madcap Market* happen, so it is imperative that contestants are prompt. Inability to arrive on time could result in immediate dismissal.

"We're closer to the studio from here. Why don't you stay the night?" I ask Leo, positing it as convenient when really, it's to satiate my libido.

He stops checking himself out in the mirror—such a sexy show-off—and asks, "Afraid I'm going to oversleep, aren't you?"

"Yes. A little. But you have a toothbrush here, our sweatshirts are here, and you can borrow some of my clothes for tomorrow." I love the idea of sharing clothes with Leo. No matter how clean you get a garment, there's always that unique scent that stays behind, imbedded in the warp and weft. I want Leo to carry a piece of me as close to him as possible, especially after our awkward run-in at the market and all he shared with me in the car. Our intimacy has extended beyond the sheets. I want to continue that and see where it leads. "Plus, if you stay here tonight, we can have some pre-stressor fun, and we can be as loud as we want."

After the run-in with Carter, we helped make pajeon

with Mrs. Min, ate in front of the TV, and ended up binging Mrs. Min's favorite K-Drama—a show that reminds me a bit of *Grey's Anatomy*—for the rest of the day. With the subtitles on, I became engrossed in the storytelling, falling completely for this bunch of med students sharing love and friendship.

It was the perfect comedown after the utter excitement of the morning and the terse conversation with Carter. Now that I have a better understanding of Leo's dating history, I feel closer to him, and all the more like I might be falling for him, too.

When I tune back in, Leo is looking at me with a devious light in his eyes. "Oh, so you want to get loud tonight, huh?"

"Yeah." I openly ogle him—one, because I know he likes the way I eye him up and two, he's just so damn enticing to look at. "I want to get loud."

"What if you couldn't get loud?" he asks, voice pitching deeper, one eyebrow rising with intrigue.

"I'm not sure I know what you mean." I run a finger down the outside of his arm. My heart feels like it's on a trampoline.

Leo crouches a bit so we're exactly eye to eye. "I want to try something. Do you trust me?"

As someone who had his heart shattered a month ago, I assumed trust would be a transient visitor for a long while. That's why I'm surprised to find it knocking on my front door with a U-Haul parked in the driveway right now. I don't know if it's here to stay, but it's moving in, and I'm moved by that. "Yeah, I trust you."

He bares his teeth in a sexy way. "Strip down and get on the bed."

Excited, I do as I'm told, folding my *Madcap Market* sweatshirt and tucking it safely in a drawer. Shucking my underwear, I splay out on the bed, naked and waiting for further instruction, already growing harder by the second, wanting to curl up inside that devious mind of his.

Leo takes his time, inspecting the strips of fabric we cut away from our *Madcap Market* sweatshirts before. I'm surprised when he uses his bare hands to rip one of them apart. What is he doing, and why is it spiking my pulse so much? Eventually, he holds up four long pieces—two thicker and two on the thin side.

"Spread out," he instructs, crawling onto the bed and positioning his knees on either side of my hips. I starfish for him, noticing that every time he praises me for following directions, I become more and more erect. "Lift your head."

Gently, he wraps a thicker piece of fabric around my skull, covering my eyes and tying a loose knot in the back. The loss of sight heightens my other senses making every subsequent touch even more arousing.

"Is that okay?" he asks using his everyday voice, perfectly playing the caring dominant.

"More than okay."

He focuses on my wrists next, positioning the backs of them against the bedposts and twisting the fabric around. I can sense how meticulous and tight his knots are, making me assume he was either a Boy Scout or he's done this before. Either way, the tug of my muscles is titillating.

Straddling my hips once more, Leo traces his fingers down the insides of my arms toward my armpits. The featherlight touch tickles me. I laugh and writhe, never having felt touch this delicate or intentional.

The pads of his forefingers do an ice-skating routine across my abdomen; they perform figure eights and tiny leaps that excite my breath. A huge moan rips out of me as he finds my navel, circles it, tantalizes me.

The bed gives out an exhausted creak as the mattress dimples in. Something hot and wet arriving at my lips lets me know that Leo's lunged north. "Open wider."

I'm rewarded with saltiness. A gradual thrust stretches my lips and offers a fullness that goes unmatched. I begin to rock my head, suctioning to him, but he tells me to stop, reminds me that he's in charge. I nod wordlessly and lay my head back giving him as much access as he wants.

The pressure of his palms crushing down the duvet to hold himself upright makes me loll as he takes off, grinding in and out of my eager mouth. I moan around his length, knowing the vibration will carry through him. He reacts by thrusting harder, faster. I grow louder, until he backs away suddenly.

The loss of stimulation leaves me panting.

"There's one last component if you're up for it," Leo says. I can almost hear the twisted pleasure he's getting from denying me his cock and his calculated touch. "This last strip is for your mouth. It'll muffle your cries and moans and sighs." Then comes a light brush of something soft—the fabric strip, probably—across my right nipple. I let out what will likely be my final groan. "Some people love it, removing the ability to speak. I'll be in control. I'll cater my touch solely to your physical reactions."

This whole time I've had my eyes closed, but now they rush open only to be met with blurry blobs of dark purple. I'm having a hard time deciphering if the pounding in my chest is anticipation or fear of this last element.

This is all new to me, so my limits aren't set.

Leo, clearly taking my extended silence seriously, says, "If this is too much, we can stop. You say the word and I'll untie you. I want this to be enjoyable for both of us."

"It is," I say. "It will be. At least, I think it will. I just…"

"What? Tell me."

I gulp back my own reservations. "What if I don't like it after you do it? How will I let you know?" Buckley was very consistent with sex and in life. He rarely deviated from the tried-and-true formula that made his world march on at an even, steady pace, which was to be expected from an accountant.

This newness for me, all at once, is confounding, yet I don't want to let the opportunity to explore, especially with someone I know I can count on, slip away.

The rebound of the bed lets me know he's shifted. His hand finds my right one. "Can you snap?" I try from this position and, sure enough, I can. "Snap at any point. I'll ungag you."

My worries ripple away and get replaced by bravery. "Let's do it."

A ball of fabric lands on my tongue first and the ends of

the fabric get strung over my ears, pulled taut around the base of my neck. There is a comfort in the restraint. The lack of motion lays me bare, drains me of apprehension.

Am I doing this right? Am I making him feel good? The insecurity can't find me when Leo's making my body his personal play toy. Respectfully, of course.

The wet lap of his tongue starts between my nipples and runs down through my happy trail. At the base of my erection, he kisses, causing my groin to pulse and grow larger. "Somebody likes that," he says. All I can do is grunt into the gag because he's right.

I listen as he slicks his palm and grips my shaft. He pumps me in his fist, evidently relishing the stop and start, the tease and retreat, until his hand wanders lower, parting me with efficiency. His already slippery fingers find my hole, tease the rim, tip inside but only slightly. Still enough to make me bite down on the gag in ecstasy, so engrossed and needy.

After a few minutes, he plunges his fingers into me. My head rolls back as I let him penetrate me farther, deeper, gloriously. The blindfold is no longer a hindrance. It's spangled with starlight, constellations of Leo and me in every position imaginable, as if our union was predestined by the sky.

Leo hikes my legs up with a growl and tongues me where his fingers were. He performs slow, luxurious circles at my entry point, similar to the ones he did with his finger around my belly button. He knows where all my hot spots are, and he doesn't hesitate to push them time and time again.

How does a man I've known for only a handful of days understand how to uncork me so expertly?

He answers that question by lifting my legs up over his shoulders with ease. The tip of his lubed, condom-covered erection presents itself at my hole. If I weren't gagged, I'd beg. I'd barter. I'd steal to have him inch closer to me, let me feel that exquisite stretch I desperately want.

But the gag demands my patience, and my patience pays off because Leo whispers, "It's time to take me inside you, baby."

I can't help but surrender completely and think: I never want to give this up.

Nineteen

Sex works up an appetite.

The hotel bar stays open late most nights, so after showers, Leo and I sit at the mostly empty counter downstairs, nursing beers and splitting a cheeseburger.

It's incredible how natural this seems, as if we've been doing it for months or years. I thought after what transpired between us, how heady and kinky and wild I felt all bound up and gagged, I'd be too embarrassed to look Leo in the eyes. When he took off the blindfold, I swore I'd blink back the light and turn away from him for fear he somehow saw me differently. That he unlocked a part of me that he wouldn't like.

It seems the opposite is true.

We knock elbows side by side at the bar, laughing over stupid jokes and melty cheese and making up backstories for the patrons who sit in booths across the way. I haven't felt this carefree since I don't even know when. I want to say since Buckley and I split, but a part of me senses that isn't true.

"Aside from your student loans, what else do you plan on doing with the winnings?" Leo asks with his mouth half-full.

"Like you, I guess I'll get my own place," I say. "Give my dad a break after four weeks of crashing at his bachelor pad. Oh, shit!" I reach into my pocket for my phone and check the time. "I can't believe I didn't tell him we got cast on the show. Do you mind if I do that now while I'm thinking about it?"

"Not at all," Leo says with a smile. "But I can't promise the rest of the french fries will be here when you get back."

"They're all yours." I venture back into the lobby with my beer, wave to Annabelle, the desk attendant, and find the least craggy chair in the quietest corner to sit in. When Dad picks up, he sounds groggy.

"Holden, what's wrong? Is everything okay?"

The time difference rears its head. It's only 8:00 p.m. here, but it's eleven there. "Crap. Sorry, Dad. I didn't mean to wake you. I forgot that you're three hours ahead. I can call tomorrow if that's better."

"Nonsense. You know me. As soon as we hang up, I'll crash again." He chuckles to himself. I hear the rustling of sheets as if he's sitting up. "What's going on?"

"I have some exciting news..." The exhilaration makes my head rush. "I'm going to be on this week's episode of *Madcap Market*!"

"Wow! That's incredible. You got a ticket to the taping?" he asks.

"No, I'm going to be on it as an actual contestant."

"I thought you said your friend wouldn't audition with you." His confusion is palpable, even across the country.

So much has happened in such a short span of time that I forgot he doesn't have any idea about Leo. Not that I can tell him the truth of the matter. One blanket lie is easier to contain and maintain. At least that's what I'm telling myself as I battle off a wormy feeling. "I auditioned with someone else. Someone I knew from online that I met while I was out here. Someone that I'm sort of…seeing now?"

"Oh, that's news to me," he says. "Does this someone have a name?"

"Leo. Leo Min."

"What does this Leo Min do?"

I pause momentarily, debating how to answer. A huge chunk of me wants to confess everything to Dad, spill all my sparkly feelings over the course of this phone call, but I know I can't for the sake of everything. So, I keep my response brief. "He's between gigs right now."

"Gigs? Is he a musician or a dancer?" he asks.

"He *is* a dancer just not in a professional capacity. He was working as a concierge, but that didn't pan out for him, so we're doing the show now and, yeah." I've run the course of what I should divulge, which makes my throat itch with irritating guilt. "That's it! I just wanted to tell you to tune in on Thursday night at eight. I'll let you get back to bed."

"Thanks for calling, Holden. I'm excited to watch," he

says, but he sounds more excited to get back to sleep. I don't blame him. The sex and the carbs are combining to become the world's best sedative for me. Before Dad hangs up, he says, "Oh, and, Holden?"

"Yeah?"

"This Leo, he's nice to you?"

This question hits me in a weird spot. "Yeah, he's nice to me. Why?"

"Just asking." He lets out a yawn. "You deserve someone nice."

His words make me more emotional than they should. "Thanks, Dad." I'm tearing up.

Before I can backtrack, confess all the lies and the true feelings, he says, "Good night, Holden."

"Night."

I sit there for a moment longer. Was Dad insinuating Buckley wasn't nice? I would hope if he felt that way that he'd have told me when we were together. Though, thinking about it now, I probably wouldn't have listened. I was and still am stubborn. My life with Buckley was regimented.

I flip over to Leo. While he may be a fan of fucking with me, he's also caring and thoughtful. He checks in with me and makes sure I'm okay. Even if, like when we ran into Carter, he clams up and goes cold, he warms up again and talks it out.

The differences between Buckley and Leo are more pronounced than ever. So are my feelings for each of them respectively.

When I walk back into the bar, it's even clearer because

Leo has left me the very last french fry and a smidgen of ketchup. "Figured it was only fair."

I was set on fighting off my feelings for Leo, but now, as they encroach on me in this bar, I kind of want to cuddle up with them and stay locked in their embrace, even if that makes me more nervous than ever before.

I happily eat the final fry. "Miss me?"

"Terribly." He swivels his bar stool into mine, bumps our knees. "How did your dad react?"

"He was half-asleep, but excited," I say, thinking longer about the conversation and zeroing in on when Dad asked if Leo was a dancer. "Humor me, have you ever thought about being a dancer?"

"What are you talking about?" He sips his drink.

"As a career. The crowd loved your moves at karaoke. You took all those classes when you were younger." I reflect on those adorable photos and the one video Mrs. Min kept of Leo doing hip-hop. "You clearly love it. What's stopping you from pursuing that?"

"Money." His tone is flat.

"If that wasn't an obstacle," I say. "What happens if we win? You get your cushion. Would that be something you're interested in?" I don't know why exactly I'm questioning him like this. The only reason I can think of is that I've seen the way his whole aura heightens each time a song he loves comes on. "Wouldn't it be amazing to get paid for something that makes you so happy?"

"It would, but leaving your livelihood up to chance is a major risk."

"Isn't that what we're going to do on *Madcap Market*?"

He bobbles his head. "I suppose you have a point."

In the bar lighting, dim and a bit blue, Leo looks younger, more innocent. He's not masquerading as someone who uses charisma and his good looks as a front. With cheese crusted in the corner of his mouth, he reminds me of the kid in the dance recital costume from the scrapbook.

I grab a bar napkin, dip a corner in my water glass, and wipe his lips clean. It leaves behind a light, enticing sheen. I want to kiss him so badly. I don't care who sees. But this conversation feels too important to derail. "I think this risk has proven successful so far, don't you?" I ask it softly; I'm afraid he might hear too many emotions wedged inside the words.

Whatever happens at the rehearsal tomorrow and the taping on Thursday is out of our hands for the most part, but what transpires between us after is ours to direct.

"I do." He bites his lip.

Replaying Dad's sentiment about me deserving someone nice, I decide to take another risk. "Sorry if I sound like a fifth grader passing a note in social studies, but I like you, Leo."

"In case it wasn't obvious from the past couple days and what we just did upstairs, I like you, too." Leo's sincerity unmasks itself. It's beautiful. He's beautiful. All sharp lines and strong muscles and sweet brown eyes and caring words.

"You mean this hasn't just been about the sex and the show for you?" It was easy to think that. He was a place for me to pour my trip-based desires. I was a place for him to lean on and get off with.

"I'm not going to lie," he says, pushing our plate away. "It's mostly been about the sex and the show, but my mom likes you, I had fun cooking with you, and our sex has been good."

"Just good?"

"Shut up," he says with a light, playful nudge. "It's been great. There? You happy?"

"Very."

"I guess what I'm getting at is that I can't say any of that stuff about half the guys I've gone out with in the last few years," he says. "Aside from…"

He doesn't even want to say Carter's name now, which I get. "Dating is hard. Meeting people. Testing compatibility. Making sure they laugh at your jokes even if they're horrendously cheesy and unfunny."

"Is that one of your relationship must-haves?" he asks, looking a bit skeptical.

"Yeah. You don't have any weird ones? Everybody has weird ones."

"I do," he says, sounding bashful all of a sudden.

"Uh, okay. So, spill."

"It's…" Why is he hesitating? "It's karaoke. The guy has to be willing to sing duets with me at karaoke."

A card flips over in my mind, revealing a truth I hadn't been anticipating. "Wait, so last night you were…"

"Testing you? Yeah." His posture closes off as if he's been caught.

I can't suppress my smile. "That's supremely adorable."

"Adorable? No. Uh-uh. I'm not *adorable*." He traces his hands down his body. "Look at me."

It's crystal clear that his body—as gorgeous as it is—is a tool for working out his insecurities. Whether it's dancing in his room or lifting at the gym, he must use physical activity and his body as a means of deflecting negative emotions. I get it. But I can see past it.

"Yes, you're a hunk. But even hunks can be adorable," I say, sweetly condescending. "I like that I passed your test. It's a good test, too. Not many people are willing to be that silly in front of big groups. I almost chickened out."

He shrugs. "Some guys have turned around at the door. Some guys have made it inside with reservations. Only two have had the balls to sing with me."

He doesn't need to tell me who the other person is because it's written all over his face, but I ignore it because we've given him too much talking space today already. I can tell Leo's ready to move on. I lean over and kiss him on the lips—quick and sweet.

"I was thinking," he begins, voice wavering a little. Damn, he's adorable. I don't care what he says or how ripped he is. He's a muscley plush toy I can't wait to take back up to my room and cuddle with. "Once the show is over and the pretending is done, we could agree to consider trying this. At least talk about it."

The offer is possibly the sweetest I've ever received. My heart rate ratchets up, knowing the level of risk there is. "I'd like that."

Leo grabs a ring-stained bar napkin and steals a pen off a receipt plate two seats away. He begins writing. "Right now, we've got to keep our head in the game. 'In it to win it,' right? We need the money, but after? After, I think maybe there's a bigger conversation to be had." His hand domes over mine, and a sudden heat whizzes through my body.

"What is that?"

"We signed something when we agreed to fake it. If we're proposing something real, I figure we ought to sign something, too." When he slides the napkin to me, he's written out, in fake legalese, the terms of a new agreement.

Big conversations usually scare me, but the prospect of this one doesn't. Maybe it's because it feels like fate had a hand in this, and even if there are a million reasons to say no, I don't because he makes me happy, so I sign his silly-sweet napkin.

Twenty

Leo and I are the first set of contestants to arrive for our rehearsal day.

My sheer level of excitement had me awake before the sun. I took my time showering, getting dressed, lazing around the hotel room while Leo slept peacefully, sprawled out and sheets spilling onto the floor.

We didn't have sex again last night, but made out naked, rolling around and laughing into each other's mouths, which sounds weird but was blissful. Leo has a way of making me feel like the outside world is a zillion miles away when he's holding me in his arms, when he's exploring my mouth with teeth and tongue, when he's making me harder than I've ever been in my life.

But we fell asleep cuddled up close. Facing the world and this day beside Leo is both manageable and exhilarating.

"And this is the main set." The production assistant waves in front of the soundstage where an exact replica of a grocery store has been built. There are four bisected aisles, a coffee spot, a deli counter, and a produce section. Overwhelming joy rains down on me.

This is my Oz. This is my Wonderland. "This is amazing!" I cry.

"Feel free to..." I'm off before she can finish. "Look around." She stalks off, clearly used to contestants geeking out over this realistic grocery store where the boxes are filled with weighted Styrofoam instead of cereal.

"What happens to all this perishable food once the show tapes? Doesn't it go bad between episodes?" Leo asks.

"They donate it to food banks," I say, loving the charitable way they make the place look real without creating waste. "They've been doing it a long time. I'm just amazed how much you don't see on-air."

The fake grocery store is smaller than it appears in an episode. When I look up, I can barely see the ceiling between the crowded grid of lights and equipment blocking it. In front of the grocery store are the risers for the live studio audience. It's amazing that in two days that whole area will be filled with eager viewers, cheering us on as we compete.

I stand there thinking of Mom, how she would've loved this, and how I hope she's proud of me. That wonky feeling of guilt I had over Leo's and my deception is erased now that, in my pocket, I have a promise printed on the back of a napkin. A promise we both signed in blue pen. Once the chaos of our game-show-extravaganza is over, we're going to explore our connection, see if it works.

Our story is inching ever closer to the truth, minus a few details, which is enough for me.

Spending time with him, learning about his past, and having mind-blowing sex with him has unboxed emotions I didn't think possible. The plan wasn't to come to Los Angeles and fall for someone. Then again, the plan never panned out at any juncture so maybe I should've expected the unexpected.

I look over at him in his eggplant-colored crewneck, and realize that even in my wildest dreams, I couldn't have come up with him.

In the back of my mind, I realize that we live on opposite coasts and Leo's never been in a relationship before. Bad signs that would be hard to ignore under different circumstances, but I'm choosing to see the light at the end of this tunnel.

My stomach gurgles, anxiety manifested.

"You didn't eat a lot at breakfast this morning. Do you want me to grab you something from the craft table?" Leo asks, striding up beside me. The production assistant had given us a full tour of the surrounding areas, including the long, fully-covered table of wraps and eggs and protein shakes. My eyes were eager, but my stomach wouldn't come to the party.

Today is the day all my dreams start coming true. When that much is riding on something, it's hard to take care of yourself.

"No, thanks," I say. "It's just nerves. I'll be okay."

"Are you sure?" he asks. "Don't want you passing out

on the first day. I'm sure they've got something small like a granola bar."

The more I consider it, the more I realize he has a point, but instead of letting him go for me, I say, "You're right. I should have something. I'll get it. Can I bring you anything back?"

I think the walk and the distance will help me parse out some of this.

A tall man with long sandy hair wearing all-black comes barreling through with a cart covered in inflatable pool toys shaped like food. "Out of the way!" he shouts. I jump to the side before he pancakes me, and I nearly knock the whole catering table over in the process.

When I turn, I notice I've startled a man so much that he's dropped half of his everything bagel. When I pick up the part that landed by my foot, I notice my hand is covered in scallion cream cheese. Buckley is the only person I know that used to eat that. It always weirded me out because it felt like onion overload, but he loved it and had it almost every Sunday, which meant he walked around for hours with bad breath.

The memory blurs into reality when that familiar scent hits my nostrils, and Buckley blinks back at me from one side of the catering table. I shake my head certain I'm imagining this. Maybe Leo was right. I should've eaten more this morning because now I'm hallucinating. Only, when my vision sharpens once more, Buckley's still there, still holding half a bagel, still…smiling?

What the actual fuck is happening?

"Buckley?" I ask, feeling and sounding stupid. I'm tempted to reach out and touch his face to make sure, but he steps closer and I'm far too certain.

"Hi there." He wipes his cream cheese hand on a napkin and then offers it to me to shake as if four weeks ago we didn't kiss on the mouth and have sex and sleep in the same bed. I grimace at his outstretched hand, and he awkwardly tugs it back. "Surprise!"

"Surprise? What's going on right now? How are you here?"

"A car and then a plane and then a car," he says. There's no humor to his words. He's being factual, answering the question at face value. I'd forgotten that quirk about him. He fixates on the minutia to make sure you know you've asked a ridiculous question.

"That's not what I meant." I backtrack. "Why are you here? What are you doing?"

"Remember when I said 'surprise'?"

"Yeah, that was two seconds ago!"

"Well, that's why I'm here. I'm surprising you," he says so matter-of-factly I could scream. Los Angeles has been a fever dream as it is, but this has turned it into a diabolical nightmare. My worlds should not be colliding like this.

Buckley made a choice. He left me. I left New York for this trip without him. And now he's here. On the set of *Madcap Market*. A show he openly detests. My heart palpitates with all this conflicting information. The screeching and shouting around me as the crew preps for rehearsal is adding to the cacophony inside my head.

"They just let any person waltz onto the set like this?" I

ask, incredulous. Leo and I had to go through many levels of security. Scans and pats and checks. How is Buckley here and eating from the bagel platter meant for cast and crew only?

"No, I'm here for my call time," he says as if I should've known this. "I'm competing. I figured you'd have seen it on the email we got sent last night and my surprise was ruined, but by the look on your face, I assume that's not true." He's receiving sick pleasure over this, I can tell.

Nearly catatonic, I shake my head slowly. "I—what? A month ago, you told me this show was an abomination!"

"Shh," he says, sharply demanding, which knocks me the wrong way. "Keep your voice down. As far as everyone here knows, I'm a fanatic like you."

Anger and confusion are helixing in my chest. "You're telling me you flew out to LA and auditioned for the show?" I don't remember seeing him at the audition, but then again, that casting call was mobbed. He could've been in any of the groups before or after us. There's no way I could've kept track of everyone coming and going.

Though, if I hadn't been so wrapped up in Leo last night, both physically and metaphorically, I might've seen Buckley's name on the call sheet and prepared myself for this emotional upheaval.

My mind flashes to Leo flexing in his sweatshirt, to him tying me up, to him saving the last greasy-yet-delicious french fry for me at the bar. I didn't miss it. I willfully wasn't looking. Leo has a way of making me stay present, so I'm not reaching for my phone when we're together.

I think suddenly about Leo back on set. I'm supposed to

be bringing him something small to eat. There's no way to avoid my teammate from meeting my ex-boyfriend when we're competing against one another. Everything is all jumbled up.

Which leads me to another gnarled thought: Who is Buckley's teammate?

I'm about to ask when a familiar face appears behind him.

Alexia stands there looking flush and beautiful in brand-new athleisure (God, I can't escape it). When she sees me, she smiles a friendly smile that reads as so deceptive that she could be cast in a film noir as the murderess. "Fancy seeing you here," she says with a little tap on the shoulder.

This situation gets a thousand times worse.

Buckley was easily aggravated and sometimes standoffish with me when we were together, but he was never devious or mean. Showing up here, out of the blue, after publicly reaming me in front of an entire restaurant over these exact plans seems crueler than I know him—knew him?—to be. And to do it all with Alexia by his side makes it feel like he's hurling the culinary-grade knives I saw in the cookware aisle at me as I'm trapped to a spinning target.

"Holden, what's the holdup?" comes Leo's voice from around the corner.

This situation gets a *million* times worse when Buckley extends the hand I refused to shake earlier. "Hi, I'm Buckley."

The shock on Leo's face is apparent. "Nice to meet you, Buckley. I'm Leo. Holden's boyfriend."

The downpour of awkwardness soaks through us all. Leo obviously wouldn't expect this to be the same Buckley who dumped me and made me move out back in New York. Buckley obviously wouldn't expect me to have moved on so quickly. Also, he'd have no reason to believe Leo is lying as part of an elaborate ruse we constructed to get on the show.

An immaculate, sticky spiderweb has been spun around me. I'm starting to think I won't find a means of escape before the arachnid of my mistakes eats me for lunch.

The production assistant appears out of thin air and shouts right in my ear, "All contestants are needed on set for a safety walk-through! Again, that's all contestants!"

We haven't even begun rehearsing and this is already proving to be a shit show.

Twenty-One

The cotton-polyester blend of this shirt is warm under the bright television lights.

Leo and I have been taken aside into a smaller studio where two stools are set up against a green screen backdrop that unrolls in a smooth, clean wave. There's a condensed crew in here with only one camera.

Two makeup artists check our foreheads and noses for unwanted shininess. I keep trying to catch Leo's eye through the blur of hands and brushes, but he either doesn't notice or doesn't want to look at me. Both cause my hopes to droop.

"You have such amazing skin," the tall man with swoopy hair doing Leo's makeup says with a dash of flirtation, barely doing anything with his sponges to even Leo's tone. "What's your routine?"

"Washing my face and moisturizing," Leo says with a half laugh and a one-shoulder shrug.

The makeup artist raises an eyebrow. "Yeah, right. I wasn't born yesterday."

Leo laughs harder. "I'm being for real. I wouldn't lie about that."

The guy's painted-in left eyebrow goes, somehow, even higher. "I guess I'm just supposed to believe that you're blessed then, huh?"

"In more ways than one," Leo says back.

Jealousy mixes in with the bewilderment and upset already overwhelming me. In my pocket is the napkin Leo and I signed last night. It felt wrong to leave it behind in the hotel room this morning. I was too afraid Mrs. Min would see it or another housekeeper would throw it out by accident.

Besides, it made me smile. I knew today would be hectic. I assured myself that anytime I needed a pick me up, I could look at that crumply napkin and think about what was on the other side of this.

Now it serves as a wishing token—a physical reminder of how badly I wish I could go back to last night before complicated became downright convoluted.

"Hello, gentlemen," says the breezy white female assistant director with auburn hair. "Once makeup is finished, we're going to get some good banter out of you with some prepared questions. I'll be back in about ten. Can I get you anything—water, tea?"

"Water, thanks," Leo says.

"I'll have the same."

I know *Madcap Market* by heart. This is the part of the day where we film our package materials.

Some contestants share sob stories, others funny stories

or heartwarming stories. I know, from us, they're looking for a sweet, make-them-say-aw love story, and I'm sorely selling it short today. My smiles are mannequin-esque and my laughs sound waterlogged. We've had barely a second to pause, let alone have a decent conversation dissecting why Buckley is here and what we do about it.

As if they can hear my thoughts, the makeup team announce that they've finished. Before they disappear, Leo's guy slips him a business card. "If you ever decide to come clean on your skin secret, hit me up."

Leo pockets the card as the door closes.

I don't think I expected him to throw it out. Or laugh it off. Or tell me not to worry. Except, in my right pocket, I've got that napkin! Which makes me feel a little stupid. It could've been a post-sex, post-burger haze we were stuck in. Buckley's arrival might've knocked us out of it.

"He seemed nice," I say, testing the waters. Not wanting to play this role but needing to say something that isn't a swirling garble of gibberish.

"Really?" Leo asks, sounding annoyed, and again, I don't blame him for that.

I take a deep breath before diving in. "Yes, that Buckley out there is my ex. No, I didn't know he was coming out here or competing. You have to believe me on that."

Leo's head bows a bit. "Then, what is he doing here?"

"I wish I knew!" I shout before realizing we could blow our cover if anyone on set overheard us. Good thing we haven't been mic-ed yet. "He said him being here was a surprise, that he thought I'd have seen his name on the email, but we got…sidetracked."

I catch Leo's blush, spotlighted in these complimentary yet blazing lights. "Well, why do you think he's here, then?"

I think back on the night in Manhattan and what I said to him as he left me high and dry in the restaurant. "I think I might've offended him the night we broke up. I said something to the effect of him being a stick-in-the-mud and that I couldn't have won the show with him."

It sounds dramatic and ridiculous, but the longer I consider it, the more I think it must be true. Buckley came out here to get back at me.

It's hard to admit that toward the end there Buckley and I weren't on the best terms. I was sad half the time. He was irritable half the time.

I started saving money, fixating on this trip, booking plane tickets and a hotel, all to block out the noise of the one stable relationship in my life that I didn't know for certain but maybe sensed was crumbling down.

"Are you trying to tell me we're in the middle of some sick revenge plot?" Leo asks, sounding disgusted.

"God, I really hope not." I bite my nails just as the crew return to take their places.

"All set, guys?" the assistant director asks, holding tight to a clipboard.

We both shake our heads in stupefied synchronization.

Lights. Camera. Kill me now.

We need to talk.

That's what Buckley's text message reads when Leo and I arrive back at the hotel room, sweaty and run-down from a day of lying and worrying and running and jumping and, wow, it all looks so much more effortless when it's someone else on TV.

Too spent to speak, I hand Leo my phone.

He considers the message longer than I do. "I guess you should go." His eyes cast down but his jaw looks locked, as if sadness and anger are fighting an unseen battle that I have no way to put a stop to.

So, I don't argue. I shower, change, and head back out, already dreading whatever awaits me.

The address Buckley sent me ends up being a bowling alley, one where the overhead lights are off, the neon lights are on, and the rental shoes are glow-in-the-dark. Orange orbs hang from the ceiling and star fixtures shoot across the walls.

I would like this place if I weren't intensely nervous.

There's a full-service bar across the way and an old Madonna music video is playing on big screens hanging down over the play area.

This is not the kind of place Buckley would ever suggest for a date night back when we were together, so I'm rattled when I notice him sitting on a faux-leather couch at a central lane. A pair of shoes sit on the seat next to him; two hot-pink balls are waiting in the return.

"You made it," he says, but he doesn't sound happy to see me. He passes me the shoes. Checking the heels, I notice he got my size wrong, like I got his shirt size wrong the night of our disastrous breakup. At least these shoes are too big and not too small, so I can be extra careful where I step and not have to call attention to the snafu.

"Where's Alexia?" I ask. I assumed she'd be here. Back in college, they traveled as a pair almost everywhere, completely inseparable. Sometimes, on dates, it even felt like I was the third wheel because Alexia monopolized so much of the conversation, ate so many of the appetizers, and insisted on sitting between us at the movies so nobody whispered a thought without her hearing.

When she moved out to Los Angeles after graduation and Buckley and I moved in together, I always felt a bit like a consolation prize for her absence. Clearly, I'd misremembered all of that when I came out here and convinced myself she'd compete with me. My mind has a sneaky way of latching on to my worst ideas sometimes.

"Oh, she's back at her place. I've been staying with her. She's resting up for the taping tomorrow." Buckley bends over to tie his shoe and every twist of the laces is so methodical, so precise.

"Isn't that what we should be doing?" I ask, taking a step and trying desperately not to trip as the shoes slip in the back. I look up at the scoreboard where Buckley has already input our names and bowled his first frame before I even arrived. A power move.

"I figured we could unwind and have some fun," he says with a smile that doesn't reach his ears. "Didn't you say I wasn't any fun?"

Hearing it back, I realize how childish it sounded, but in my defense, I was caught off guard. That breakup was nowhere on my radar. We'd survived almost four years together. I thought we could overcome anything. Everything about that night went off the rails and I didn't have the control to right it or filter my words. He doesn't need to throw them back in my face at me like this.

"I honestly can't remember. It was so long ago, and I met Leo. I haven't thought about it since." The lie dances so easily off my tongue as I pick up a bowling ball, line up my roll, and sail the ball down the lane, striking the pins right in the center but without enough umph. I end up with a split.

Buckley slides down a seat so he's in my peripheral vision, outlined by hazy, neon red that gives him a devilish quality. A new Madonna song comes on—"Hung Up."

"Right, Leo. Your *boyfriend*. We got sent everyone's B-roll cuts today. Leo doesn't seem like the type to frequent nerdy, game show fan forums."

I don't give him the satisfaction of shock. Instead, I bowl my second shot yet only hit one pin. I tie up the score, though it's not as rewarding as I'd hoped. "Looks can be deceiving."

I'm seeing that exemplified right now. Buckley seemed like such a sweet, innocent guy when I met him in college. Here, in this bowling alley, he's got the smarm of a Disney animated villain come to life. "Regardless, clearly you moved on pretty fast."

"Was I supposed to be mooning over you this whole time? You dumped me." I've known the sting of it, but it's only now that I inspect the chasm where closure should be. He didn't come home. I packed up and left. There was no further communication until now.

He edges around me, leaning over to grab his ball in

near slow motion. Such a performance. "I thought you'd at least give it some time to cool, some thought." I can't see his face, but from his stillness, I sense a discontent. Has he reconsidered since? "That hurts, Holden. I thought I meant something to you. We were together for nearly four years. We have a history."

"A history that includes laughing in my face and then leaving me all alone in an expensive restaurant while I cried," I say, controlling my tone so the teenagers in the next lane don't start listening in. "Did you forget about that?"

"Of course not," he says, peering over his shoulder, almost wounded-looking. From behind, I wait with bated breath as he takes his turn. Never have I seen him so focused on anything other than his work.

The pink ball pendulums back with perfect form and coasts down the lane with a near sensual spiral. When it crashes into the pins, it takes them all down in one fell crash.

Buckley turns back wearing a wide, toothy smile that I can't quite read.

Is he here to win me back, or is he here to win the breakup?

"I know you and Leo are faking it," he says, unintentionally answering my unvoiced question. "It didn't take long to search up Leo's supposed fan account and see when it was made or to find out where he worked, call to file a complaint about his service, and find out he no longer worked there. Fired, I presume?"

"I think you know where you can shove your presumption," I say, growing fiercely protective of Leo, no matter what trump cards Buckley thinks he holds. I may have

earned backlash, but Leo certainly didn't. What kind of villain stoops that low? "Leave Leo out of this, and keep his
name out of your mouth."

Buckley rolls his eyes, half shrugs. "Tell me if I'm wrong.
You took this trip without me, begged Alexia to audition
with you, which she declined and promptly told me about,
giving me the idea to go through with this. And then, un-
beknownst to us, you got the hotel concierge to play pretend
with you. He needed the money, so he agreed." Buckley
sounds proud of himself for deducing all of this. I'm sure
I'm not hiding much on my face. You don't date someone
for as long as we dated without learning their tells.

Damn, Alexia. "So, you assumed I wouldn't audition,
wouldn't get cast, and then I'd see you on the latest episode
and you'd get your comeuppance?"

"Something like that..." he says. "It's your turn."

At first, I think he means to speak, but then I look up
at the scoreboard. I ignore it. "What is it you want here?"

"Give me one good reason not to tell the producers you're
in a fake relationship and have you cut from the show." He's
practically snarling.

"Because there has to still be a smidgen of love left for
me in your heart. Almost four years doesn't disappear over
four weeks." Though, looking at him, I wonder if it could.
If our love was evaporating long before the break. "What
could I have possibly done to deserve this?"

"You made a fool out of me the night we broke up,
Holden. Yelling and carrying on. We were the laughingstock of the restaurant," he chides.

I rock back on my heels, confused. "That's it? You were embarrassed one time. That can't be the only reason you came all the way out to Los Angeles. It just can't be."

Buckley stops what he's doing, looks me square in the face and with no irony says, "Can't it? You claimed I wasn't spontaneous, wasn't fun, couldn't win. I've been thinking about that a lot these last few weeks, and I'm here to prove that wrong."

"Prove it to me or prove it to yourself?" I ask, stalling. Trying to find a way out of this that isn't never-ending mortification. For me and for Leo. Leo needs that money to springboard into a new life. I refuse to let him down.

"I can send an email right now. I have all the proof ready to go," he says.

One final idea hits me. "You'll just be proving my point."

He arcs an eyebrow at me. "What?"

"If you get me and Leo kicked off the show, you're admitting you think we're worthy opponents," I say, heart ramping up. "You're scared we'll beat you, and if we don't get the chance to go head-to-head, well, I think you and I both know we'll spend the rest of our days assuming who would've come out victorious."

His face flushes crimson. "That's not true."

"Fine," I say, growing bolder. "Send the email, then. See if I care. I'll always know the truth and that's enough for me." It's a bluff. I hope he can't see the sweat at my hairline as I start taking off my bowling shoes, ready to leave this setup.

Buckley huffs, evidently annoyed I've bested him at his

little game. "Okay, have it your way. We'll settle it on the show. I hope you like nationwide humiliation."

"And I hope you like eating your words." I stomp out of the establishment, shaking with adrenaline and happy I've halfway put a stop to Buckley's fiendish plan.

Twenty-Two

"I'm going to wipe the floor with him!" I shout-grunt, performing bicep curls with fifteen-pound weights to Leo's expert count.

"Eye of the Tiger" blares on a loop across the room. This is my Rocky moment. This is the training montage to end all training montages. Leo, seemingly unrattled by most of my dramatics thus far in our fake relationship, was befuddled when I got back, changed into workout clothes, and told him—no, barked at him—that we were hitting the gym.

If you can even really call this a gym. It's a green-carpeted room on the basement level of the building with one tiny window touching the ceiling, letting in barely any light. There's an elliptical, a rack of weights, and a bench. And it's devoid of other people. Which is perfect. Because I'm pissed.

"Are you feeling okay?" Leo asks, pumping heavier weights directly in front of me, providing ample motivation. We're only twenty minutes into this forty-minute workout.

I'm sweating, and in the reflection from the mirror across the way, my eyes are intense lasers.

"I'm fine," I say, which is met with visible skepticism. "Okay, I'm enraged I spent four years of my life with a mega-jerk who would do all of this just to spite me. What does that say about me, about my judgment?"

The fizzling anger I'm experiencing makes me want to punish my body. I unload the fifteen pounders and reach for the twenties.

"Whoa there, champ," Leo says, stepping between me and my demise. "Let's not blow out our arm muscles before the show, okay? You're already going to be sore in the morning."

"Because you're going to fuck me so hard and good that I'm going to forget my ex hates me so much that he'd fly across the country to compete on a TV game show he despises?" My tone is hopeful.

He laughs, but it's rueful. "No."

I boo back at him, trying to fake him out and grab for the weights anyway.

"Maybe!" He beats me again. "If you listen to me. You were young, right? You said you met in college. Your brain wasn't fully mature yet. You shouldn't beat yourself up—literally with weights or emotionally—for outgrowing someone."

"Easy for you to say," I huff out before taking a swig from my water bottle. "At least with your ex, you know why it all went to shit. With mine, he just, what? Woke up one day and decided I wasn't good enough to be with anymore."

Leo's weights clunk back down onto the metal rack. I

can tell by his gait as he grabs his sweat towel from his bag that I've upset him by being a rude, selfish gremlin. The last thing I want to do is jeopardize what we're building with the wrecking ball that is my past.

"Sorry. That was completely insensitive of me. I know this is affecting you just as much." I face the mirror but close my eyes, unable to look at myself right now. The person stuck there in the glass feels unmanageable, unworthy of Leo's support. "When I ran into Buckley on set this morning, it's like this sadness I've been harboring mutated into hot rage. It's like I have this heartbroken werewolf clawing around inside my stomach and I just want to… I want to…let him out!"

I strike the nearby stand-up punching bag. The sound makes Leo flinch, but relieves me a little, even if my fist hurts.

Leo peers over, eyes inquisitive. I throw another punch, and then another, alternating hands and shouting. "Eye of the Tiger" circles back to the start. Eventually, Leo comes and steadies the bouncing bag from behind, which creates some tension and makes the impact of the hit more satisfying. So much so that I get my legs involved.

In the mirror, I look like a windup toy that's malfunctioning, but I don't stop. And I truly don't care. Because Leo's not judging me and I'm trying hard not to judge myself.

I key into the song instead. Those guitars burrow into my soul as I pick up speed, letting a feline instinct take over. As the chorus comes around, I switch from primal grunts to shouty singing.

Leo, seemingly loving this, joins me.

We get loud and rowdy, until my skin is on fire and throat is raw.

The outro plays. I abandon the bag, grabbing Leo's sweat-soaked tank by the collar and tugging him into me, pressing our lips together with force and fervor. He kisses me back, latching his hands onto my hips, sinking his fingertips into the flesh.

"What's going on in here?" comes the sound of Annabelle, the desk attendant who gave me my bag the other day. Leo and I break apart as we notice her standing in the doorway looking about as pissed as I feel. "Why am I not surprised it's you?"

"Sorry," I say, rushing over to turn down the music. "Just letting off some steam."

She shakes her head. "There are plenty of places in this city to do that that won't disturb my guests." I was on her bad side before, but I can tell I've marched my way onto the abysmal side. "This is your second warning. One more and I'm going to have to cancel the rest of your reservation and have you seek accommodations elsewhere."

"No, no. I'm sorry. This is the last time. I promise," I say. "We won't be around tomorrow and then, the day after next, I check out. I'll be out of your hair." It hits me that this trip is about to come to a sudden end. We'll either win or we won't, but one thing is for sure: in two days, I fly back to New York.

Even if we do go home with the grand prize, it's not like they're going to direct deposit my half into my account as soon as the cameras stop rolling. There will be a lapse and taxes taken out and paperwork filed. I can't just extend my trip. Not with all the money I've spent so far.

That means leaving Leo.

"Well, good," Annabelle says, fixing her blazer with an exaggerated sigh. "Regardless, given the volume of complaints, I think it's best we lock the gym for the night."

Checking my phone, I realize it's well past 10:00 p.m. I need my rest for the competition tomorrow. We've got an early start. "No trouble. We'll go."

Feeling like teenagers caught smoking in the graveyard after hours, Leo and I go back up to my room, which is becoming more like our room as the days pass.

Unselfconsciously, we both strip out of our sweaty workout clothes. We stand there, naked in the lamplight, exhausted from the day but growing hard at the sight of one another. I reach out a hand as a peace offering to Leo, which he takes.

I stop up the drain, fill up the tub with water, and dig through my toiletry bag. "I never travel without these. We don't have a tub at home, so I always hope for one in hotels." I pour out a little liquid from the tiny bottle and watch as the bubble mountains begin to form.

Leo looks at me with stars in his eyes. Suddenly, the sudsy mounds are filling up my heart, too.

We step in and immediately my muscles relax. We each claim a corner, sinking down into the foam and the bliss and steam billowing up. Leo dunks his head under and when he comes back up, he's got a pointy bubble hat and a matching beard. "Ho, ho, ho!" he bellows, and I laugh and splash him. So, he splashes me back.

It's calming, sitting here like this in the silence and slosh. Leo smiles across from me. His hand finds my ankle under the forest of bubbles. He brings my foot to his chest and slowly massages the sole. His hands are strong. I knew that, but I didn't fully appreciate it until right now.

My eyes close in pleasure. "I'm sorry again for conflating our situations before." If Annabelle hadn't interrupted us, I would've said it sooner.

"I know you didn't mean it literally. I understand that feeling," he says, not stopping the massage for a second. "The werewolf-inside feeling. I had it right after Carter broke it off with me. I still have it sometimes, but most of the time it's more like a Yorkie. Yappy and annoying, but the worst it's going to do is tear up the furniture or pee on the carpet. Yours is newer than mine, though. It took me time to tame it, and seeing Carter in the store the other day didn't help the situation at all. I can only imagine what you must feel being confronted by your ex in a place that you thought was safe from him."

Leo grabs my other foot and starts in. The kneading of his thumbs is purposeful. "That doesn't make my heartbreak more important. Just because it's newer or bigger. I shouldn't have said what I said."

"Holden, someone you loved threatened to blackmail you. Out of character reactions are okay when that happens," he says, laughing but more to himself. It is ridiculous, hearing it spoken aloud.

"You're implicated in that blackmail, too," I point out. "How come you're not riding this anxiety spiral with me?"

"Because, despite everything, I want to see the good in people." His gaze is supercharged. That moral thesis explains why he didn't write me off as some sad sap that first night. It would've been easier to make that call and cast me aside. Instead, he stayed. "I think he'll do the right thing here, even if he's already done the wrong thing. If that makes any sense."

"Sort of," I say, still trying to make heads or tails of the situation myself but feeling a growing pitter-patter for Leo inside my chest. I scoop up a handful of bubbles and blow, letting them go airborne. One by one, they pop. I wish I could get rid of my problems that easily. "I just wish he'd been honest with me tonight. We were together for a long time. I know when he's holding back. Or, at least I thought I did. Something about this whole scheme of his isn't adding up. The breakup can't be the sole reason."

Leo sets my foot down, so to return the favor and distract my mind a bit, I start in on his. It's okay if I'm not as good as he is because I can tell by his expression that he appreciates it already. "Maybe he was holding on to some hidden resentments you didn't know about."

I ponder this. Part of me believed Buckley wore his annoyance for my quirks on his sleeve, but did he have cards slipped up inside them too that I didn't know about? I always assumed living with someone meant secrets have nowhere to be stashed. I suppose you can never fully know another person.

Yet, it's only been a few days, and I feel like Leo's vulnerable parts have all been laid out for me like the pieces of pre-construction IKEA furniture. I may not be able to pronounce all the names, and I don't know what all the parts are for just yet, but I'm aware they're there and that they're important.

For his care and the comfort his presence brings me, I kiss the side of his foot and then up his smooth calf. He wiggles a bit, probably surprised. The water drips over the edge of the tub. I ignore it. I venture farther north, bodily radar honing in on his perfect lips which crest into a smile.

"Thank you," I say before giving him a quick kiss. "For going on this wild ride with me." I snuggle in closer and notice he's sporting an erection that brushes the inside of my thigh and makes me come alive just the same. His cock is exactly the distraction I need right now.

"Oh, you haven't experienced how wild this ride can be yet."

His voice is brushed velvet, his hands are silk, and despite the laws of thermodynamics the bath gets hotter and hotter the longer we stay in.

Even still, hours later—when we're drained, dried off, and Leo's fast asleep in the bed beside me—I lie awake unable to shake a rising dread that starts low in my gut, snakes through my sternum, and puts my heart in a choke hold.

Twenty-four hours from now, will I be popping champagne or regretting I ever dared come here?

Twenty-Three

When I hear the *Madcap Market* theme song played live by the full band for the first time, my eyes well with tears.

Mom's not here. I'm leaving Leo tomorrow. Blackmail looms larger by the second.

I don't know which one of these is bringing on the most tears, but I fight them all back. I can't cry on camera. There are plenty of them pointed right at me behind the persistent, disorienting glow of the bright lights ready to capture me at my best. I need to leave my worst in the wings.

Leo and I stand behind our Team Eggplant podium in our purple sweatshirts. Jessica and Darla—who magically got cast this go around—are wearing blue, and Buckley and Alexia settled on a salmon pink that washes them both out. It's petty, but it gives me a smidgen of satisfaction. Especially since their glitter glue additions look like a fourth grader did them.

Leo made good on his promise of a wild ride last night,

and it was a fun distraction, but now, faced with my competition, the reality zips back into sharp focus. I have to get my head in the game.

The dread from last night hopped on my back and followed me here. It whispers over and over again: this could all go up in smoke so quickly.

"And now, here's your host, Paaaaaaat Crumskyyyyy."

The studio audience goes wild as the salt-and-pepper star emerges from behind a black curtain. Wearing a white shirt and a tie with potatoes on it, he waves at the crowd as they cheer him on.

I grab Leo's forearm to remind myself that this is real. It's happening, and I'm here with Leo, and I won't let a conniving ex or niggling emotions stand in the way of making good on my promise to Mom.

"Welcome to *Madcap Market*, the game show where we turn an everyday grocery store into an adult playground." Pat Crumsky flashes the crowd a natural-born showman's smile. I can't help it. I fawn. Despite his age, he's even handsomer in person. "For those of you who are new to the program, here's how it works. Our teams of two will participate in three rounds of physical competition and trivia. The winners will earn advantages such as coupons and gift cards for the final round, *Madcap Mania*, where the store becomes a minefield of obstacles as the teams race to complete the ultimate shopping list. The team with the lowest receipt total gets to go on to our finale where they'll be put to the test to win one hundred thousand dollars. Let's meet our teams."

When the main camera lands on me and Leo, heat rises

to my cheeks and my tongue ties up, so Leo, probably sensing this, speaks first. "I'm Leo Min. I'm from Los Angeles, California. I'm a gaming enthusiast who loves to dance, and I plan on going home with one hundred thousand dollars." All that practice paid off. He flashes a charming, boyish smile that gets a good laugh out of the audience.

"I see you've taken the sleeves off your sweatshirt. I take it you frequent the gym in your spare time?" Pat asks, knowing his audience is going to love the response.

"Thanks for noticing, Pat. I do work out pretty regularly," he says. "But I did a little extra just to get in shape for your show." Leo, as he always does, lifts up his arms and flexes to a near unanimous swoon throughout the room. I'm not immune to it. Neither is Pat clearly, even though he has a gorgeous supermodel wife and two kids at home.

All those episodes I made Leo watch primed him for this. Not that it will necessarily help us win—there's luck and skill involved in that part—but being winsome on national TV nets you social media followers, maybe free gifts from brands who want you to post about them, and on rare occasions, an invite to compete on an all-star episode of *Madcap Market*. Our performances aren't limited to this sole taping.

But I can't think about all that right now. My only aims are grinding Buckley to dust and getting out of debt.

"How about you?" Pat pivots to me.

"Well, Pat, my name is Holden." My eyes flick over to Buckley behind the opposite podium. There's a slight upward twitch of his right eyebrow. Almost imperceptible. But I'm still, even after the breakup, so attuned to his shifting moods. I know what he's thinking. He's thinking about exposing me on national television. I clam up.

"Cat got your tongue?" Pat asks.

Leo leans over. "He's so excited, Pat. He's been a fan since he was a kid. I think he's too starstruck to speak."

"Yeah," I blurt out. "This is a dream come true."

"That's lovely, young man. It's always wonderful to have a superfan on the show. Tell me, who introduced you to *Madcap Market*?"

The tears I fought back before return, especially when I notice a familiar face in the audience. Mrs. Min sits behind one of the main cameras. She's not frowning, but she's not smiling either. She looks uncomfortable squished onto the bleachers with so many hyper, excited fans.

She's been so kind to me. She's given me cooking lessons. She raised such a respectable if somewhat cocky son whom I'm growing fonder of by the second. It's all overwhelming.

If I believed in ghosts, I could almost imagine Mom sitting beside Mrs. Min shooting me a big thumbs-up.

I croak, "My mom." Then, the tears fall.

As if he expects this to happen once an episode, Pat pulls a monogrammed hanky from a pocket inside his suit jacket and hands it to me. "Is she no longer with us?"

Unable to get out any words, I shake my head. Leo's arm wraps tightly around me. I should've known this would happen.

"I'm sorry to hear that. I'm sure she's smiling down on you right now. Team Eggplant's number one fan!" I'm mortified we went with that name now. A little, surprising laugh chirps out of me and stops the crying in its tracks. "Care to explain that team name?" Pat asks, trying to transition smoothly back into the show's fun tone.

Leo takes the question. "Well, who doesn't love a little eggplant in their life?" His eyebrows waggle to win the laugh. "In seriousness, we're a little cheeky, but mostly we were online friends who recently met in person. We're egg-*planting* the seeds of our relationship on the show tonight."

An *aw* sounds off that tickles its way into my heart. Leo stole my line, but delivered it better than I ever could. The cheesiness doesn't negate the sentiment.

Pat Crumsky moves on, and the lights on our podium blink off, but the heat wave I'm experiencing doesn't subside because Buckley is still glaring at me. Even if the mention of my mom lessened its intensity, it's still there, menacing, re-minding me that even if there's truth to our tale now, there wasn't when we started this.

When Buckley begins speaking, I hold my breath. Leo, once again, sensing my emotional distress like it's his god-damn superpower, lassoes one arm around my waist. It's below our podium so the crowd can't see. He tugs me into his side so we're hip to hip.

The studio slides away until Leo whispers, "We're in the clear."

The camera has panned away from Buckley and Alexia. There were no gasps. No producers running onto set de-manding to know why Leo and I would lie like that. Buck-ley zipped his lips, but that doesn't mean he's thrown away the key.

Everyone breaks for commercial. The smile I didn't even know I was wearing drops.

"Seems like we have nothing to worry about."

"I wish that were true," I say, unease becoming our third teammate.

Round one, a single product scavenger hunt, starts off with a bang.

Pat Crumsky reads out the first clue. "It's a frosted menagerie for your mouth!"

"Frosted Animal Crackers!" I whisper-shout frantically in Leo's ear, cupping with my hand so our competition can't read my lips.

Leo bolts out from behind our podium like a racehorse. My heart pounds erratically as Leo disappears into the aisles. Bulked-up cameramen with heavy-duty equipment strapped to their torsos run after Leo, Alexia, and Darla.

Leo beelined straight for snacks. I have to watch on the monitors to see where he swerves next. With a plastic basket swaying from his muscular arm, he goes sheet-white panicked when he charges down the aisle and sees Alexia coming in from the other side.

I grip the sides of my podium, leaning forward, praying and hoping and cursing under my breath. Is this what a premature heart attack feels like? I could honestly pass out with nerves.

Leo lunges in front of Alexia grabbing a red box and causing a smattering of others to fall. Alexia, with catlike reflex, slides away before getting hit and grabs a pink box.

No…

Leo rounds the corner running back to me with his arms outstretched and a smile on his face not knowing he's made a losing mistake. I'm shaking my hand, waving him back. I'm not allowed to speak or we lose automatically, but if he runs around one more time maybe we can still cinch this.

But Leo isn't looking. He bypasses me and slams our buzzer.

Bzz. Alexia slams the buzzer on her Team Salmon Sliders podium second. Darla is way behind.

Pat comes over to us. "All right, Leo. The clue was: *A frosted menagerie for your mouth.* What product did you come up with?"

Leo's smile falters when he holds up the box and registers his mistake, too. "Animal Crackers."

Pat scrunches up his face. Or, gets as close to scrunching up his face as he can because of all the Botox. "Oh, no. I'm sorry that's not the product we were looking for. Team Salmon Sliders buzzed in next."

Alexia, flipping her hair out of her face with one hand and holding up the box with the other, says, "*Frosted* Animal Crackers here, Pat."

After they're crowned the winners and given a twenty dollars off your purchase of one hundred or more for the final round, Buckley and Alexia hit me with matching sneers. I should've known, even back in the day when I felt like the third wheel despite being Buckley's boyfriend, that this is how everything was going to shake out. I was the guy with the dead mom. I was never going to get happily-ever-after. The universe foretold that.

A bell rings and the director yells cut. Commercial jingles pipe in from overhead.

Leo leans in. "I'm sorry. I reached for the first box I saw."

It's like we're back in the grocery store on that first day. I'm trying not to be annoyed with him over something out of his control. This set is overstimulation city. No wonder he had tunnel vision. Had I been the one running, I might've done the same thing. Except, it's hard to sand off the edge to my voice when I say, "It's fine."

I can sense Buckley's and Alexia's smugness from across the room. It's overpowering like the aroma of garlic in an Italian restaurant.

"We'll get the next one. You're going to crush the trivia round," he says reassuringly, undeterred by my unwarranted exasperation.

Round two is more evenly matched than you might expect.

Flummoxed by us fumbling the bag in round one, my head is garbled, making identifying blurry produce and unscrambling animated alphabet soup even more daunting.

When Leo taps in, I can tell that he studied, but the cousin duo (Team Artichoke) to our left has this down to an art. All those times they auditioned must've really given them the training they needed because they hit the button with robotic superspeed.

"Celery!" Jessica shouts.

"Clam chowder!"

"Wagyu beef!"

They are an unstoppable right-answer machine, and we're falling far behind.

But then, Pat Crumsky says, "On to our next trivia challenge: The Mighty Mascots."

I perk up. My mind races with memories of Mom, to the silly voices she did when she pushed us down the aisles on a crisp December afternoon picking up snack foods and cereals.

When our monitor shows the first picture—a round-faced man with a mustache and a bow tie—my memory produces my mom's terrible Italian accent.

"What is this Mascot's full name?"

"It's-a-me, Julius Pringles," she said, dropping her favorite kind— sour cream and onion—into our cart.

I slam the buzzer and answer the question.

"That's correct!" The celebratory ding sounds. The audience cheers. Leo jostles my shoulder with approval as we switch spots.

During his turn, the trio of cherubic, hat-wearing cereal hawkers show up on screen. With pride, Leo announces, "Snap, Crackle, and Pop."

Pat repeats himself. "That's correct!"

Leo whispers as we pass each other again, "*ers.*"

I laugh, my mood lifts, and we start slaying this section. Question after question, we're buzzing in fastest and providing the right answer. So much that Pat Crumsky cries, "These guys are on a roll! Team Salmon Sliders and Team Artichoke, you do know where the buzzers are, don't you?"

By the end of the round, we've amassed a couple cou-

pons, a gift certificate, and a rebate (as if those are still relevant). After the last question is asked, we're crowned the
winners, which knocks Team Artichoke out of the game
completely. They throw major side-eye when the cameras
cut, and they're walked off set.

I would be peeved too if an out-of-towner crushed my
one chance on this show after so many failed attempts. I try
to look as apologetic as possible as Jessica and Darla pass by.

"Talk about a comeback," says one of the younger production assistants as she passes us on the way to hide some
bonus items throughout the store.

The real test of physical stamina comes next. I'm amped
up, practically vibrating.

We're ushered into a side room so we can't see the crew
as they booby-trap the store. When the automatic doors
open, the third round, the all-out frenzy, will begin. One
at a time, we'll push carts into the store, grab as many items
as we can until we hear the buzzer, and then race back to
tap out. We must:

☐ Clip coupons from the circular
☐ Complete the shopping list
☐ Avoid obstacles
☐ Snag bonuses

It's a lot to accomplish in six minutes, but I'll be damned
if I don't try my absolute best. I accept the electronic scanner
and prop fanny pack from a wardrobe person with poofy hair.

In the holding room with a few cameras set up in the

corners to catch our preparations , Leo leads me through a warm-up, so I don't pull a muscle or collapse into a pile of bones in the freezer aisle. Alexia, noticing us, does the same for Buckley who has been pacing, chewing on his lip.

When he catches my gaze, there isn't malice there. It's concern. Concern that he might not come out victorious after all. I like instilling that fear in him. It fuels me.

I read Alexia's lips as she tells Buckley he should run first.

"I'm going to take first shift," I tell Leo, standing and brushing myself off. I want to go up against Buckley.

"You sure?" he asks.

I take another look at the list we got sent to our scanner apps.

1. Wicker basket
2. Cucumbers

I can't help but laugh and blush at that one.

3. White bread
4. A dozen chocolate-covered strawberries
5. Reusable table cloth
6. Plastic cups

"It's for an outdoor picnic," I say quietly.

"What?" Leo asks.

I point to his scanner. "They're going to give us a bonus if we can correctly guess what kind of event the shopping list is for. It's an outdoor picnic."

My mind rewinds to spring semester sophomore year when Buckley texted me to meet him at a nearby park. I had just gotten done with a really stressful final when I saw him sitting on a large beach towel with hoagies and a gallon jug of sweet tea.

I wonder what happened to that Buckley because this Buckley, leering at me while dropped down in a lunge across the room, is not him. Maybe getting his ass kicked in this competition will show him that messing with me was the wrong move.

The countdown times out. Alexia fixes her ponytail and throws me a withering smile. "Good luck, guys," she says, then adds under her breath, "You're going to need it."

"Welcome back to *Madcap Market*," says Pat Crumsky directly into the camera. On the monitor, he looks larger than life. "Before we parted, we said goodbye to Team Artichoke. Now, Team Salmon Sliders and Team Eggplant are prepared to go head-to-head in the shopping list challenge. We've staged our store with a multitude of fun tricks and tests for our competitors to overcome. Who will go on to the finale? Let's find out! Contestants, are you ready for some *Madcap Mania*?"

Buckley and I throw thumbs-ups to the cameras as we approach the doors. Our first carts are greased and ready. I grip the handle as if it were a luxury sports car and I were about to drag race my way to fame.

"Better stay out of my way," Buckley says snidely while smiling for the cameras. We were told there's no audio recorded in this room, so no one will hear our trash-talking.

"That won't be a problem because I'll be so far ahead of you," I say. "Try not to choke on my dust."

"On your carts, get ready," Pat announces. "Shop!"

Twenty-Four

Four and a half minutes later, I'm desecrated.

Whipped cream glops down the side of my face. The front of my sweatshirt is soaked with lemonade from a sample stand I accidentally knocked over and then fell into. But heaven knows I won't let a little mess stand in my way of winning that prize.

Leo and I performed the penultimate handoff, and now I'm racing toward the tablecloths. I have to remember: the lowest cart total wins the money.

Buckley is only marginally in the lead. He's taken a shortcut through the chip aisle only to be greeted by the lemonade spill. The wheels of his cart spin unprompted, rolling away without him while his arms flail and he falls into the table.

God, how has nobody died doing this before?

I shake away the morbid thought as I ditch my cart so I can army-crawl beneath a sign that is hanging from only one chain, blocking most of the aisle. I hope the audience at home is having a good laugh because this is far less fun from the inside. I feel like I've been put through the ringer. I still need to grab the tablecloth, get it into the cart, and get the cart over the finish line.

My body protests—fully pushed to the max—but I must press on. For me. For Mom.

Leo's encouraging voice cuts through the store, "You got this, Holden!"

For Leo. Sweet, deserving, hopefully-going-to-be-my-boyfriend-when-this-is-all-over Leo.

Finding my strength again, I stand and begin scanning the shelves. My eyes gravitate toward the red-and-black-checkered fabric cloth with the shiny SALE tag beneath it that reads: 50% off with Club Shopper Card.

I can't remember for the life of me if we collected that one in the previous rounds or not. Unzipping the fanny pack they gave me, I quickly skim through the coupons I've clipped and our various winnings. I'm not seeing the Club Shopper Card, but after doing the quick mental math I know this tablecloth will end up being cheaper than the budget plastic tablecloth by at least a dollar if we do have it.

This game can come down to pennies. We can't bear that extra dollar.

The Club Shopper Card is probably in the pack. I'm just too stressed to see it like Leo was too stressed to notice he grabbed the wrong Animal Crackers.

Risking it all, I scan the cloth and rush back to my abandoned cart.

Of course, as soon as I return, my cart isn't where I left it. I crane my neck down the nearest aisle and, sure enough, Buckley's playing dirty. He's sent my cart off on its own, crashing into cases of Coca-Cola which topple with loud, fizzy splats much to the audience's delight.

Ever the adult, Buckley sticks his tongue out at me.

"Real mature!" I shout.

Fuming with the checkered tablecloth under my arm, trying desperately not to crumple it in transit, I resist the urge to flip off Buckley. I know Dad is watching at home. Shaking it off, I turn back to Leo.

He's right across the line, jumping up and down, smiling despite the setback. It's all apropos. Leo's the one I'm running toward. Buckley's the one I'm leaving behind in a puddle of spilled drink. The future looks bright.

As I tap him in, Leo cries, "We're killing this!"

With my hands on my knees and my heart in my throat, I catch my breath and think: hell yeah, we are.

Except when the bell sounds and the round ends, I find out, for sure, that we didn't have the Club Shopper Card after all. My naive optimism kicks me in the ass.

I'm standing on my mark next to Leo, combing through my fanny pack and Leo's fanny pack, and waiting for Pat to come back out and reveal which team is going on to the finale.

"Didn't we win the Club Shopper Card during trivia?" I frantically ask Leo, knowing the answer but needing to hear it aloud for it to register completely.

"No," he says, using a cloth to wipe at his sweaty brow.

"We won the five-dollar gift card and the three-dollar-off coupon."

"Looking for this?" Buckley's grating voice comes from a few steps away. He's holding the Club Shopper Card in his hand. As he wiggles it, the piece of plastic catches the light like it's a goddamn golden nugget.

I grow cold. I might've just cost us the game.

"We're back in two!" shouts a production assistant.

Leo and I snap forward. "We're screwed," I mumble, furious with myself.

"You don't know that." Leo's conviction isn't sound.

"I took the most expensive tablecloth thinking we had fifty percent off when I could've taken the cheapest one. The difference would've been like a dollar. Now, who knows how off we're going to be." My pulse ratchets up. I can sense Mom here with me. Was coming on this show and losing a fate worse than never knowing if I could hack it on our favorite game show?

Leo rubs a reassuring hand up and down my inside arm, which comes off as placating. I don't like it. "We won't know for sure until Pat comes out and announces the totals. We did our best."

"But—"

"We did..." he says, stepping closer. "Our best."

I want to breathe in those words, not let the panic win, but my mind won't let me.

Then, in front of the audience, in front of Buckley, in front of his mom, Leo kisses me. He kisses me with a passion that should be exciting and reassuring like it was at karaoke, but this time it's neither. My skin crawls, and my negative thoughts continue to crank out. One rises above the rest: he's doing this for the audience and the producers. He's selling the lie.

A kiss off camera is worth just as much as a kiss on-air. Maybe more. It solidifies our story and mortifies me.

What was I thinking? Why did I do this?

I've lost us the show and even if not tomorrow or a year from now, one day, I'll lose Leo, too.

Once a loser, always a loser. I thought this show would help me shed that, but the dread on my back grows larger and heavier the longer we stand here. "Save it for the cameras!" cries the production assistant as she passes us to count the cameras in once more.

Flushed, I pull away. I'm lost in the haze of horrible thoughts that I don't even realize when we've begun rolling again. Pat Crumsky has appeared with the special envelope that contains our fate.

"Our teams' final receipt totals were separated by a mere fifty-six cents," Pat says. My stomach evacuates into the bowels of the earth. "Could one coupon have cost the competitor a chance to play for one hundred thousand dollars? Let's find out."

The lights dim and the music skews dramatic. My heart keeps time with the persistent, ominous drum line.

I want this to be over. I want to be home. I want Mom back.

"The winner of round three is…" His pause is a major test of my patience. "Team Eggplant!"

The bright lights blink back on. I'm too stunned to process. Leo's yelling excitedly in my ear. Buckley looks like he wants to murder me. Mrs. Min is in the crowd sporting the biggest smile I've seen from her yet, which breaks my heart because we lied to her. Because, despite what I believed before, I feel as tangled as I did when I arrived in Los Angeles.

"Team Salmon Sliders, thank you for playing. We loved getting to know you," Pat says.

Buckley and Alexia both look about ready to blab my secret, but before either of them gets a chance to speak, I notice they're being consoled by a background actor in a grocery store uniform.

I'm not even relieved. A twisted part of me wishes Buckley and Alexia would out our lie. I would bow out in disgrace but at least I could wash my hands clean of this whole scheme. But then I look at Leo who is so genuinely thrilled to have almost won his way out of unemployment hell, and I can't torch it all.

Leo doesn't deserve that. He deserves better than the lot he's been given.

He definitely deserves better than me: an emotionally messed up, stuck-in-life nobody. Right?

As a show of good sportsmanship, they always ask the losing team to shake hands with the winning team before the finale. Alexia does so, eyes narrowed but not maliciously. She had no serious skin in this game. She got her screen time.

Buckley, on the other hand, bypasses my friendly outstretched hand and pulls me in for an overly familiar hug right as they cut to commercial again to ready the set for the finale.

Buckley's right hand slithers up between us and does its best to cover both of our microphones. He whispers in my ear, "I figured it out."

"What?" I ask as he continues to hold me.

"The other night you said I couldn't have come all this way because of the restaurant fiasco," he explains. "Well, you were right. You put all your love into the past. Into this show. Into your mom. There was no place for me. Do you know what it's like being in a relationship with someone, living with someone who is barely there, a ghost?"

"I—" I want to protest, but a part of me knows when the chaos and excitement of college ended, I fell into a depression. The grief tsunami tugged me into the undertow once more. My jobs weren't fulfilling, I hated our apartment, and I can now see clearly that Buckley was pulling away from me. That tension I felt that I thought was just growing pains—acclimating to a new normal—was a serious warning sign that my insular, avoidant life was about to collapse.

"I hope you've worked it out. For Leo's sake," he whispers. So earnest it's cruel. I almost wish he were still playing up the mustache-twirling villain. It was easier to hate him. Easier to pin my neuroses on his antagonism. Now he's handed me my faults on a silver platter. Where am I supposed to hide them when I'm on the set of a national TV show?

I swallow a thick wad of spit as he walks off the set arm linked in Alexia's. I'm crying. I try to wipe the tears away faster than Leo can spot them, but he's too perceptive for his own good.

"What did that asshole say now?" Leo asks, totally ready to throw fists if he needs to.

"Nothing," I say, mustering up a sense of self-preservation. "He wished us luck. That's all." For a second, I consider reaching out and touching Leo, but instead, I keep my hands to myself. This devastation feels private. Something I can't drag him into when I've already unloaded so much on to him.

The makeup artist who has been working with me all week rushes onto the set. "This part is always overwhelming. Don't worry, sweetie. I'll fix you." Externally, he erases any evidence of upset. Internally, I'm unspooled, and there's no fixing that.

When the show returns from commercial break, the monitor shows Leo and me all primped and made over in our interview from the other day. Instead of the green screen, they've dropped in a generic backdrop of the produce section. This was the video Buckley watched and deduced we were lying.

Watching myself now, it's not the obvious holes in our story that get to me. It's the fact that, in my grief, I don't even recognize myself. The guy on the screen is empty-eyed, spouting off rehearsed lines. My posture is rigid. That's the face of a man who's deluded himself beyond reality. A man who's convinced himself that reality TV was the answer to all his problems.

I seem to have only created more for myself.

The video ends, and against all odds, I couldn't care less what happens next.

"Team Eggplant, how does it feel to be going on to the final round?" Pat asks.

Leo jumps in. "Amazing! We trained hard, we played hard, and we're going to take home that grand prize."

"Holden, anything to add?"

With the microphone in my face, my mind goes blank. Shouldn't I be stoked to be making good on that long-ago promise to Mom? Shouldn't this be an accomplishment—the last stage of grief completed? Chip collected? Life moves on?

To save my last shred of dignity, I flick on the false charisma and say into the camera, "Only that we're blessed to have this opportunity, and I hope our efforts were worth it."

Twenty-Five

"Where's the best place to put this?" Leo asks of the absurdly large prop check the *Madcap Market* crew insisted we take back with us even though it won't fit in my suitcase no matter how hard I squish my stuff.

"Anywhere is fine." I close the door to my hotel room for the final night, pick a stray piece of confetti off the shoulder of my crewneck. How can a festive piece of paper feel so hefty?

We won, but I don't feel like celebrating.

Actually, I feel just as bad as I did the night Alexia frienddumped me at the tapas restaurant. If Leo wasn't here, I'm sure I'd be elbow-deep in the mini fridge by now.

Buckley's words are like that errant piece of confetti; they've trailed me all the way back here. After the final round and the hugs and pictures, without the excessive external stimulation of a TV set, my mind can't escape the loop it's stuck in.

Leo sets the cardboard monstrosity down inside the unstable closet and looks at me. No, not at me. But through me. Maybe I am barely here. A ghost—transparent, floaty, not awake in this world.

Until I landed in Los Angeles and Leo leaped into my life, I can't say I was ever very present. I was often wishing events to be over, social interactions to fall through, life to pass by. I would live it up when it felt right, and I wasn't missing Mom with every fiber of my being.

It's occurring to me, only now, that perhaps I'll never stop missing her. That maybe I'm one of those people who's not meant for romantic love because of the constant Mom-shaped empty space in my life.

"I expected you to be more excited," Leo says while tugging off his sweat-stained top. Even the sight of his exquisite torso in touching distance doesn't break me out of my obsessive spiral. "Is it because your mom's not here?"

"Something just feels off." My words taste like a straight shot of vinegar. It's not something. It's everything. I'm one unruly mess of emotions, and I can't stop shaking my head.

"You're probably just in shock," Leo says, crossing to the swag bag he left on the table. As a parting gift, the *Madcap Market* associates gifted us a grocery store chain gift card, fancy chocolates, and a pricey bottle of wine on top of our winnings. Leo begins unwrapping the cork. "This was a goal of yours since you were young, and you did it. We won one hundred thousand dollars."

"Minus taxes."

"Yeah, okay," Leo rebuts. "Minus taxes, but still. That's got to be hard to wrap your head around."

"Yeah," I say with little umph. "Maybe. But we lied to get it." I know this isn't my primary concern, but it still weighs on me.

Leo scoffs a little. "It's reality TV. They're interested in ratings, not truth. Have you ever seen an episode of *The Real Housewives*? I would say the only thing real about those women is their bodies, but even that's not true!"

I nod, unconvinced. "Fair point, but..."

"Once you have a glass of this, I'm sure you'll be feeling better." He grabs the paper cups from the bathroom and unwraps them. It's the least classy receptacle possible for such an expensive bottle and vintage. "To our success, to our windfall...and to our conversation tomorrow."

Leo's blush reminds me of the napkin we signed at the downstairs bar. Where did I put that? Tomorrow we're supposed to hash out how we can make this work as a long-distance, official couple.

After what Buckley said to me, there's no way I can entertain a relationship with Leo beyond what's transpired already. Can I?

My ghostliness turned Buckley from a boyish nerd into a vengeful ex. If that's the effect I have on men, I want to leave Leo unscathed before I diminish any of his light. Sure, he was snarky when I got here, hardened by growing up without his dad, but he's still optimistic. He has a world of opportunity waiting for him.

He'll get his own apartment, a new, satisfying career, and

he'll find a partner who can cook without lessons and sing karaoke without the help of alcohol. He deserves a happy ending.

If this whirlwind has shown me anything, it's that endings, I'm good at, but happiness, not so much.

"About that," I begin, unable to find the words to let him down easy. A napkin signed over beers isn't binding. He'll understand. He has to.

"No," Leo presses a stern finger to my lips as his domineering bedtime voice comes out to play. With his other hand, he gives me a cup of wine. "Tomorrow we can talk more. Tonight I want to make love to you."

"Love?" I choke out.

He looks as surprised as I sound, but then his eyebrows fall, and a small smile tickles the edges of his lips. "Yeah. I'm not jumping the gun here. I promise. Before we were fucking. Intense and deep but still separate. After today, I feel so connected to you."

I want to say I feel that, too, because I do in some ways, but my tongue won't allow me and mostly I just feel numb. Instead, I ask, "Sorry, but you're in love with me?"

His eyes bulge. "Oh, God. No, not exactly. Not yet. I'm just thinking, uh, that maybe I could be? In the future?"

The same sentiment lives inside my heart, but if I let it out, I'm only leading him on. According to Buckley, I don't have the emotional capacity for an intimate relationship. My frazzled brain won't string together anything coherent.

Leo sips his wine, smiles shyly. "Sorry, can we forget I said that? I was only trying to say that we did the damn thing. We're tired from a long, hard day. But, I'm so, so horny for you, Holden. Seeing you shine out there, all this adrenaline inside me. I want to edge you and tease you and make you cry my name. I want to slowly slip inside you." He steps closer to me, brushes a stray strand of hair from my border-line-watery eyes. "I want to feel you grip me as we lie on our sides. I want to be depleted before I fall asleep with you in my arms. Tomorrow will be tomorrow."

His lips find mine. It's like the kiss on the show but some-how more loaded. I pitch into him, allowing myself one last moment, one last night even. This was all fake from the start, right? What's one more evening of playing pretend—one last stellar act of avoidance from Holden James?

"Tonight," he says as he breaks the kiss. "Can we do that?"

Hesitantly, I nod.

Then, we do.

We do all of it. We do it languidly and with intention. We do it quietly and then loudly and then quietly again. We do it as if the world is about to end and, in a way, it feels like it is. I won't make believe that one hundred thousand dol-lars is going to change the way we live overnight, but it is a golden key of opportunity for guys like us.

To get me out of debt. To get Leo a better living ar-rangement.

However, later, as I lie beside a gently snoring Leo, star-ing up at the popcorn ceiling in the darkness, I'm reminded that it's not a magic potion. I can't drink our winnings and forget that Mom is gone or that the grief I experienced in her absence hasn't hurt others.

I won't hurt Leo. I couldn't live with myself if I did.

I love him too much to do that.

Whoa. It's fast and ridiculous, but it's true. In the future. In the present. I do love him. And that love is what leads me to the ultimate sacrifice.

At 5:00 a.m., Leo still fast asleep on the other side of the bed, I slip into my clothes, collect my toiletries, and stand my suitcase up on its wheels. I know what I must do.

In the darkness, I go searching for the hotel stationery only to find it full up with Leo's notes. All the details of my life he committed to memory. Various pieces of strategy for the game show we crushed only last night. A single tear spills from my eye and lands on the paper. I set it back down.

There's a plane leaving LAX in a few hours that will ferry me back to New York. I've decided that I need to be on it.

There are too many dangling threads of my life that I thought I could snip off with a single, diverting trip. I was wrong. Los Angeles isn't another universe. Buckley is proof that my old emotions could follow me here.

If I don't deal with them, I'll never be able to be someone worthy of loving Leo for real. Better to take the loss, like I'm so good at doing, than face the rejection later. Maybe, hopefully, one day, when I'm better, we'll find each other again, and he'll forgive me, allow me one more chance.

But for now, my eyes land on the Monopoly box from the very first night. Silently, I slip a paper bill from the plastic packaging inside. Using the hotel pen, I write Leo a goodbye note:

Leo,
This trip has been amazing. YOU are amazing.
But, I have to leave.
You don't deserve to fall in love with a ghost. You deserve to be with a fully invested human man who appreciates you for the caring, talented, goofy person you are.
Maybe that will be me, but I can't ask you to wait for a miraculous transformation that may never happen.

I run out of space on the first slender, slip of paper, so I grab another.

Please don't try to reach out to me. It'll only make this harder on us both.
I hope you use your half of the winnings to chase your passions.
You deserve it.
You deserve the world.
Love,
Holden

Twenty-Six

"Happy to have you home, son." Dad hauls my suitcase out of the trunk of his black, midsize Mazda.

"Oh, I got it. You didn't have to do that." After the long flight, my back is tense and my neck keeps cricking, but he's already letting me stay here again. The least I can do is move my own luggage.

"Nonsense. You just won a nationally televised TV game show yesterday!" he cries. "You hear that, neighbors! My son is a *Madcap Market* champion."

"Let's not bother the whole complex," I say, embarrassed and trying not to think about Los Angeles, trailing behind Dad as he fumbles in his jeans pocket for his keys.

When we're back inside the apartment, Dad says, "I've got leftovers in the fridge if you're hungry." He pulls out the remnants of a rotisserie chicken and slaps it on the counter of the in-need-of-an-update kitchen. His special cheesy mashed potatoes come out in a serving dish. The same ones we'd have every Thanksgiving. The ones Leo will likely never get to try. The ones Buckley asked for seconds and thirds of the first year he came home with me.

Dad asked, four weeks ago, when I arrived here to stay, what happened with Buckley. He was concerned and paternal. I clammed up. I told him, "It didn't work out." Dad didn't push.

Mom would've, though. She would've pried answers out of me in the kindest way possible; she knew how to ask the right questions and which bribes to offer that would get me to talk.

I don't begrudge Dad for not taking on Mom's role when she passed. Overnight, I was an adult, and he was a single parent and the world kept unfairly spinning.

We sit down on the hard, high-top chairs pulled into the chipping breakfast nook. Our elbows bump each time we pick up our forks. He's left-handed while I'm a righty.

"Sorry, son," he says, the third time it happens. There's a graveness to his voice that wasn't there a second ago. When I look over, I notice there are tears rimming his eyes. "I know I always try to look on the bright side and when it came to your mom, there was no other way I could face the day-to-day without optimism, but last night, watching you all alone, it hit me how unfair it is that your mom couldn't be there to see you. I know she was smiling down on you and cheering you on, but I just wish she could've been there to see you."

I push my plate away, appetite upended. "I don't." The confession sends a chill through the room. Despite how I felt on set, the plane ride and the sad in-flight meal helped me realize the truth of the situation.

"What?" Dad asks, evidently surprised. "Why not?"

"Because Leo and I were lying," I tell him. It doesn't feel so leaden now that it's out in the open. "He was working at the hotel I was staying at. He lost his job and we agreed to fake a relationship so we had a better chance of getting cast on the show. Somehow, it worked." After I say it, I realize that *somehow* isn't quite right. The *somehow* was us falling for each other, and others catching on to that quicker than we could.

"I have to admit, I was a bit caught off guard when you told me," Dad says, surprise in his voice. "Even more so when I saw you were competing against Buckley."

"That part was a shock to me, too," I say. I fiddle with the napkin on my lap, remembering the napkin contract I voided by leaving the hotel last night. In the moment, it felt like the right decision. Now, I...

My mind switches tracks before I can complete that thought. "Have I been a ghost?" I ask.

"You haven't been going around shouting 'boo' at people, if that's what you're asking." He chuckles, tears subsiding. "I will say that when you moved back after school you did, uh, shrink a little."

"Shrink, how?"

He strokes his chin, obviously searching for the right words. "Your life force got smaller, I'd say."

I blink rapidly, unable to compute this. "Sorry, I'm not following."

"I've probably been watching too much sci-fi TV since you've been gone, but I noticed when you moved in with Buckley and you took the job at the boutique that you downsized everything. You got a little quieter and a little less social," he says. He stands and moves to the fridge, pulls out another tray. This time it's a blueberry pie. He did this a lot in childhood—brought out the dessert to sweeten even the most difficult situations. We had a lot of these when Mom first passed. Chewing away our sadness because speaking was too challenging.

"I'm sure you're right."

He cuts and plates us both a hearty slice. "My hope for you was that after school you'd move someplace new where the memories wouldn't be so hard to handle."

"Why haven't you done that?" I add a dollop of whipped cream to my plate, waiting to hear the answer to a question I probably should've asked a long time ago.

"Because my life is here. The love of my life is buried here. Every week, I still carve your mom a small figurine that represents something exciting that happened during my week and I switch it out every Sunday when I visit," he says.

"Really? I had no idea." My heart lurches knowing this tradition existed for so many years without my knowledge.

"Do you want to see this week's?" he asks.

Leaving behind our pie, we go into his room. Dad picked this building because at some point in the seventies they added a woodworking shop for resident recreation. He's really the only person who uses it these days.

He slides open his closet door and flicks on the light.

There, on the shelf above his clothes, are what have to be hundreds of wooden figurines of all sorts and shapes.

"Whoa." I start picking up the ones that are closest to the door. One is a graduation cap and when I flip it over, on the bottom he's carved the date. This was the week of my college graduation. There's one of a dollar sign.

"That's from when I got a raise at the furniture store," Dad says, a note of pride underpinning his words. He points to a music note. "That's when you got certified for Cardio Dance Fit."

"Don't remind me," I say with a laugh. "Is this all of them?"

"Only some. Some get ruined after I leave them due to weather or animals," he says. "Some I gift. On more than one occasion, someone else visiting the cemetery has seen one of my figurines and told me some story or another about how what I'd made represented a loved one they lost, so I've given it away. Some I simply don't have space for so I repurpose them for other projects. These are my favorites."

These remind me of the scrapbook Leo's mom proudly showed me. It's strange that I had no idea Dad did this. Sure, I knew he woodworked in his spare time, but these mini trinkets dedicated to Mom never crossed my mind.

He pulls down a rudimentary unfinished one of two people pushing something square.

"Is this me, Leo, and a shopping cart?" I ask, accepting it from him. Cringing at a physical reminder of the man I thought I had to leave behind to right myself.

"Yeah, it's not finished yet," he says, taking it back from

me. "I got some more whittling to do this week, but when it's done, would you like to come with me to the cemetery?"

Only now does it dawn on me that I haven't been in a year or two? Maybe more. It says a lot that I can't even remember. The act of driving past the cemetery was always painful for me. Going in felt like ripping out infected stitches. I couldn't put myself through that.

"Does visiting help?" I ask.

"The grief? No, the grief is always going to be there, but visiting gives me routine. It reminds me that she was here. She's still here." He's looking at me now, cradling the figurine he's working on. "When I saw your face on my seventy-five-inch TV last night, I thought, 'Wow, he looks so much like his mother.'"

The tears come quickly. "I'll come with you on one condition."

"What's that?"

I point to the figure in his hands. "Teach me how to make my own?"

He agrees, and I spend most of the rest of the week in the wood shop taking tiny blocks of wood and turning them into memories. It reminds me a bit of peeling an apple but with more dexterity needed. Each rolling cut allows me to shed more and more of the pressure that's been mounting inside me.

I'm bad at it, mostly. It's not like I've uncovered a hidden talent. There's no denying my novice skill set. I'm impatient and not the safest with the small, sharp blades Dad entrusts me with, so I end up wrapped in a myriad of waterproof Band-Aids, but it's worth it because by Sunday I've created a figurine that's at least somewhat close to the shape I intended it to be.

I even paint it for added flair—using the craftiness I picked up out in LA with our *Madcap Market* sweatshirts. While this piece may look more like an abstraction, it encompasses the big feelings I've been carrying with me all this time. I've packed it in a bag alongside Dad's weekly figurine and we ride over to the cemetery together on a crisp, overcast day. Dolly Parton sings on the radio.

The parking lot is mostly empty. Dad leads us on foot to Mom's headstone—past angels, flower arrangements, and a frisky squirrel holding a nut.

Mom's burial spot is marked by a gorgeous granite mound with a curving tree carved into it, which nearly mirrors the one a few paces away that is swaying in the breeze, giving the sunlight a dazzling effect.

Dad's offering from last week sits on the lip near the ground. It's a small airplane. "I wanted to make sure you had safe travels."

I don't know how I got so lucky to have a dad like him. Patient, supportive, always looking out for me.

Dad swaps out his figurine. The likeness of me and Leo are true to form and make me go misty-eyed. "Hey, Julia. Hope you don't mind but I brought company with me this time."

Dad's speaking to Mom's headstone like it's a person. This should probably weird me out, but it doesn't. He sounds so relaxed, at-home, normal. So why every time I try to speak do my words get caught in my throat?

"Holden just got back from Los Angeles. Thanks for looking out for him while he was away." Dad's always been steadfast that Mom is our guardian angel, even after I grew too old to believe in divine intervention. "He went through a lot of trouble to get to compete on your old favorite TV show and guess what? He won."

I shake my head at that. How had winning still left me feeling like a loser?

Dad pauses, maybe choked up, but he's facing away so I can't fully tell. "I'm sure you knew that already, and it seems like it was quite the experience. Maybe he'd like to tell you a little more about it?"

Dad looks back at me, giving me permission to step forward. I'm scared and shaking. He reaches out a hand, pats my shoulder, then nudges me closer.

A chill rattles through me as if I've passed through an invisible portal.

"I'm going to take a little walk," Dad says. "Give a shout if you need me."

Dad disappears in the direction of the whistling tree. Part of me wants to call after him right away. Being alone with this is frightening. I have no idea where to begin. Then, I notice I've been fidgeting with my wooden figurine in the bag.

I pull it out, hold it up to the light, and inspect it from all sides. It took a couple failed attempts and a lot of cursing, but I was finally able to make a semi-re-creation of Mom pushing a young me in a shopping cart.

When I think of Mom, there are so many ways I could remember her. I could remember her on bring-your-child-to-work day reading a picture book to a room full of eager students. I could remember her sick and frail, hooked up to machines that made scary noises. But most of the time, when I think of her, I think of this.

"When Dad showed me all his figurines, I knew I needed to make one for myself." I offer up my creation. "As you can see it took some trial and error, but I'm happy with how it turned out. It's not perfect, but neither am I, so." I sit down in the grass, careful not to disturb the neighboring grave. I dig my fingers down into the soil to ground myself.

"I chose to make us like this because you had a way of making even the mundane magical. A trip to the grocery store with you was a visit with friends—you doing all those voices for the brand mascots, getting me my favorite snacks from the candy aisle, reading the age-appropriate articles aloud to me from the latest issue of *People* in the checkout line. I was a kid. I shouldn't have looked forward to trips to the grocery store but somehow, I did," I say. I take a sharp inhalation of breath, ready to launch into everything else I've been pushing down.

"Even when I was older, you were sick, and you still made my first trip to the DMV to get my permit a game of who-was-that-person-in-their-past-life. When you left us, I thought you took that magic with you. I was mad at the world for tearing you and that joy away from me, so I did everything to avoid confronting it." I hiccup, my body overwhelmed with emotion. "I took out ridiculous loans so I could go to school far away, I obsessed over a relationship with a boy for years who I was clearly not meant to be with and I avoided coming here."

I look around, half hoping for zombies or ghouls to materialize and chase after me. For day to turn to night in an instant. For anything scary to happen to justify the way I avoided this place for years on end.

"I'm sorry it took so long for me to get out here, Mom." I'm crying now and, after rustling through my pockets, I realize I don't have a tissue, so I accept the mess I'm about to become. "I think when I was away at college, I let the miles speak for themselves. I couldn't come visit because I didn't have a car on campus and when I was home for holidays, we were too busy visiting Nana and Jeff to make the trip. Then, I think when I moved in with Buckley, I became obsessed with making my new life with him work, even if it was hurting me. But I see now that my biggest mistake was thinking a game show could put a spear through my grief."

Thank God nobody else is around because I'm sobbing now. My body lurches forward as I climb up onto my knees, place my hands on the slightly chilly stone. "Winning *Madcap Market* didn't make me miss you any less. I think I'll miss you forever. You're my mom. One of the greatest loves of my life. And I'm so fucking mad that our time together was so short, but I'm so grateful I got that time at all. I love you."

I collapse onto the stone, tears falling faster than I can catch them with my hands. A massive burden wisps up and off my shoulders. Instead, I feel the gentle press of a pair of hands there. "It's okay, Holden. It's okay. Let it out."

Finally, I do. I let out the grief I've been white-knuckling back all these years. I tucked it inside a relationship that couldn't last. I buried it inside a false dream of reality TV stardom. I sat on it and kicked at it and did anything I could to keep it caged. Now, out in the open, I can accept it.

"She's with us always," Dad says like I'm a teenager again and I'm in the fetal position in my childhood bed. "After everything that happened out in Los Angeles, you have to feel that."

I blink back a few tears while hugging Dad and my eyes zero in on his figurine—Leo and me on two edges of a shopping cart. The fact that his shopping cart is a million times better than mine aside, I think about Mom, guardian angels, and messages from the universe.

A game show may not have expunged my grief, but in a weird way, it did gift me Leo. I wonder if the happenstance of it all wasn't so coincidental. Maybe Mom was putting in a word with a higher power for me—assisting with lining up the dominoes so they'd all fall exactly as they were supposed to.

I don't know if that's true, but in this moment, I choose to believe it.

Twenty-Seven

The *Madcap Market* winnings hit my account on a Monday a few months later.

I'm sitting in a coffee shop waiting on someone when the notification from my bank rolls in. I laugh a little to myself.

After a lot of thought, I've finally decided what I'm going to do with the fifty thousand dollars. One half of it is going to go toward paying off my student loans. I may have lied to get the money, but the lie turned into real feelings. Besides, Leo's justification from after the taping still rings true to me. If they were interested in the truth, they would've dug deeper. I have to believe that they didn't care. We made good TV, and I deserve to keep living through this.

The other half is going toward a breast cancer charity—a donation in Mom's name.

Originally, I thought I'd selfishly use it all. I'd pay off my loans, quit my jobs, and use the extra money to pay rent on a place all my own while I focus on finding a career that satisfies me. My plans changed pretty quickly.

I sip my iced chai with oat milk and think back on how well living with Dad has been these past few months. Since we're both busy working, we don't see a ton of each other, but at night, when we sit down to homemade dinner, we get to talk about our days and share stories about Mom and do all the things we didn't get to do right after she passed because I went away to college and I thought time plus a new environment would fix the unfixable.

It's been nice.

The bell over the entrance door rings. Buckley enters. I wave him over.

"I ordered you a horchata latte and an everything bagel with scallion cream cheese," I tell him. "Hope those are still your favorites."

"They are," he says, slinging his satchel over the back of the wooden chair. "Thanks. It's good to see you."

"You, too. Thanks for meeting me here." I picked a convenient spot close to his work and chose an hour prior to the start of his workday. Routine is important to him and deviation puts him on edge. I can see now how my chaotic ways when we were together created unwanted tension in his life. We weren't a match.

"I was pretty surprised when I got your text," he says, spreading his cream cheese so that it's evenly distributed. "I figured we said everything we needed to say out in Los Angeles."

Buckley was a day or two behind me. Part of me worried

that morning I left the hotel with Leo still sleeping soundly in bed that Buckley and I would end up on the same flight. Then, I remembered he'd probably have sprung for an Economy Plus seat and I'd be at the back of the plane keeping company with the toilets, so it wouldn't matter.

"Not everything, not exactly," I admit before sipping my drink to fortify myself. These days, I choose tea over alcohol when my emotions overwhelm me. It's one of the many intentional changes I'm making to be more present. "For the past few months, I've been attending a grief group. Try saying that three times fast. Grief group. Grief group. Gree *goop*. See? Not easy. Anyway, we talk a lot about the Cs when it comes to losing someone and I won't bore you with the details, but one of them is communication. I want to apologize for not communicating with you."

"Apologize?" he asks, midchew.

"Yeah," I say, nodding. "When we met at college, I was stuck in denial. I was pretending that I wasn't hurting and I pretended for so long that you believed me. The longer we were together, the more I started to believe me, too. But inside, I was in a lot of pain, which caused me to withdraw and become a ghost."

"H," he says. My breath catches at the sound of the disused nickname. "Sorry, Holden. I—I was out of line saying that."

"I don't think you were. I think maybe you were a little harsh, but you told the truth and I appreciate that," I say, thinking about ghosts. Many of us assume that when someone passes, they either float on to a greater afterlife or they remain tethered here to haunt, but much like funerals, ghosts aren't a form for the dead, they're a mode of the living. "Because if you hadn't said it, I think I would've tried to continue pretending. I'm much happier now that I'm not."

I smile to myself. I may not love what I do, but I've started finding tiny ways to find joy in the necessary. At the boutique, I turned doing inventory into a game where I hide small prizes in the stockroom, so my coworkers don't find it to be such a slog. During my Cardio Dance Fit classes, I sneak in one unapproved song per week that I absolutely adore be it old or new, hip or out-of-date. It always gets the class jumping, and the monitors could care less.

"That's great to hear," Buckley says, mirroring my smile. "Though I do think flying out to Los Angeles only to get a glittery sweatshirt as a parting gift was a bit much. It's thrown my sleep schedule and my finances completely out of whack."

"Sometimes big emotions make us do zany things," I say with a hearty laugh that's a bit too loud for this small café. Oh, well. I'm following my positive impulses more these days and trying my best not to judge them.

Buckley nods. "I'm glad you're doing so well, Holden."

"Yeah, thanks. Me, too." I pause for a moment. "And I just wanted to say, thank you for helping to keep me afloat all those years and I'm sorry that sometimes it seemed like I was trying to hold your head underwater while doing it. I hope you know it wasn't intentional."

"Of course." He sighs. "We needed each other. We just

weren't meant to be. We had some good times—TV game show rivalry notwithstanding."

"Yeah, I can imagine I won't be adding that episode to my list of regular rewatches." Which reminds me: "Here." I pull a wooden figurine from my bag. It's Buckley. The way I saw him back in college. Lanky. Glasses. In his hand, he holds an *H* to represent me.

"Did you make this?" he asks. My skills have improved over the intervening months. Dad's guidance (and willingness to step in when I can't get a part right) has done wonders. Maybe this was a talent of mine after all; I just never thought it a worthy channel.

"I did."

"You whittle now?"

"Yeah, I guess I do?" I shrug. "It's been a really good outlet."

Buckley appears touched. "Thank you. This is...wow. I love it."

"Just something to remember me by." What he doesn't know, and what I won't say, is that there is a hole carved on the bottom. The figurine is hollow. When and if he figures it out, inside, he will find a check written to make up for that fourth of the rent I unknowingly never paid. Maybe it's a little over-the-top, but I don't want to owe anyone anything, and at least if he wins the game I've set out for him by discovering it, in a weird way he'll have earned it.

Buckley checks his watch, clearly marking how much time he has left before he needs to head to the office. "This might be overstepping, but are you still seeing Leo?"

Immediately, I shake my head. "No, it wouldn't have been fair to him or right. I had a lot to work out."

"Seems like you're doing that pretty well." He shakes the figurine.

"True, but I left Los Angeles without saying goodbye."

"Oof." You know it's bad when your ex that flew all the way across the country to best you on live TV thinks what you did was brutal.

"I left a note! Well, two, technically."

"Still." He makes a face that has yikes written all over it.

I hang my head in my hands. "I wasn't feeling my bravest."

There's a stretch of silence where the whirr of the nearby espresso machine fills my head.

Then, Buckley says, "I know you two may have been faking it for the cameras, but the way he looked at you was real. Believe me, it ignited some latent jealousy. Why do you think I sent your cart down that aisle? Feelings like that don't just disappear in a matter of months."

"Can't they?" I ask, fishing for any excuse not to have to put myself out there emotionally and possibly get rejected by the guy I've been thinking about nonstop since that day in the cemetery with Dad.

"No. Trust me, they can't." Buckley stands and grabs his bag. "But I think you're going to have to find that out for yourself."

I stand and we give each other an awkward yet reaffirming hug. We're going to be okay. I don't think we'll be in each other's lives. I'm not sure there's room anymore after everything. Yet I know in my heart, I'll always be silently rooting for him, wishing him the best.

As the bell jingles over his head once more, I sit back down and finish my latte. I look at the email from my bank again and, on a whim, I open my text thread with Leo.

I type: The prize money hit my account today. It made me think of you and how much I loved spending time with you in LA and how much I miss you. (A lot.) I'm sorry I ran off in the middle of the night. I had a lot to work out for myself. Thanks for giving me the space I needed to do that. If at any point you'd like to video chat, so I can see your face again and apologize in a better way, let me know.

Send.

I type a second message: PS. Tell your mom I said hi and that I've caught up on her favorite K-Drama and I can't wait to see what happens next!

For the first time in months, I've placed the ball in his court. If he doesn't want to connect with me again (one of my *C*s), I'll respect that. I'll always have the magical memories which I can turn into carvings which I can cherish forever or choose to forget, but either way, I'm grateful to have made them in the first place.

Twenty-Eight

The song I snuck into the Cardio Dance Fit playlist queues up—a Taylor Swift throwback jam we'd never get licensing clearance for.

It invigorates me and the room. All the moms are mouthing along to the words as they pump two-pound weights to the beat. Ever since I started giving this job my all, my classes have been better attended and the vibes have been largely more positive.

"All right, everybody, grapevines to the right!" I instruct into my headset. It's always a little trippy hearing my voice through the speakers. Now that I've stopped viewing this as a dead-end gig and accepting that this is just where I am in life, I've begun to enjoy the sense of community it has brought me.

The packed class moves in unison like a health-conscious school of fish. It's nearly mesmerizing until I notice the door in the back of the room open. A medium-height man with jet-black hair ducks into the class late. I can see him in the reflection of the mirror as he puts down his duffel bag and grabs a set of weights.

Cardio Dance Fit is a nonstop exercise class, so I don't have a second to scrutinize the newcomer, but my heart senses what my eyes can't confirm.

In the blur of bodies, I try to keep my hopes in check and my expectations low, which is hard to do when at every song change, I get another peek that throws my systems off. A muscular arm doing a bicep curl. A pair of blue Nike sneakers in a kick. A butt I could pick out in a lineup underneath a pair of five-inch-seam running shorts.

It's not until the class is over, the music has stopped, and we all gather in a circle for a cooldown that I finally see Leo's sweaty, smiling face and know for sure.

Well, not entirely for sure.

I could be imagining this because Leo lives on the other side of the country, right? He wouldn't be taking a cardio dance class in suburban New York for no reason. Unless he's taking a cardio dance class in suburban New York for…me.

I give the class the shortest cooldown imaginable and send everyone on their way.

My regulars are the sweetest, so they all line up as I pack up and thank me for my time. Some tip me. It is gratifying. But I'm hoping these women move it along because Leo has grabbed his bag and tacked himself on to the end of the line.

When the room has cleared, it's just me and him. A few months hasn't changed much. His hair is a little longer. His arms might be a little bigger. Regardless, it's his dark brown eyes I can't look away from. There saying so much that his simple "Hey" can't cover.

"I can't believe you're here right now," I utter. "You are here, right? Because these last few months have been kind of jumbled, so this could totally not be real."

Leo, ever the cocksure stud, flexes one bicep and with his other hand, he guides my palm to the mark. "Does this feel real enough for you?" He drops my hand immediately and lets out his melodic laugh. "Did I surprise you?"

"My heart is racing, so I'd say yeah, you surprised me."

He dips his head, voice going all bashful. "I got your text a couple weeks ago."

I had been wondering. Leo left his read receipts on. I knew he'd seen it, but he never responded. I needed to respect that he wasn't interested in reopening us. "So instead of responding you flew all the way out here?"

"Don't let it go to your head," he says with a cheeky wink. "You're not the only reason I'm out here."

"I'm not?"

"You're not," he says, coyly not divulging any more.

We're back on our banter-y bullshit. Maybe I didn't dash us to smithereens when I left after all.

"Why else are you here?"

He shakes his head. "Oh, no. You're not getting answers that easily. I only came here to give you this." From the front pocket of his duffel bag, he pulls out a small purple envelope. "You're not allowed to open it until I leave, got it?"

A smile overtakes my face. "Got it."

"Good luck," he says before giving me a quick kiss on the cheek and then dashing off.

I pack up the rest of my belongings, all the while my mind is on what's inside that secret envelope. Once five minutes have passed, I sort through the contents. One is a folded piece of paper. The other is a Go Directly to Jail card from Monopoly.

Is this his twisted way of saying he wants nothing to do with me? That I'm in relationship jail or something?

I open the note:

Holden,
You've got 24 hours.
Happy hunting.
Love, Leo

Love. My heart thuds.

I don't know where this leads, but he's pressed one of my buttons. There's no way I'd turn down a game, especially not a scavenger hunt.

This must mean the Go Directly to Jail card is my first clue.

I puzzle over it as I exit the workout room, reentering the bustling main gym where people grunt and heave with earbuds in. I'm about to head toward the parking lot when I notice a large green GO square stuck to the wall in front of me with tape. The arrow points toward the main gym.

My mind regurgitates the rule: Go directly to jail. Do not pass GO. Do not collect $200.

He must want me to walk the opposite way. I find myself

heading toward the locker rooms. Hooking a right, I head into the men's. I start noticing more Monopoly properties and try not to notice the fit men in tiny towels walking out of the showers. I follow the printed pieces to a grated locker with a key in it.

When I open it, I find a second purple envelope.

Inside, I find the orange New York Avenue property card. The word *Avenue* is scratched out and the word *City* is written over it. There's a jumble of numbers below. First, I think I need to add them up. Then, I realize, if I reorder them. They are a date and a time. Tomorrow. 2:00 p.m.

Leo wants me to meet him in New York City tomorrow at 2:00 p.m.?

The next day, I plan to board the 1:07 p.m. train into New York City. When the ticket attendant asks what my name is and I tell her "Holden James," she rolls her eyes, grabs an envelope and says, "Someone left this for you?"

Once I find a seat to myself by the window, I open the envelope. It's the card for St. James Place.

As soon as the train lets out, I march into Midtown and find the St. James Theatre. Assuming this clue is like the last, I head inside to the box office where a smiling man asks if I'm looking for a ticket to the evening performance.

"No, sorry. I'm Holden James. I think something was left here for me?"

He smiles. "One second."

This time, it's not an envelope. It's a plastic hotel piece from the Monopoly set.

Back outside, I fiddle with it. There are hundreds of hotels in this city. This can't be the only clue.

That's when it catches the light at just the right angle and I notice there are tiny, thin numbers etched onto the sides: 3989

Another number clue. It's definitely not a date this time.

I wander over to the street corner and stop. Looking up before I get trampled by a feisty walking tour, I catch sight of the street sign and the numbers.

That's when it clicks: Leo's left me cross streets. 39th Street. The block between 8th and 9th Avenues.

Luckily, I only stumble upon one hotel and once inside, I explain my situation and am directed to the concierge desk which is more of a cart and, of course, part of the East Coast chain of Traveltineraries. The place where Leo used to work. This is all starting to make sense now.

The handsome man behind the cart offers me a flier for the Karaoke Lounge and Bar.

It isn't hard to find, but I've been running all over the city so now I'm sweaty and flustered and I don't want Leo to see me like this, except the hostess must've been briefed on what I look like because she immediately says, "Leo, party of two," and leads me to a private room.

A private, empty room with the haze of pink neon lights playing with my eyes.

When they adjust, I notice the hostess has shut the door behind me. The screen with one microphone in front of it has "Me Against the Music" by Britney Spears featuring Madonna queued up on it.

"Grab the microphone," says Leo's disembodied voice through the room speakers. I jump at the unexpected and loud sound.

"Leo? Where are you?" I ask, confused.

"Just start the song."

I press Play, taking the spoken-word Britney lines for myself. Leo, still hidden, does the Madonna ones. As I sing and he does backup, I start looking around for him, checking behind the couch and under the table.

It's not until the catchy chorus loops in that a glittery curtain gets thrown back and Leo stands there in a flawless re-creation of Madonna's white suit and vest combo from the music video. In classic Leo fashion, he breaks into the music video dance moves flawlessly and, once again, I'm in awe of him.

I'm in awe that he put this scavenger hunt together. I'm in awe of his skill. I'm in awe that there's nary a stain on his well-fitted all-white suit even though I spot a platter of chicken wings in the corner.

"Did you use part of your winnings to get that suit?" I ask during an instrumental break.

"Duh. Now shut up and sing with me!"

Twenty-Nine

"All right. I played your scavenger hunt," I say, flopped onto the couch beside Leo. Breathless, both from a whirlwind day and this sexy man in the dapper suit. "How long were you waiting here for me?"

"An hour." He shrugs. "Maybe two. Time flies when the guy you like is out having fun."

"Who said I was having fun?" I ask, raising my eyebrow at him. I don't make any comment about: *the guy you like.* I let the warm, fuzzy feeling take me over.

"Did you not?" he asks genuinely.

I drop the snark. "No, I did. A lot of fun, actually. The most fun I've had in a long time."

"Good. I hoped you would." Leo's shoulders are drawn back yet relaxed, and a smile takes up his handsome face.

I take a deep breath. "I'm sorry I was a coward and left a note instead of saying goodbye."

"I know you are." His hand casually falls onto the seat between us in an offering.

"I was so conflicted," I confess. "I should've been ecstatic, yet I hadn't confronted my grief, I hadn't gotten over my ex, and suddenly I was falling in—" I stop myself but the grin inching onto his lips tells me he gets the hint. "I needed to be alone to sort that all out."

"I understand," he says, grinning fully. "I forgive you."

I scoot closer to him, wanting our closeness from Los Angeles back. I crave skin-to-skin contact. Now that I have his forgiveness, has he come to give me his heart again? I ask a different question instead: "Ready to tell me the other part of why you're here?"

"When I woke up and realized you'd left, I was pretty hurt. Not gonna lie. It was like Carter all over again." My stomach sinks. Because my misguided attempt to save him from hurt caused it anyway. "But I started thinking about what you said, how something felt off. I wanted so badly for our last night together to be special that I was ignoring the fact that something felt off for me, too."

"Oh, yeah?" I ask, very curious. "What was it?"

"The lies," he says, turning off his microphone and setting it down between us.

"The lie we told to win the money?"

"No, the lies I told my mom." He sighs a heavy sigh. "Admittedly, it was good that you left. It forced me to go home and talk to her. I told her why I did all of this in the first place. I let her know that I love her and want to take care of her and be close to her, but I also need more space and independence."

I shift into him. "How did she take that?"

"Not great at first." He takes an audible breath. "She was mostly mad that I got fired from another job, so she iced me out for a few weeks. After some extensive home cooking on my part, she broke her silent streak and finally spoke. She told me she was hurt that I felt I couldn't be honest with her. Since it's always just been me and her, I've never had the option to keep her in the dark when it came to my life, but then Carter happened and I felt ashamed and I started keeping secrets."

"You told her what happened with Carter, too?"

"I did."

"Was she understanding?" I could imagine Mrs. Min being rigid in her stance. She obviously holds firm beliefs about life, the world, and relationships.

"Surprisingly, she was." This makes me relax. "And then, she opened up to me about my dad because she was keeping secrets, too. We never really talked about him. He left, she told me that he wasn't coming back, she let me cry about it, and then we went about with our lives. This time, she admitted that she kicked him out because he was embarrassed that he had a gay son."

"Leo." I say his name as if it cures any of the hurt he must be feeling right now after learning this information.

"In a way, I should've known." He shakes his head. "As soon as he left, I was able to start taking dance classes like I'd always wanted to, and I was allowed to listen to my music at full volume around the apartment. For the most part, I grew up without a dad, but I got to grow up as *me*. I can't be mad at my mom for giving me a gift like that."

"That's a great way of looking at it." I reach out a hand, and he takes it. I summon all the pride I feel for him into my palm. I'm utterly impressed at the man sitting in front of me. Still Leo, but Leo 2.0. Leo leveled-up. It's a miracle that our journeys have synced up like this.

"Yeah. I'm glad she was honest with me." He squeezes my hand. "And, in the spirit of honesty, she calmly told me I need to call *Madcap Market* and tell them the truth."

Dropping his hand, I grow scared the longer the silence stretches on without explanation. "Well? Did you?"

He bites his lip and nods. "I was raised to do what my mom tells me to."

"Oh, my God!" I stand and start pacing.

"It was an awkward conversation."

I tug at my hair. "What? Are they going to retract our win and make some public statement on the next episode? We're going to be a laughingstock. I already spent some of the money. I can't just go back to the Breast Cancer Association of America and be like, 'Hey, sorry. That actually wasn't my money to spend.' Why didn't you call me and tell me?"

"You explicitly told me not to contact you," he says firmly.

"Okay! But this is an emergency situation. I would've understood. I would've—" In my panic, I register what Leo's wearing again. "Wait, how could you afford that suit if—"

That shit-eating smirk from the very first day we met stamps itself onto Leo's face. "I'm fucking with you."

I gasp and throw one of the nearby decorative pillows at him. Gah, I'd be madder if he weren't so infuriatingly handsome and here and wonderful in every way but this one. "So you didn't tell them?"

"No, I did," he admits. "But they said to me what I said to you, they don't care. As long as we weren't going to go blabbing about their less than scrupulous casting process, they didn't see a problem. They said others have fudged their relationships before, too. It's about looks and chemistry, not history."

"Oh." I start to wonder how many of my favorite contestants over the years weren't actually who they said they were to each other. I suppose the artifice should've been more obvious. It's a fake grocery store after all!

Even still, it warms me to know they cast us because of chemistry. The chemistry that's reprising itself now that we're back in the same room.

"Seriously, they said we were the most talked about contestants online this whole season. We're the reason *Madcap Market* was trending on socials for the first time this year. They loved us. Didn't you see the influx of followers we both got?" He turns so we're eye to eye. "We're good. If this whole experience taught me anything, it's that telling white lies and withholding information are fine with people who don't matter like the mega-wealthy producers at *Madcap Market*, but they have no place between you and the people you love."

"Love?"

"Yeah, love." Leo smiles. "You signed your goodbye note with it, and even though you were running away—maybe *because* you were running away—I knew you meant it."

Huh. I honestly don't remember doing that, but maybe my subconscious did me a solid favor by putting the word I was most afraid of out there.

I can't rip my gaze away from Leo. He has a way of locking me in, and I love it. I love *him*. "I did and still do mean it."

"I mean it, too," he says, appearing a bit bashful.

"Okay," I say a little breathless over this massive revelation but not wanting to rush this important conversation. "You came all this way to see me, to let me apologize in person, but I have a feeling there's one more thing left. What is it?"

"Know me that well already, huh?" he asks.

"Honestly? Not as well as I'd like to."

He blushes at that. "Your note told me to use my half of the winnings to chase my passions, so yesterday morning I had an audition."

"An audition?" I ask. "Oh, my God! For what?"

"To be a background dancer for a newbie pop singer going on her first tour," he says, sounding proud. "Don't get too excited. I got cut third round, but I made it pretty far and I got some good feedback. I think I'll try again the next opportunity I get. I promised my mom that if I was going to forgo a nine-to-five to pursue a passion, I had to go all in. I couldn't half-ass it like my other jobs."

"That's incredible, Leo!" I want to throw myself on him and kiss him, but I know we're not there yet. Forgiveness was given and love was broached, but that doesn't mean we're automatically going to try again. "Wait, isn't there more of an industry for that out in Los Angeles?"

He half shrugs. "Yeah, but your note said chase my *passions*. Plural." The back of his hand strokes down my jaw. I could break into a million happy pieces when I fully digest his meaning. "I couldn't pass up the opportunity to knock out both in one trip." Like he's a magician, he snaps the napkin up between us. "What would you say if I told you that I—Leo Min—was your prize for winning the scavenger hunt?"

I pretend to consider this. "I—Holden James—would say that I graciously accept."

Our lips collide, and it's like our hearts merge. As our tongues tangle up, I've never known two hungrier mouths. Leo's palms scoop up around my ass until he's hauling me off the couch, holding me tight, my legs wrapped around his sturdy waist. It's distilled paradise.

In our closed-eyed frenzy, Leo bumps the remote that controls the karaoke machine. The electronic beat and ghostly backing vocals for "Breathe On Me" by Britney Spears filter through the room.

I laugh into Leo's mouth. "Could a hornier song possibly have come on?"

"No, but let's leave it on," he says before trailing his teeth along my lower lip. "It's doing something for me."

"Oh, yeah?" I ask, bucking into the new bulge in his thin suit pants. "Your hotel isn't far if we run."

"Fuck running, we won one hundred thousand dollars.

We're getting an Uber!" he shouts triumphantly, frantically grabbing our stuff. "An Uber Black! Only the best for us."

After calling a ride and settling the tab, we step out from the dark neon of the karaoke bar and into the bright spring sun of New York City, kiss-drunk and happy off our asses.

The game of life is hard, and the rules are always changing, but with a good teammate by your side, it's always worth playing.

Epilogue

My ass is on the edge of a makeup station. Bright marquee bulbs frame me. Leo's hands brush up the tops of my thighs before wandering beneath the hem of my dark purple polyester blend crewneck.

His hot palms crest up my stomach until his fingers find my sensitive nipples. He tweaks them, grinning into my mouth because he's learned how wild that makes me. The press of his lips and the softness of his hands have me gasping as I wrap my legs around him until our bulges are flush, frotting.

He grunts in approval. Our erections knocking, I slip my hand beneath the elastic of his athletic pants, pushing them out of the way to get a view of the dark blue, bikini-cut briefs he's got on. There's a noticeable dark spot where the tip of his penis is begging to be let out and licked.

Slipping down off the counter, I plant my knees on the plush carpet and kiss him where he wants it. Smartly, he turns up the pump-up playlist we've been blasting so nobody hears me pumping *him*. My tongue dances over his length through the fabric, and Leo lets out an expletive that would never be allowed on network TV.

It's amazing that after a full year of togetherness—of planning and airplanes and budgets—we can still fall into a sneaky, sexy rendezvous so easily.

Wide-eyed, I blink up at Leo as I take him in my mouth, starting a rhythmic suck with an added hand to apply pressure. We don't have a lot of time, but we both need this release.

"That's how I like it, baby," he whispers before cupping my chin and guiding me up to standing. We kiss. I know he can taste himself on my tongue, a dirty little treat he likes more and more.

He brings us over to the couch. He lies down first and I lose my pants before getting on top. The fullness in my mouth mixed with the sensation between my legs is enough to light me up like a studio set. I'm burning bright and fast for him.

I moan around his shaft. He does the same for me.

In my periphery, I notice our reflection in the mirror—Leo's muscular body curved beneath my wiry frame. A perfect sixty-nine. Synced up and nearly there.

"I'm so close," I tell him, coming up for air.

"Same," he says on a heavy exhale.

Almost exactly in time, Leo's shooting into my mouth

as I am his. I'm swallowing ropes of him—salty, delicious. Not a drop wasted.

Spent and breathless, we demount only to be jarred by a knock. "This is your ten-minute call! Ten minutes!"

"Good timing," Leo says, smacking me playfully on the bare ass as I wander back to my pants.

"Now we can really focus on securing a second victory."

Leo stands, naked as all hell, still semierect and gorgeous. He cups one ass cheek and tugs me into him, possessive but not overly so. "We've already won, baby."

He gives me a kiss that goes straight to my heads. Yes, both of them.

"No time for a second round right now," he says, heading into the bathroom to brush his teeth and get show ready.

Ten minutes later, we find ourselves on the updated *Madcap Market* set—same layout, new products, extra challenges. We've been prepped. Leo and I reprise our roles as Team Eggplant behind the familiar podium, our names proudly displayed on self-written name tags on our chests.

This time, my head isn't overflowing with conflicting emotions, and we're not faking anything. Today, I'm present and ready to play. I link my pinkie with Leo's out of sight of the cameras. A tiny tether to amp myself up.

Pat Crumsky appears at the end of the theme music. "Welcome to a special all-star episode of *Madcap Market*. We've collected three of our favorite teams from last season to come compete a second time. We've got reigning champs like Team Eggplant here to secure a second jackpot and underdogs who almost made it big like Team Biscuits here to try again. Let's reintroduce ourselves, shall we?"

Pat saves us for last, chatting with the other teams before making his way to us. After reading off a brief bio and showing a highlight clip reel of us from last season, he flashes his Emmy-winning smile at us and asks, "So, tell me. Last time we saw you, you two were considering a real relationship. Can you showing up here this season mean what we think it means?"

I take Leo's whole hand in mine and hold it up. "Does this tell you anything, Pat?"

The crowd cheers, including Mrs. Min and Mr. Park who are seated over to the left wearing big smiles right next to Dad who holds up a small GO, HOLDEN AND LEO pennant he made himself.

"Young love! Warms my aging heart," Pat says sincerely. "Leo, what would a second hundred grand mean for the two of you? What would you do with the prize money?"

"Well, Pat, we've been a bicoastal couple for the last year doing long distance. Airplanes are expensive and the relationship has gotten significantly more serious. Wouldn't you say, Holden?"

I nod excitedly. "One hundred thousand dollars would help us to relocate to a more permanent place that we can share." Leo kisses the back of my hand. My heart flutters for all to see.

Pat opens his arms to the audience as if saying: Could these guys be any cuter? "We wish you luck. We wish all of our teams immense luck as they gear up to play America's favorite grocery-themed game show—say it with me now—*Madcap Market!*"

As the lights dim, I kiss Leo and then whisper alongside Pat, "Let the games begin."

★ ★ ★ ★ ★

Look for Timothy Janovsky's next novel from
Afterglow Books by Harlequin,
You Had Me at Happy Hour,
available Summer 2024.